THE
MISADVENTURES
of a
PLAYGROUND
MOTHER

THE MISADVENTURES of a PLAYGROUND MOTHER

CHRISTIE BARLOW

Bookouture

Published by Bookouture

An imprint of StoryFire Ltd.
23 Sussex Road, Ickenham, UB10 8PN
United Kingdom

www.bookouture.com

ISBN: 978-1-910751-32-9

For my family,
Christian, Emily, Jack, Ruby, Tilly, Mum and Dad.

ACKNOWLEDGEMENTS

As always, a huge thank you and much love to my family, Christian, Emily, Jack, Ruby and Tilly (Mop) for all your patience and support while I've been locked away for hours writing in my cave. Woody, my best friend, my life is complete with you in it. You are all simply the best.

Many people have helped in the writing of this book, my heartfelt thanks to my agent Madeleine Milburn for her faith in me and I am beyond blessed to be working with such a fantastic team at Bookouture. Kim Nash who is everyone's Fairy Godmother, I simply adore her. Claire Bord, Olly Rhodes and all the fantastic editors are incredible people who have turned my stories in to books; I thank you from the bottom of my heart. I am both proud and honoured to be called a Bookouture author and everyone's encouragement and enthusiasm for my writing is heartening.

Huge love to all of the Bookouture authors for their warm welcome to the Bookouture family. The support from all of you has been truly amazing.

A special mention to my wonderful friends, Anita Redfern, Lucy Davey, Chantal Chatfield, Nicola Rickus, Catherine Snook, Louise Speight, Suzanne Toner, Sue Stevens, Alison Smithies, Sarah Lees and Bev Smith, Sarah Yeats and Ilona Hampson who have always been on hand in person or at the end of a telephone listening to plot dilemmas. Their everyday support has not gone unnoticed. Thank you.

Many thanks to Sue France, Sarah Pickles and Susan Miller who are genuinely some of the loveliest people I know.

Finally to some very special people, all the wonderful readers, book bloggers and followers who's tireless cheering, retweeting, sharing of posts and continuous excitement for my books have enabled me to get this far. You have all kept a smile of my face throughout my whole journey and I couldn't have done it without you, big love to Lisa Smith, Janet Baldwin, Allison Marsh, Deborah Turner, Claire Hall, Michelle Dobson and Sarah Ansell, You have made Twitter a joy and one day I am sure we will meet! I hope you all enjoy *The Misadventures of a Playground Mother.*

Dreams can come true,

Warmest wishes,
Christie x

INTRODUCTION

My sleep was unceremoniously interrupted as the bedroom door was flung open and three loud pops erupted to sound the start of a new day – the unmistakable sound of party poppers! The kids had clearly managed to lay their hands on some left-over mini pyrotechnics from the previous night and after letting them off within a foot of my left ear, they simultaneously shouted, 'Happy birthday'! This could only mean one thing – it was my birthday – my thirty-fifth birthday!

I bolted up and tried to create a gap between my upper and lower eyelids in a vain attempt to loosen the grip of the mascara holding them together. As I began to recover from the shock of the artillery barrage going off in my bedroom, I felt a relentless throbbing in my head. It was as if the cast of *Riverdance*, the band of the Coldstream Guards, and that noise-making stage act that made a living kicking bin-lids and banging other metal paraphernalia with hammers were all shamelessly trying to win the Making-the-most-noise-at-a-stupid-time-on-New-Year's-Day award.

I assumed it was a stupid time; I still hadn't managed to open my eyes wide enough to read the display on the clock radio. My tongue felt like a pharaoh's sock so I fumbled around looking for the glass of water that routinely sits on my bedside table but I was unable to locate it. The vivid red numbers on the digital display finally reached my retina and my brain slowly interpreted the image. It was 6.17 a.m.!

I muttered something – probably unpleasant – at the kids and they gave me a hug and began to filter out of the bedroom. Samuel, my son, offered to make me a cup of tea, at which point Matt – who would be able to hear the offer of a brew from the other side of the country – finally began to stir and added his name to the tea round before climbing out of bed.

I allowed my body to sink back down towards the bed, every fragile movement causing my head to throb even more. Finally, it touched the pillow and I detected the distinctive smell of stale alcohol and a hint of mint. Mint! Why on earth would my pillow smell of mint? A little dribble of saliva – probably the only liquid left in my body – evacuated my mouth at the corner so I quickly licked it up in a hopeless attempt to rehydrate my tongue. Curiously, my taste buds also detected a hint of mint so I licked my lips again and before you could say 'Miss Marple,' the mint mystery was solved; I must have climbed into bed with toothpaste smeared around my mouth, which had now dried into a crusty film. On the plus side though, at least it proved I had brushed my teeth before I passed out.

Samuel aged eight appeared with my mug of tea. He looked as if he had slept well with his mass of curly blonde hair sticking up like a mad professor. I sat up again and took a small sip, but as the hot liquid hit my stomach, I immediately began to feel sick. I spotted a bucket at the side of the bed. A bucket that Matt must have strategically placed there, knowing full well I would need to be sick.

I mustered up every ounce of energy to heave myself out of bed and made my way tentatively towards the bathroom. I reminded myself that I was a mother of four and not a teenager, and partying to the early hours always took it out of me.

CHAPTER 1

There was no doubt whatsoever that this birthday would be spent in exactly the same way as so many previous birthdays – with my hair tied back and my head permanently positioned over the toilet. I tried to recollect more memories from the night before but everything seemed to have been erased. Apparently, it's called selective amnesia – in my case another year older but certainly not another year wiser.

My phone started to beep – no doubt Facebook messages wishing me a happy birthday - but I wasn't quite sure what was happy about it so far. After reading numerous birthday wishes on my profile page I flicked to the newsfeed and immediately began to feel even more nauseous; the profile picture of a mother from school, Botox Bernie, was gawping back at me. She appeared as though she was in the middle of a mid-life crisis with her push-up bra catapulting her artificially enhanced chest so high above her low cut top that it was hitting her chin. On a positive note however, her forehead was wrinkle free, she was still living up to her Playground nickname of Botox Bernie.

Facebook hadn't improved my mood so I gingerly made my way over to the window, trying desperately to keep my head still to avoid triggering the motion-sensitive organs in my ear, which would make me feel even dizzier. I parted the curtains to view the rest of the world; the sky was grey and white flakes were falling thick and fast. I stared out of the window at a spectacular sight. A fresh blanket of snow covered the fields that spanned for miles and miles, with not a single tyre mark or footprint to be seen. There were a few cottages either side of us but I could tell no one had ventured out yet as the snow that lay on their gardens was undisturbed.

Matt had ushered the children downstairs and had fed them. I could hear the television blaring from the playroom, which would suggest he had kindly sat them down to watch a DVD. I could hear conversations filtering from downstairs. Jane, Mark, and their daughter Poppy had stayed over and joined in our New Year celebrations. They were our good friends from up North. The scraping of the kitchen chairs across the stone floor and the banging of the cupboard doors suggested breakfast was being prepared. The clatter of knives and forks and plates crashed onto the table, the sound amplifying all around me.

I slowly made my way downstairs, carefully stepping over the carnage from the night before – empty beer cans, party poppers, streamers, and leftover sausage rolls that had been trodden into the carpet – when my eyes fell upon a most unexpected sight. There at the foot of the stairs lay a pair of shoes; not just any pair of shoes but shoes belonging to one Rupert Kensington, the philanderer of a husband married to Penelope Kensington.

I peered inside the cloakroom cupboard, looking for further evidence that Rupert Kensington was alive and well and had not been driven over the edge of a cliff in my make-believe bus. Every month I would allocate a seat on my pretend bus to particular people; all those that boarded would hopefully never cross my path again, but his coat was still there, hanging on his own personal peg, the peg to the left, was vacant. That left Penelope's name clearly visible on the sticky label Matt had fashioned when we thought we were going to be joined by a full complement of Kensington lodgers after a relentless run of Saturday night get-togethers. Penelope and Rupert had never been good at taking no for an answer and had no qualms about taking up all of our Saturday evenings. We had given up trying to fob them off because it simply did not work.

My mind drifted back to the game we had amused ourselves with, the previous evening, as midnight approached; the game that revealed Rupert's drunken desire to marry the lovely Annie and avoid his wife at all costs. Annie was Penelope's friend; well ex-friend now; Rupert had fallen in love with her but had dutifully stayed with Penelope due to the two children they shared, Little Jonny and Annabel. Shortly afterwards, my friend Jane, from the north, was brave enough to secure Rupert in a vice-like grip planted an over-zealous New Year's kiss directly on his lips. This had understandably pushed Penelope to breaking point; she was last seen bounding out of the lounge, knocking me off the settee, in her hurry to leave the room. No one could blame Penelope for storming out of the room, she must have been sick to the back teeth of Rupert and his Lothario tendencies.

I opened the kitchen door forcing an insincere smile on my face.

'Happy New Year everyone; hope the hangover isn't too appalling,' I announced.

Matt, Jane, Mark and Rupert peered at me as I placed my backside firmly on a chair and slid my legs under the table. I needed to sit still to stop the motion that was trying to convince my body I was bobbing around in a rowing boat in the middle of the ocean. Matt pressed another cuppa in my hand and placed a bacon sandwich on the table in front of me. I took a slurp of my tea as he moved forward and planted a kiss on my forehead.

'Take these,' he commanded, and forced headache tablets into the palm of my sweaty hands, 'and Happy Birthday, sweetheart!'

I glanced over at Jane and Mark who somehow appeared as fresh as daisies; they were showered, dressed and quite happily tucking into sausage and bacon muffins. Due to the weather conditions, they wanted to leave as early as possible to avoid any hazards on the motorway. The kitchen was invitingly warm, but to me it smelled far from delicious. Rupert was hugging a mug of tea too, as if his life depended on it – well I suppose it did – at some point he would need to return home to face Penelope. Death Row would probably seem more appealing to him right now.

I was convinced Rupert would provide another Oscar-winning performance to win back Penelope.

His current predicament made me think of all the characters from the Wizard of Oz rolled into one; in the film, Glinda the good witch tells Dorothy to follow the yellow brick road to the Emerald City. On her way, she meets and befriends the Scarecrow who wants a brain, the Tin Man who desires a heart, and the Cowardly Lion who is in need of courage. Rupert would need lots of courage, like the Cowardly Lion, to face Penelope, and he certainly needed a brain to have even contemplated his revelations of the night before, and surely he lacked a heart, as his numerous dalliances, which had almost destroyed his family had been entirely influenced by the goings-on in his trousers. Still dressed in his New Year's Eve ensemble, he looked full of misery and very bedraggled. His shirt was stained with beer and sweat patches. An unpleasant smell left nothing to the imagination.

Rupert was probably praying that this year would be better than his last. During the past year, his various affairs had been uncovered; his double life with Charlotte had been busted, and his love for Annie revealed. Rupert's short stay in rehab for his obvious sex addiction had humiliated Penelope. The year ahead potentially offered Rupert a fresh start.

Jane and Mark started to pack up their belongings and round up their daughter Poppy for the long journey back up to Cheshire. Jane was still breaking into fits of giggles, clearly amused that Penelope, Rupert's long-suffering wife had knocked me off the sofa just as I was about to give the air guitar performance of a lifetime to Queen's 'Fat Bottomed Girls'.

'It was the moment when you heard the taxi beeping, and were convinced your make-believe bus had arrived to take them out of your life forever,' she chuckled.

In that split second I remembered receiving a drunken text from my best mate Fay wishing me a happy birthday along with the bad news that the bus had been delayed due to bad weather. 'I'm really sorry,' it read, 'you will have to go on holiday with the Kensington's after all.' The holiday with the Kensingtons was something I wasn't looking forward to this coming year. Last November, they'd invited us round to share a meal on their anniversary and like the Spanish Inquisition had interrogated us on our holiday plans for the following year. Before we knew it the laptop had been whipped out, plugged in and they were booked on the same flights as us. They'd only invited themselves to stay at our villa.

That the 'bus had been delayed' was apparent since Rupert was sitting in my kitchen, larger than life and on my birthday too! That surely meant that all the other people I'd allocated a seat to on my make-believe bus were also still breathing and more than likely nursing their own hangovers on this snowy New Year's Day.

Suddenly, the shrill of a siren cut through the atmosphere and the kitchen was bathed for a moment in blue swirling lights. Samuel rushed into the kitchen, waving his arms wildly.

'There's something going on at Mr. Fletcher-Parker's house,' he yelled. 'There's an ambulance parked outside and a woman wearing a tatty fur coat and high-heels is standing there wailing.' Mr Fletcher-Parker for the last year had been my pensioner stalker; he was my very own geriatric ninja who Matt and I had named Frisky Pensioner due to his energetic frolicsome tendencies.

Jane bolted to the window followed by Matt, Mark and Rupert as though they were in an Olympic 100-metre race. Jostling for position and standing on their tiptoes, they strained their necks for an improved view. The window was rather crowded and I wanted to see what all the fuss was about. Still in a very delicate state, I headed gingerly towards the front door. Grabbing my coat, I stepped outside, and instantly the freezing air blasted colour into my dehydrated hung-over skin. The rest of the household – spotting my obvious vantage point – put on their coats and shoes and crunched their way through the snow to the bottom of the drive, and peered around the hedge in a vain attempt to appear inconspicuous.

Standing together at the bottom of the driveway, we could hear the wailing woman. Other neighbours had started to gather in the street, agog to discover the reason for all the commotion.

I surveyed the area, looking for the source of the wailing. When my eyes finally fell upon the woman in the fur coat, my jaw nearly hit the ground. She was standing in white stiletto heels, not classy by any stretch of the imagination. They looked scuffed and had certainly seen better days; they were the ubiquitous hooker heels, the kind you would see adorning the feet of the less-than-glamorous lead female in a typical low-budget porn film. They were certainly not the proper footwear for this type of weather – whatever was this woman thinking?

My eyes now focussed on the fur coat, which looked more like a flea-ridden chinchilla. It was difficult to be absolutely certain but she didn't seem to be wearing a great deal under the fur coat – the plunging neck line revealed her ample and not unfamiliar cleavage. Surely not! I immediately turned my attention to her face and for the second time today, I was confronted by the face of Botox Bernie. It was one thing lording it around on the school playground every day, as she did, but BB (Botox Bernie) was now standing in the street being just as vocal as she was in the playground.

Her expression didn't falter – which was no great surprise as her face had been injected full of poisonous fillers – but as the volume of her howls increased, I could hear the dog beginning to whine from inside the house. The onlookers were beginning to mutter; clearly still unsure as to why there was an ambulance parked outside Frisky's house and why BB was dressed like a hooker. We had plenty of time to find out though; It was too icy and slippery to move anywhere at speed, so we were not going anywhere in a hurry.

BB suddenly dropped to her knees and her moan reached new intensity levels. A wry smile began to spread across Rupert's face and his face was flushed with embarrassment. I concluded from his reaction that this was not the first time he had witnessed her in this position. My hangover was still hanging onto me for dear life, and as she sat there on her haunches, I tried to stop my mind running wild with thoughts of what she may or may not be wearing under the flea-ridden chinchilla. One thing was certain, if she didn't rise back onto those unclassy heels soon, there would be a beaver with a severe case of frostbite.

At that moment, two men dressed in paramedics' uniforms emerged through Frisky Pensioner's front door. The gathered crowd were straining their necks trying to establish whether they were the real deal or leftover visitors from a fancy dress

New Year's Party. Any doubt as to their integrity was soon dispelled as the two men wheeled out a stretcher, its cargo completely covered by a blanket. It looked like a dead body, but because it was covered in a blanket, it was difficult to work out who it was. That puzzle was soon solved though when BB began sobbing, 'It's the end, it's the end. I'm so sorry Mr Fletcher-Parker.'

She pulled herself wearily to her feet and made her way towards the trolley. As she did so, her coat slipped open for a split second, briefly revealing a furry relation of the flea-ridden chinchilla. 'Jesus,' Matt remarked, 'she's got more bush than the Australian outback!'

Frisky Pensioner was dead, snuffed out like one of the candles on my birthday cake. This time last year, he was my very own pensioner stalker who had tried to kiss me on quite a few occasions. It now appeared that he had breathed his last breath. I knew it was unethical, but I had the urge to peel back the blanket to double check it was actually him underneath. Rumours began circulating amongst the onlookers that Mrs F-P had walked out on him the previous night; she hadn't gone to look after an ill relative as she had told us. She'd finally had enough of his years of constant womanising and decided it was now or never if she was to venture out into the world on her own, in the hope of finding a few years of companionship with a more devoted partner. To console himself, Frisky Pensioner had rung a low class budget stripper agency to try to cheer himself up. Unfortunately, due to it being New Year's Eve, there was only BB left on the books – the only stripper that couldn't secure a booking on the busiest night of the year.

On their way to the ambulance, the paramedics discreetly revealed that he had suffered a massive heart attack.

There was nothing more to see as the ambulance manoeuvred its way down the snowy road. The rest of the neighbours began to disperse, excitedly chattering about the prospect of a post-funeral buffet to attend. They clearly all loved a good wake – the local post-office would be buzzing with excitement on Monday, when they all assembled to collect their pensions. We filed back towards the house for some warmth but not before I was entertained by BB's impression of Bambi as she slipped and slid down the lane on her high heels through the snow.

CHAPTER 2

So this was the village life that I had craved so much only twelve months ago. To be honest, I'd already had a bellyful and began to mull over my New Year's Resolutions.

1. I will drink less alcohol.
2. I will not be subjected to peer pressure in the playground.
3. Always remember it's quality not quantity of people on Facebook.
4. I will learn to say NO to Penelope.

Those would keep me going for now, even though I was fully aware that the majority of New Year's Resolutions are broken by the end of January. I had every intention of holding onto these resolutions for a lifetime.

As we all approached the front door, we wiped our snowy shoes on the mat and were relieved to be going back into the warm, inviting house. 'Get that kettle on,' I shouted to Matt who had already started to fill it up with water. Rupert was right behind me so I turned to him and suggested it would probably be a good idea to head back to his own house now. He didn't look thrilled at the thought of facing Penelope, his furious wife; in fact it was safe to say he turned a sickly green colour very rapidly. He nodded at me obediently, and retrieved his coat. Reluctantly, he set out into the cold, raising his right hand as a gesture of thanks before stuffing both hands into his pockets and heading down the path. He probably spent the whole journey mulling over in his mind how he was going to convince Penelope to let him back in.

So this was my birthday, uneventful as ever! Frisky Pensioner was dead but at least the evidence suggested he had died a content man in the clutches of BB. I shuddered as I tried to imagine the expression on his face as he started his journey towards the pearly gates. Matt laughed and suggested that perhaps BB had been wearing a pearl necklace a few minutes before which immediately made me gag. Rupert was heading home to the lovely Penelope with his tail between his legs, but the opinion of the party-stragglers – which to be precise, was only Jane, Mark, Matt, and myself – was that perhaps he shouldn't have wagged his tail in the first place.

After we had all defrosted and had a brew, Jane and Mark began to gather their belongings ready for the long journey home back up North, trying to prepare themselves mentally for the lines of cars on the motorway. That was something I didn't miss, queuing in traffic for hours on end, of course I was always sad to see my friends go back home, but I was never tempted to return to the routine of the rat race. Waking up each morning at a reasonable hour to the spectacular views out of our windows always won easily. On her way back in from the car, Jane noticed a small figure trudging through the snow on the path to our front door. She hollered towards the kitchen that we had a visitor. Who now? I needed a shower and I was desperate to tuck into some of the leftover Christmas chocolate to satisfy my hangover sugar cravings.

I was hoping the birthday fairy would appear and transform my house back into some sort of habitable state. The trodden-in sausage roll was beginning to look like a fur ball the cat had sicked up. I marched towards the front door to meet the mysterious visitor. On the positive side, I knew it couldn't be Frisky Pensioner, but it would just be my unfortunate luck if he had a twin brother.

Opening the door, I was confronted by the familiar figure of the Farrier; he was the long- suffering husband, now separated from, Camilla Noland, a fellow mum at the school gates. In the last twelve months, they had both seemed unhappy with their marriage and had clocked up numerous affairs between them. He looked very forlorn peering out from under his oversized hood.

'I've missed the ambulance,' he declared. His voice was shaky.

I looked at him blankly.

'Do you know where my father has been taken to?' he continued. 'Did the paramedics give any indication?'

I tilted my head to one side like a puzzled puppy while my hung-over brain continued to process his words. I was definitely a bit slow on the uptake; did he say father?

'F-f-father?' I finally managed to stutter back in response as the penny began to drop. 'Did you say Father?'

'Yes, Mr Fletcher–Parker is … I mean was … my father.'

It doesn't happen very often but I was totally flummoxed. The Frisky Pensioner was the Farrier's father! My very own pensioner stalker, the same man who would spontaneously pop up behind hedges and wander around my garden at ridiculous hours of the morning was the Farrier's father which would make him Camilla Noland's ex father-in-law.

Although there was, no love lost between Mrs Noland and I (her refusal to sell me a saddle from her saddlery early last year and the continuous gossiping in the local shops, which I have witnessed on many occasions revealed her unpleasant ways), the Farrier had always seemed a pleasant chap and I had no axe to grind with him. It wasn't his fault that he had been hoodwinked into marrying Camilla to secure her place in the horsey world and he certainly couldn't help the fact that Mr Fletcher-Parker was his father. I couldn't leave him freezing on the doorstep another moment so I did the decent thing and invited him inside whilst bellowing again for Matt to put the kettle back on. I peered around the playroom door to check on the children; they were all exhausted from the previous late-night activities and hadn't moved a muscle, all faces were still glued to the television screen.

He stepped into the hallway past Jane and Mark, who seized this opportunity to finally say their goodbyes and to escape with Poppy back to the relative sanctuary of their own home. As we waved them off, the Farrier removed his coat and trotted behind me into the kitchen and parked himself down on a chair. Matt handed him a brew. I did wonder whether I should offer him something stronger – his father had just died after all – but in all honesty we had drunk the house almost dry the night before and I'm not sure whether leftover Malibu would have been his tipple. I wasn't sure it was anyone's tipple!

Matt took this opportunity to grab some fresh air; his head was beginning to feel a little heavy. Enticing the children away from the television, he encouraged them to wrap up warmly in their coats, hats and gloves. He clipped the lead to the dog's collar, and within five minutes they were all heading out through the front door to enjoy a New Year's Day walk, leaving me alone with the Farrier.

The next two hours were like story time with the Farrier. I couldn't believe I was spending my thirty-fifth birthday with him, hearing his entire life story, but what could I do?

I sat back and listened.

The Farrier had lived in the village all his life; he was the only son of Iris and Bert Fletcher-Parker. Overall, his childhood had been a happy one until the day he decided he wouldn't follow in his father's footsteps and become a factory worker. He wanted to live his own dream; he wanted a country farmhouse with a beautiful wife and family.

As a lad, the Farrier had often sneaked into the local farmer's field where he taught himself to ride the horses that grazed there – which was where his love of horses originated. When he left school, he decided he would take himself off to college and train as a farrier, much to his father's disappointment. He thought he was the luckiest person alive when he graduated, and then secured a position at the local stables, but that was where all his troubles began.

There were numerous stable girls employed there and as a young man with a good job, he could have his pick of the lasses. He was particularly taken with a girl called Melanie. The Farrier thought she was lovely, very feminine. Her long curly locks flowed beautifully down her back and her striking blue eyes that always sparkled with kindness were just perfection. She was exquisite – kind and funny – the type of girl he wanted to make a life with; the type of girl he wanted to marry. One day he was determined that she would be his.

Then the day Camilla, his current wife, started to work at the same stables it all went wrong. Overnight, Melanie disappeared without saying a word. There was no trace of her. His heart was broken, and he had no idea why she'd suddenly vanished.

It didn't take a genius to know what was coming next; even with my hangover, I was able to surmise it was none other than the lovely Camilla lurking behind the stable doors waiting to pick up the pieces of the Farrier's broken heart. The Farrier was vulnerable, and unfortunately fell into the arms of Camilla.

The story didn't end there, which was unfortunate for me but I suppose I wasn't going anywhere; after all, how else was I going to celebrate my birthday? It couldn't get any better than a dead Frisky Pensioner and a day spent with the Farrier. 'Sod it,' I thought to myself as I poured the leftover Malibu into a tumbler and took a swig – hair of the dog and all that, it was my birthday after all.

'I had no idea Bert was your father,'

He nodded.

'Not many people do, it's a long story,' he answered taking a sip of his drink then making a weird sound which sounded like a sob.

'Well, I'm not going anywhere,' I encouraged. Matt would most definitely be out for a while with the children so I might as well listen to him, he looked like he needed a shoulder to cry on.

'All communication with my father had become strained, he was disappointed in me.'

I shifted in my chair and tucked my feet under my body, making myself more comfortable. His eyes were sad. He continued.

'I had ambition, I wanted a career, I didn't want to follow in my father's footsteps to become a factory worker in a mundane job doing the same thing day in and day out, I love the outside, that is what makes me tick.'

I didn't interrupt him, I stayed silent while I sipped my drink.

'He never listened to me, and when he was angry he would thump his hand on the table and order me to do what he said, but when I stood up to him, he didn't like it. I always had the desire to work with animals so I persevered. It caused numerous arguments between him and my mother, she would often tell my father to calm his temper down and that would make him worse. I would often hear her sobs from the living room late at night while he was out working the night shift.'

'How awful,' I agreed.

'The bottom line is we tolerated each other, he had no qualms in reminding me who the head of the household was and to be honest when I became close to Camilla this was my escape route.'

'What do you mean?' I enquired tentatively.

'It meant I could set up house with Camilla and move out of my childhood home.'

'Did you see much of your parents after you had moved out?'

'There was the odd Sunday lunch, or special occasion like Christmas. This one Christmas, seven years ago, was when all communications halted. I remember it like it was yesterday.' The Farrier looked down at his drink and paused.

'I noticed Camilla had been gone for a while after lunch. I was chatting with my mother when I was aware my father wasn't in the room either and both of them had now disappeared for some time. I went in search of my new wife and entered the study to find them both in what seemed like a rather compromising position. Camilla swore blind that her frisky father-in-law had made numerous passes and that he was very domineering and she told me she felt intimidated by him.'

From what I had seen of Camilla Noland in the past year, I was very much surprised that that woman would feel intimated by anyone.

'Camilla was very convincing, we were still in our honeymoon stage of marriage and I knew my father could be very persuasive and somewhat scary so I believed her, I stood up for my wife and ultimately this led to the complete breakdown in the relationship between me and my father.'

Nooo! He was kidding me; I was sitting there believing Camilla had played a blinder.

'What was your mother's take on all this, if you don't mind me asking?'

He shrugged his shoulders.

'She blamed Camilla and supported my father. There was no love lost between the pair of them due to an argument that took place on our wedding day. Camilla's stubborn nature refused to take on the family name of Fletcher-Parker; she wanted to keep her maiden name.'

I gasped in astonishment and gave a tiny shake of my head. Ah ha, I thought to myself, no wonder it had never crossed my mind that these people were related.

The Farrier continued for a while longer explaining that his mother had also had to contend with the reputation of her own husband; she wasn't daft and knew her husband was a serial womaniser, but she lived in fear of his temper and his manipulating ways, and so divorce simply wasn't an option. Bert would have made life so difficult for her that, in order to keep a roof over her head for the next thirty years, she chose to grin and bear her husband's antics and to take his side in the rift with his son.

However, Iris had often threatened that she would disappear one day, and years ago, the Farrier had discovered numerous bank statements in his mother's name with regular deposits of money. He had no doubt she had been planning her escape route for some time and had secretly been scrimping, saving, and siphoning off her house- keeping money without his father's knowledge. Her best friend Jean had upped and left the village a couple of years ago to begin a new life in Spain and had successfully started up her own café business and he knew his mother had kept in touch with her by email. Jean had often tried to persuade his mother to run off and join her, and start a new life in sunnier climes.

It was now approaching late afternoon; there didn't seem much point in my getting dressed today, and the Farrier didn't appear to be leaving anytime soon. By this part of the story we had moved into the living room; the Farrier was beginning to make himself at home, plumping up the cushions around him then sinking into the leather bucket chair while he continued his tale. I heard the front door open and the chatter of the children; Matt's rosy-cheeked face peered around the living room door 'Anyone for a cuppa? I'm parched.'

In sync, the Farrier and I nodded our heads.

The Farrier's plan was to move into his father, the Frisky Pensioner's house. Well, I suppose that made sense now his mother was gone too, the property was standing empty. Since his split with the delightful Camilla, due to her adulterous ways with the gentleman named Elvis from the local eatery last year, the Farrier had moved out of the family home he had shared with her, and resided in a rented property not too far from the village.

That property was nothing special; it was a flat, a bachelor pad. The décor lacked a homely feel with its dull grey and black colour scheme and brown shag pile carpet which no doubt had seen more than its fair share of action over the years. It required a woman's touch but it was a temporary stopgap until their family home was sold. It was simply somewhere to lay his head away from the drama of his marriage breakup.

'It will make life easier for me if I move back to the village as I'm looking after my daughter Rosie on my own now; at least this way she can remain at the same school and have a permanent home now her mother has also gone.' explained the Farrier. I knew Rosie; she was the same age as Samuel, and in his class at school.

Had I just heard him right? I felt my hangover completely lift as I drained the last remaining traces of Malibu out of the tumbler; did he just say Camilla Noland had left the village?

Sitting upright, 'Wait, did you say Camilla has left the village?' I asked.

'Yes, the silly woman has accumulated enormous debts from her saddlery business that was linked to the mortgage. She took care of all the financial arrangements when we were together.'

Gosh, that was certainly unlucky for the Farrier, who wouldn't receive any financial benefit from that situation. Things couldn't get much worse for him at the moment.

It would seem that the bailiffs lacked festive spirit and had hammered on her door the day after Boxing Day. They had stripped the house of all her belongings and reclaimed the property. The lady of the manor had well and truly fallen on hard times.

At school, her false, doting mother routine that she liked to put on in front of the teachers and headmistress did not fool anyone. She would ostentatiously smother Rosie in kisses and boast about her private violin tuition and drama lessons. Yet it was a known fact that Camilla hadn't turned up at any school functions since Rosie started at primary school. It wouldn't surprise anyone that Camilla had no qualms in abandoning their only daughter on the Farrier's rented doorstep with a note scribbled, 'Rosie's all yours.' It was suggested Camilla had ridden off on the back of her horse without a second thought about anyone or anything but of course she had driven off in her car with very few possessions to her name.

It had only been a few hours since the body of the Frisky Pensioner had been removed and we had already become acquainted with our new neighbours – The Farrier and his only daughter Rosie, who was currently enjoying herself at a friend's birthday party.

Suddenly I heard the front door open and we were hit by a blast of freezing cold air. We looked up to find a tear-stricken Penelope standing in front of us.

It had only been a few hours since Rupert had returned home to make peace with his wife and judging by the look on her face it hadn't gone too well.

The Farrier was up and out of his chair faster than a horse racing in the Grand National and took this opportunity to scarper back to his new home, as she announced, 'I've left him, I've finally left Rupert.'

CHAPTER 3

Penelope looked exhausted and not at her best, as might be expected under the circumstances. She plonked herself down on the warm chair; the same one that the Farrier had just vacated. I anticipated an interrogation on why the Farrier was visiting me on my birthday but surprisingly she was preoccupied and no questions were asked.

Matt popped his head around the door to see who it was and then swiftly decided to retreat to the playroom with the children. He rolled his eyes when he saw it was a tear-stricken Penelope.

'I've left Rupert,' she repeated.

I'd heard her very loud and very clear the first time. I wasn't sure why I needed to know any of this; what business was it of mine? Not only had Penelope gatecrashed my New Year's Eve party she also seemed hell-bent on wrecking my birthday. I had expected 'a happy birthday,' at least but it was obvious I was expecting a little too much, for the next words that left her mouth made me sit up and question whether my brain was functioning correctly.

'Could I possibly stay here tonight?'

I felt my whole body go into some sort of weird seizure, I started to sweat uncontrollably – I hoped this wasn't the beginning of the menopause; I'd heard about women starting really young but surely not at thirty-five. Why in God's name did Penelope want to stay here? What about Little Jonny and Annabel, their children? Where were they? Surely, she would want them with her. And why couldn't she have kicked Rupert out and forced him to find a bed for the night? Let's face it, Rupert was quite the ladies' man, and there would have probably been numerous warm beds where he could have spent the night.

Penelope, clearly, was eagerly waiting my reply. Frisky Pensioner would not be the only man in the village dying of a heart attack today if I suggested to Matt that we had an overnight guest. It was at this precise moment that I made the conscious decision to change the date of my birthday and not reveal it to anyone. I lost myself in a massive daydream as I imagined myself sitting on a beach sipping a cool beer, eating cake with not another soul in sight. I was brought back to the real world when Penelope stated, 'Little Jonny and Annabel must be freezing waiting outside in the car.' I stared at Penelope in amazement, my mouth falling open. I'd assumed they were at home with Rupert.

I hit planet earth with a bump as my brain slowly digested her words. That was one of my New Year's resolutions out of the window straightaway – I will not be a doormat. However, what could I do? Penelope was requesting my help and I didn't think this was the appropriate time to upset her further so the words left my mouth, 'Of course you can stay; go and retrieve those poor children from the car and let me dish up my birthday cake with hot chocolate for everyone.'

'I knew you would say yes,' she gushed.

I paused; 'One night only Penelope, otherwise you will not be the only one getting divorced.'

After a few minutes, I wearily climbed the stairs to check on my own children; Eva, Samuel, Matilda and Daisy had been extremely quiet all day. Peering around Eva's bedroom door I could see from the corner of my eye that three of the children were snuggled under Eva's duvet watching *Back to the Future* while eating their body weight in chocolate from their Christmas selection boxes. Matt must have moved Daisy's playpen in to the bedroom because she was quite happily throwing her toys around whilst gurgling happily. I certainly wasn't going to win any Mother of the Day awards today.

Unquestionably, an early night was needed for all including me, as tomorrow was January 2nd, the day the school playground would be full of mothers displaying their range of new coats, bags and boots. This would be the day BB (Botox Bernie) would be in her element. She would have an extra spring in her step while parading her assortment of Christmas gifts such as Ugg boots, or a counterfeit designer coat, and her usual quantity of diamond-encrusted jewellery that bore a resemblance to the cheap tat that can be purchased from the local market. Nevertheless, I knew now exactly how she had accumulated her so-called gifts, and exactly how she had been earning her money if her appearance outside the Frisky Pensioner's abode was anything to go by. It was very different from the spiel she had spun, to anyone that would listen, that gave us all the impression she was a successful high-flying business woman; there had been nothing high-flying about that flea-ridden chinchilla she had been sporting this morning.

Not only would we have the likes of BB showing off her new gifts to anyone unfortunate enough to make eye contact with her but we'd also have the mothers who would enter the playground dressed in tight leggings, new trainers and headbands. They'd strut around wearing the latest Garmin watch, having downloaded the newest fitness app and raiding Tesco's shelves for skipping ropes and dumbbells. Usually after a week, these mothers had broken all New Year's resolutions, had wasted their money on their new fitness regime, and returned to doing what they knew best, ladies that lunch. Their comfort zones would be fully restored while they sipped Pinot Grigio and slated anyone with a pulse at the Petty Tedious Army (PTA) meetings. Their usual meeting place was the quaint bistro on the outskirts of the village run by a husband and wife team. The charming restaurant is loved by all the locals, and has stood the test of time; it is still popular whilst other eateries have come and gone. It is a cosy, homely scene with low ceilings and huge fireplaces; hundreds of flickering candles light up the little nooks. It is a perfect combination for the PTA to conduct their meetings away from the noise of the bar.

'Would you children like to come down for cake and hot chocolate' I asked.

I was sure with the amount of additives they had already piled into their systems today that a few more wouldn't do them any harm. 'Little Jonny and Annabel are also here,' I continued, 'and will be staying tonight.'

There was no denying that Matt had been fantastic today, he had supplied all visitors with cups of tea and snacks whilst cleaning up and now he had excelled himself with making up all the beds for our latest visitors.

Gathering around the kitchen table, the children chatted and sat down at the table. Matt poured mugs of hot chocolate for everyone whilst Eva placed some token candles on the cake. Samuel was excited about lighting the candles, and with careful supervision, he struck the match and lit each one. The candles were now burning brightly. Matilda wrapped her arms around me and gave me a quick hug before plonking herself down on the chair and I balanced Daisy in my arms. I quickly planted a kiss on the tops of their heads. Samuel rapped his knuckles on the table while Matilda raised her finger to her lips and shushed everyone.

Silence.

Eva counted to three and everyone sang a joyful rendition of happy birthday.

I can honestly say that, a few months back, if anyone had even suggested I would be spending my birthday with Penelope (we had had a big falling out the previous year), I would have thought they were very insane. However, there we all were standing in my kitchen like long lost friends. She watched me blow out the candles on my cake whilst I made my wish. I knew my wish wouldn't be granted; the genie in my lamp was on annual leave, and it was too far-fetched to believe that Rupert would knock on the door and whisk his wife and children back home so they could all live happily ever after – or at least have a peaceful night. I was deeply annoyed with myself that I had wasted my wish.

I sliced up the cake and placed the pieces onto the paper plates left over from the buffet the night before. 'It's sponge with homemade raspberry jam,' I said, handing Penelope a plate. She hesitated, taking the plate from me but with her eyes firmly locked on a larger slice still on the table. Quickly she shoved the plate in her hand straight into the palm of little Jonny's; it felt like we were playing pass the parcel. Grasping the bigger slice, Penelope completely devoured it in a couple of mouthfuls.

After all the cake was consumed and hot chocolate glugged down, the children all went back upstairs. I felt awful, not only in the physical sense, but because I had abandoned the children all day and wasn't even sure if they had eaten any proper food. Eva settled down with a book to read. Little Jonny and Annabel shared Samuel's room for the night while he lay down on the camp bed in Matilda's room. My youngest child Daisy was fast asleep before I could even kiss her goodnight on her forehead.

As birthdays go, I was glad it was drawing to a close – one dead pensioner (Mr F-P), one prostitute (Botox Bernie) and one new best friend (Penelope) who I didn't want. Taking the waste-paper basket, which was overflowing, I wandered back downstairs and grabbed the equally full recycle bin from the kitchen, and then ventured onto the drive to empty them. The snow was still falling lightly all around me. Looking over towards the Farrier's house the street lamp opposite lit up his front window. I could see him sitting in a chair in his living room; his daughter, now back from her friend's house was perched beside him hugging a warm drink; he was reading her a story. Even though today, he had lost his father, I had a feeling this would be a new start for them both. The house might be a little too big for them both, but at least there was no mortgage so they would probably have enough to live on. Over the years, he had visited his parents infrequently. Today, he had seemed a gentle, caring soul and I really warmed to him. I genuinely hoped the coming year would bring him happiness.

The dog decided to leave the cold conservatory as Matt lit the fire in the living room. Penelope had poured herself a glass of the Malibu and was looking extremely comfortable and very much at home watching television with her feet perched on top of my footstool.

Matt had a strained looked on his face as he mouthed across the room at me, 'but it's your birthday.' I knew it was my birthday, but what was with his disappointed look and sad puppy-dog eyes. I shrugged my shoulders back at him and mouthed, 'I know, it's the same date every year.'

Penelope was unaware of our silent conversation going on around her; she was glued to the television watching the New

Year's episode of Morecombe and Wise. Matt stared down at his feet sulkily. Then it hit me; I knew exactly what his sulk was about; it was his wife's birthday so what would that mean to any living bloke with a pulse? That would mean, if he was a betting man, Paddy Powers' odds would be a dead cert – he expected sex tonight. Typical bloke, it could be the anniversary of your dead goldfish's birthday, the one you won at the fairground, the one that only survived two days in the plastic bag, but was now a part of the family, and your husband would still expect sex. The pressure on any woman on birthdays, anniversaries and bar mitzvahs was just excessive.

'Well, let me tell you,' I mouthed back at his sulky face, 'it's my birthday, not yours, so huff away.'

Suddenly, Penelope bolted upright as if she had caught sight of a ghost. It would be just my luck that Frisky Pensioner had returned in spirit for one last visit before he entered through the gates up above. But no, she had remembered she had forgotten the children's bags and clothes for their return to school in the morning. I noticed she had remembered a full wardrobe for herself though, judging by the overflowing holdall at her feet no doubt consisting of numerous outfits – thinking about it – way too many outfits for just one night's stay.

'I need you to go back to the house and retrieve the children's clothes,' she piped up.

Why me? They were her children, I had not one ounce of enthusiasm to roam out into the cold, dark night. Why did I need to do anything? A hot sweat started to rise up my body again but I convinced myself it was more angry than menopausal. Penelope lifted her head to mine and I stared straight into her eyes.

'I'm sorry it's bad news Penelope, I'd rather lance off a wart than get myself dressed and go out in the freezing cold ... you are on your own.'

The cheek of the woman! She hadn't even had the grace to wish me a happy birthday. I was a little peeved at always being treated like a doormat by my so-called friend, and that's a friend in the loosest sense of the word. It was plain to see Penelope was only trying to salvage our friendship, since Camilla Noland, her latest best friend, had left the village.

Penelope was a little taken aback by my slight outburst. I had wanted to stand up to this woman for a long time; this year I wasn't going to let myself down. I was going to put myself first for a change and if she didn't like it ... well ...

Almost immediately, Penelope activated her tear ducts and the waterworks commenced – no chance of a drought this year. She and Rupert could possibly be up for joint nominations for the most dramatic performance at this year's Oscars. 'Please, please at least come with me, I can't face Rupert on my own.'

Rupert was definitely the more intelligent one out of the two of them; why had he managed to wangle staying in the family home with a fridge full of food watching the telly without any interruption?

I rose out of the chair and eyeballed Penelope. 'We had better be quick.' I growled at her.

I wasn't in the least bit thrilled embarking on operation collect children's clothing on New Year's Day at this time of night in the snow.

'Well that showed her,' mouthed Matt from the corner of the room with a knowing smile on his face. I felt a prickle of annoyance towards him and scowled at him. He needed to remember to keep his sarcastic remarks to himself, otherwise his sex ban wouldn't just be on my birthday.

CHAPTER 4

I didn't feel brave enough to drive in such appalling weather conditions. Granted it wasn't very far, but the roads would be treacherous. I located my phone and dialled the number of the local taxi firm; at least if any car was going to slide through a hedge it wasn't going to be mine. The number connected and an irate woman said, 'Yes!' Well, you could hear by the enthusiasm in her voice that she was chuffed to be working on New Year's Day.

I was just about to speak when she screamed at me down the receiver, 'It's on its way!'

'What's on its way?' I innocently asked.

'The taxi is on its way, it's just round the next corner.'

'How can the taxi possibly be on its way? I haven't even ordered the bloody thing yet.'

My patience was beginning to wear a little thin. I rattled my car keys in Penelope's direction. I quickly swapped my slippers for wellies and stomped down the path towards the car. I was still dressed in my onesie, smelling, if I'm truly honest, worse than BB's latest perfume; I hadn't been near a shower all day.

The car slid down the lane on the icy road, the sky was darkened with snow and the street lamps were barely visible through the thickly falling flakes. The only reliable light source we had to guide us back to Penelope's house was the car's headlights. There was no denying the night had an eerie feel about it. There was not a single person or car in sight. Well, there wouldn't be would there? Even the flipping taxi that was meant to be round the next corner was nowhere to be seen. Everyone else had the common sense to stay indoors, curled up in the warmth with a drink whilst munching on leftover turkey sandwiches. Mercifully, Penelope didn't speak a word on the short journey to her house.

I pulled up outside her house, well when I say pulled up, what I actually mean is the car bumped up the curb slamming straight into her recycle bin which proceeded to spill the contents of her rubbish all over the front garden. The house was in complete darkness, which was strange as Rupert was meant to be home. Penelope stepped over an empty can of baked beans in the snow as she glared at me. Placing the key into the lock, she pushed the front door ajar. We both stood like statues for a moment as we witnessed some sort of flashing emerging from the living room, then looked at each other. 'We have burglars,' she whispered. 'Bloody hell, the house is being robbed!'

So not only had Frisky Pensioner died revealing BB as a budget prostitute, or that the Farrier had moved in next-door-but-one, and that Penelope had gatecrashed my house, Wearing only my onesie, I was about to come face-to-face with a burglar on my birthday. I was not sure who would be more scared, me or him.

Penelope opened the cloakroom door slowly, and bending down, she grabbed one of Rupert's work boots from the shoe rack, the type with a steel toecap, and forced it into my hand. Why give it to me? Did she expect me to pummel the burglar to death?

We stood as still as possible; I could swear that my heart was pounding so fast it was jumping out of my chest. We listened carefully to a faint moaning sound. Maybe the burglar was in distress, wounded. Possibly, he had sliced his leg on the broken windowpane as he clambered through. We took very small steps, tiptoeing towards the living room door. We both froze to the spot. I mouthed at Penelope, 'What's the plan?' Well, she was no bloody use as she shrugged her shoulders back in return.

My instincts kicked in; I held my left hand up towards Penelope and as I practised my 3-2-1 with my fingers – I burst through the door armed with Rupert's boot in my right hand.

Penelope pushed through the door behind me nearly tipping me off balance shouting, 'Let's have him,' at the top of her voice – giving the impression she was as hard as nails.

There he was, lying on the settee with the lights dimmed. I was distracted by the slight moaning sound escaping from the television. Squinting, I witnessed a naked couple in a very compromising position. Rupert was startled and appeared to be in mid flow – his trousers and boxer shorts pushed down to his ankles. I couldn't believe my eyes as I followed the movement of his hand and realised he was right in the middle of jerking his turkey; he was having a five knuckle shuffle and we weren't talking Strictly Come Dancing!

Rupert's New Year's Day was visibly going with a bang; Penelope leaving him had noticeably not affected his mojo one bit.

'You dirty bastard,' Penelope screeched snatching the boot from my grasp and lobbing it straight at Rupert's head. Rupert tried to dodge the flying boot but with no success, he fell flat on his back tripping up over his own trousers that were tangled around his legs. The boot hit Rupert square in the face. I was quite impressed with Penelope's aim. However, Rupert's aim wasn't as accurate as I noticed he had already shot his bodily fluids at some point all over the lovely, deep shag pile carpet. In all honesty, I didn't know where to look, but as Rupert was now sprawled out on the floor trying to grab his pants I took the opportunity to have a sneaky peep. Well, I knew I would never have an affair with Mr Kensington, but I was curious to see what he had to offer.

'Wow … it's really not all that big,' I thought to myself, handing him a tissue from the box that was strategically placed next to the sofa. I didn't know what all the fuss was about; it wasn't even average which just led me to ponder what the entire population of women in the village had seen in him? I concluded it must be either his personality, or that he actually knew what to do with it. Luckily, for me, I was never going to find out.

What do we do now? The three of us were just standing there awkwardly. Rupert didn't know whether to pull his trousers up or hold his head that by now had probably begun to throb.

I was going to make a comment about the three wise monkeys, as I undoubtedly would be saying nothing after hearing and seeing all. The porn film was still playing out in the background with a woman on the screen doing; well actually, I don't quite know what she was doing. I grabbed the remote control and switched it off and the room fell into complete darkness. I was waiting for Rupert to say, 'I was watching that,' but I think at this point he didn't know where the other boot was and valued his life. As we were plunged into darkness my phone beeped and lit up with a text message, I swiped the screen to see a message from Matt.

'Where are you? You have been ages. x'

'Caught Rupert exercising his right arm whilst watching porn, not a birthday present I was expecting; it would be funny if it wasn't so tragic. x'

Penelope was seething and Rupert was not a pretty sight. I took this as a cue to abandon the scene fast by offering to retrieve the children's clothes from their bedrooms, and left the soon-to-be-divorced couple to it.

I heard Penelope screaming at Rupert while I opened the children's wardrobes and stuffed clean clothes for the morning into carrier bags. I located the wash bags and loaded them up with the children's toothbrushes, and then grabbed a couple of teddy bears off their beds.

My phone beeped with another text message from Matt. *'Well, at least someone is getting some action tonight!'*

When I returned downstairs with the children's clothes, Penelope was already outside sitting in the freezing car waiting for me. Rupert was now standing sheepishly in the living room doorway with his trousers finally pulled up. I couldn't bring myself to make eye contact. I found myself still staring at his lower regions.

'Your zip is undone,' I stated, marching straight past him and shutting the front door behind me.

We made the short drive home in the same appalling weather conditions, and in complete silence. Well what did we have to chatter about? I'm not sure we were up to comparing notes on men's body parts

We arrived back at the house and sat down in front of the roaring fire to defrost. Matt was pretending nothing had happened but I knew by the look on his face after reading my text message that he was dying to laugh at the fact Rupert had been caught. He'd rustled up a tray of leftover sandwiches and placed them down on the coffee table in front of us and poured us each a glass of wine. I was extremely hungry and seemed to have worked up an appetite in the last hour. Penelope looked worn out; give her her due, enough was enough and she had finally made the brave decision to leave Rupert, which not only meant she was single but it catapulted Little Jonny and Annabel into a new set of statistics – children that come from a broken home.

While sitting in her chair and sipping her wine, Penelope appeared agitated.

'It could only happen to me; I thought I was being burgled and what do we find but Rupert making his own entertainment. I have to say though, when I glimpsed at the telly screen I wanted to pause the movie (movie in the lowest sense of the word), but I could have sworn the woman on the screen looked like Botox Bernie, that mother from the school playground.'

That thought *had* crossed my mind; something told me we had barely scratched the surface of the great BB and what she got up to in her spare time. Blimey, I had forgotten Penelope hadn't been present to witness Frisky Pensioner's body being removed and BB sporting the 'classy look' in her flea-ridden chinchilla, and of course, she was unaware that the Farrier had acquired a new property.

CHAPTER 5

The following morning, the house was run like a military operation; there were six children to wake up, feed and get ready for school and nursery school. I woke up an hour before the chaos started and grabbed a quick shower. I was back on Planet Earth, clean and looking as if I belonged in the land of the living. That was it. The Christmas holidays were over, we were back to the same routine, taking our lives into our own hands as I survived the pretentious mothers loitering at the school gates each day – my two least favourite words: school and gates.

I needed to prepare myself mentally for the next six weeks and then I would be rewarded with a week off to recharge my batteries during half-term.

I rallied all the children round, washed, dressed, clothed them, and then dished up bowls of cereal. As I placed the empty packets into the recycling bin, I thought I had never seen boxes of Cheerios be demolished so fast. A quick brush of the teeth and we were nearly ready to go. I packed satchels with lunch boxes full of tuna mayonnaise sandwiches made with chunky malted bread, and slices of leftover birthday cake wrapped up in a serviette – not forgetting leaky water bottles – Father Christmas had failed to remember to bring new ones – it must be his age. The children were bundled up warm with their feet stuffed into snow boots, their bodies wrapped up tightly in their coats, and woolly scarves draped around their necks to keep the warmth from escaping. I opened the door to start the trudge through the crisp snow when I realised Penelope hadn't emerged from her slumbers.

'Penelope, it's time for the school run, are you ready?' I shouted up the stairs.

All six pairs of eyes looked up the stairs as Penelope appeared in her fluffy slippers and PJs, with her hair tied back in a bobble and not a scrap of make-up in sight, giving the impression she wasn't about to go anywhere.

'I'm sorry, I can't face the school run today,' she snivelled. 'Everyone will be talking about me. Will you take the children?' she asked, as she dropped her head and sniffled away her tears.

I knew from the antics of yesterday that I could presume Penelope was newly separated with a good chance of becoming divorced. It wasn't that I lacked sympathy; I did truly feel her pain – which I had a feeling would also become my pain – but the children still needed stability from their mother and walking with them to the playground on the first day of their new term at school would have been a good start. Penelope needed to grasp the fact that some of the mothers do have a life other than at the school gates, and are not interested in tittle-tattle of any sort. But yes, granted there were others who thrived on gossip. Those mothers tended to stick out like a sore thumb; the ones you knew to avoid. They would usually congregate outside the gates in their little cliques with their posh pooches. Even the bloody dog would be wearing a Barbour jacket but I was sure it would be a fake, just like theirs.

I wasn't sure how Penelope concluded she would be the topic of conversation in the school playground as there was only Matt and me who knew of the split and Rupert's leisure activity from the previous night, and I wouldn't be sharing that misdemeanour with anyone at the school gate.

Penelope was lucky that Camilla Noland had left the village, if the Farrier's account of events was true, otherwise, there would have been a possibility that the whole village would have found out by now – Camilla was a terrible gossip. Anyway, I think Penelope was worrying over nothing. Surely, the topic of conversation would more than likely be the antics of BB that had sealed Frisky Pensioner's fate. Actually, I owed BB; that was a job well done.

I hurried the older children out of the door; their arms interlocked to steady themselves and to avoid falling over onto the ice. After strapping Matilda and Daisy into the pushchair, I set off through the slush towards the end of the drive. Glancing over at the Farrier's house, I noticed he was closing his front door behind him and that he and his daughter were en route to the school playground.

I waved, and he smiled back at me. They slipped their way down the path and caught up with the train of children. His daughter Rosie tagged onto Annabel, Penelope's daughter, who was holding up the rear.

'How are you this morning? Did you both settle OK in the house?' I asked the Farrier in my most pleasant neighbourly manner.

'It felt strange at first; once Rosie had fallen asleep, I helped myself to sleep with a couple of glasses of whisky. Funnily enough, there was no ice in the freezer but I did find a set of false teeth in a glass in a cupboard,' he replied.

'New start, New Year; please tell me you didn't drink from the glass with the teeth?' I said, and winked.

He laughed. 'Of course I didn't, but I just kept thinking they were going to start chattering at me and have a conversation.'

I didn't really know what to make of the Farrier. I didn't know if he had a lady in his life; he'd probably had a bellyful after his ex-wife. As far as I could judge, from yesterday, and this morning on the walk to school, he was a caring man, who looked after his daughter beautifully.

This wasn't the impression that Penelope had given me, but we all should know never to judge a person on another person's opinion, especially when it's Penelope's fuelled by Camilla Noland.

By the time we reached the school gates, the cold had captured our noses and each of us looked like a relation of Rudolf. The cliques were gathered as usual in their usual spots on the playground, and even with the snow on the ground, you knew which territory you belonged to. I could hear BB, but took a while to locate her, now she was minus the flea-ridden chinchilla. She was dressed in a puffa jacket and was sporting new Ugg boots – probably fake – but such different attire from that of forty-eight hours ago. The Farrier tapped my arm and told me he would catch me later on. He walked off along the gritted path in the of the school office probably to inform the teachers of Camilla's abandonment of their only daughter, the death of his father, and a change of address.

I was standing in a corner of the playground, when I was suddenly aware that heads were turning in my direction. Maybe Penelope was correct, maybe they did all know what Rupert had been up to last night, and the fact she had left him high and dry.

Then I realised that they weren't looking at me, but at a woman standing next to me, who was busy reassuring her daughter that today would be okay. A new mother; the Playground Mafia would be delighted and no doubt would be desperate to subject her to a full interrogation. They would soon be firing questions at her and trying to uncover her life story – her husband, his salary and more importantly what level reading book her daughter was on. Even the mother with the small pooch wearing the fake Barbour jacket that I had passed on my way into the playground had now tied the dog up at the gate and assembled with the rest of the clique so she wouldn't miss a trick.

This time last year, that had been me. I wanted to tell the mother to run – to run like hell and get out of here. BB was straining her neck to catch a glimpse of the competition, let's face it, not much competition as this woman didn't look like a hooker and actually appeared quite normal. In a bizarre twist of events, I noticed BB turn away almost immediately after spotting the new mum. It was a toss-up as to whether BB was going to throw up, pass out or maybe have a heart attack like her love interest had forty-eight hours earlier. Something wasn't quite right; BB had become very quiet way too quickly. This to me suggested only one thing; there was history between these two women. There was more to her reaction than met the eye. If a stranger could silence BB in less than two minutes then I had an inkling she was going to be my kind of friend.

The mother was quite ordinary looking. She was of average height, and average build with plain bobbed brown hair. Her face wasn't caked in make-up; her fingernails were clean; nothing out of the ordinary to report. She would be like a lamb to the slaughter once the Playground Mafia got their claws into her. She smiled at me.

'Hi I'm Melanie, as you can probably guess, we are new. I'm not sure if it's worse for the mother or the child on the first day of a new school.'

'Pleased to meet you, I'm Rachel,' I said with a friendly smile and stretched out my hand.

'I feel like I'm under scrutiny,' she grinned grasping hold of my hand and shaking it.

She was being watched all right, except by BB. The majority of the playground mothers were twisting their heads in our direction.

'Don't worry about that lot; I was new a little while back. Are you living in the village?'

'Yes, we've moved into the house that is set amongst those beautiful acres of land on the outskirts of the village, but unfortunately the acres belong to the local farmer not us. We can't grumble though, it does provide us with some fantastic scenery. The house was repossessed from its previous owner about a month ago and I couldn't believe my luck when we purchased it at an unbelievable bargain price. Well, when I say us, I mean my daughter and me; I've been a single mum for years. Well, since the day she was born,' she added.

'Are you from this area originally then?' I enquired.

'Years ago I lived around here, it didn't work out at the time but I decided to move back recently, so here I am.'

I did wonder to myself why it hadn't worked out but it wasn't my place to ask her. That was her business. We had only just met.

Suddenly it struck me like a bolt of lightning; the property she had purchased was Camilla's old gaff, the one that had been repossessed. Therefore, the Farrier's account was true, but I'm not sure why I doubted that it would be, as what did he have to hide?

'How many children do you have?' Melanie asked.'

'I'm a glutton for punishment, These four belong to me,' I said patting their heads and naming them, Eva, Samuel, Matilda and Daisy and this is Little Jonny and Annabel who came for a sleepover.'

The children looked up at Melanie and smiled.

Wow! You have four of the little people, you must have the patience of a saint,' Melanie said admiringly.

'Something like that; luckily for me they are all very well-behaved children – must take after their mother,' I joked.

Melanie laughed.

'This is Dotty,' I have just the one daughter.

'Hello Dotty, how are you?'

'She's a little shy and probably a little anxious with it being her first day.'

Squatting down before Dotty I said 'Eva and Samuel were new last year; it's a lovely school and you don't have anything to worry about. This is Matilda and Daisy and they have their mornings at pre-school and nursery.'

Dotty looked up and smiled but still didn't say anything.

'Such an adorable name, Dotty,' I said to Melanie.

'Yes she was named after my Great Gran.'

'The bell is about to ring, but if Dotty would like to come over and play to help her settle in please feel free to let me know; we could have a coffee too,' I suggested.

'Absolutely, thank you, what a lovely idea. I will certainly take you up on the offer. It is so very kind of you,' Melanie smiled. At that very moment, the bell sounded and all the children scampered off over the brown gritted ground towards their lines.

Melanie walked Dotty towards her teacher who promptly took her hand and with a huge friendly smile welcomed her to the school.

'Don't worry Mum, she will be absolutely fine but please feel free to telephone at lunchtime if you would like an update,' suggested the kind teacher.

After kissing their children on the tops of their heads and checking out the new designer coats of other kids, the wave of mothers turned and headed up the playground towards the school gate.

Melanie was walking back towards me so I waited.

'Was Dotty OK?' I enquired.

'Yes, she went in with no trouble at all,' Melanie replied, relieved. 'It's such a worry when they start a new school.'

Just at that moment, BB passed in front of us, glared awkwardly at Melanie, and then turned away sheepishly confirming my impression that there was history between the two of them.

'Blimey! Do you two know each other?' I enquired.

Melanie raked her fingers through her hair. 'Our paths have crossed before. Do you have time for that coffee now? I can tell you all about it.'

I had things to do today: first on my list was to evict Penelope before she decided to get her feet firmly under our table, and the second was a visit to the lovely new shop in the next town that sold all sorts of crafty things. However, my interest was certainly piqued, and curiosity got the better of me.

'Of course,' I answered. 'There's a quaint little coffee shop that's just opened near the post office; it's walking distance and near the pre-school so I will drop the children off there first. You can walk with me if you like.'

'Perfect,' came Melanie's reply.

CHAPTER 6

The waitress clunked the floral teacups down onto the table that was covered in an equally floral, lace-edged tablecloth. We both ordered a toasted teacake too.

Melanie started her story; and I settled into my chair, and poured us each a cup of tea. I buttered the teacake, which melted instantly.

'I've certainly come across Bernie,' she began. 'Is she a friend of yours?'

Now there was a question. Was BB a friend of mine? At first I hesitated with my answer; it was without a doubt that she had done me a favour by bringing about the untimely end of the Frisky Pensioner, but maybe it was a little unethical to shake her hand for that achievement.

'No friend of mine,' I mused aloud.

'I bumped in to Bernie at antenatal classes, her bump was neater than mine, well in fact it was neater than everyone's and of course she liked to tell us all,' Melanie began.

'I bet she was an expectant mother's magazine dream,' I grinned.

'Exactly!' Melanie laughed. 'She was different from all us normal mums, she stood out from the crowd with her latest designer maternity wear snuggling around her bump. She must have spent a fortune in hair and nail salons during her pregnancy. Immaculately groomed she was.'

I nodded my head then took a sip from my cuppa, Melanie carried on.

'Whereas me, I had the pregnancy from hell, I fought morning sickness every day and spent most of the day stuffing my face with ginger biscuits to try to curb the nausea. My weight gain was not just baby!'

I laughed; I knew exactly where Melanie was coming from. 'You sound just like me,' I replied.

'Most of the antenatal group were the same. We were happy to turn up in our husband's over-stretched baggy jumpers, and scrape our hair back, which was permanently tied up in a bobble due to the constant view of the bottom of the toilet – those women who don't suffer from morning sickness are so lucky.'

'Most definitely,' I agreed, thinking back to all my pregnancies. 'I was all for comfort.'

'My ex-partner was always busy and rarely attended the classes with me. He was always at the gym enjoying his time before we were tied down to routine, nappies and nights falling asleep in front of brain-numbing telly.'

Typical bloke, I thought to myself.

'Bernie also attended the classes on her own. She was an extremely vocal pregnant mother and the group knew her life story after only week two of the class, well, all except the father. There was no sign of a father, she never spoke of him.'

BB was certainly vocal. My mind wandered back to the scene outside the Frisky Pensioner's house on New Year's Day.

'She portrayed herself as a successful business woman to the rest of the group.'

'I bet she did,' I smirked, knowing what type of business BB was in.

'Apparently she had built her business up from scratch, winning awards here, there, and everywhere. At first we were all in awe of her string of successes; everything she touched turned to gold. She even reminisced about her school days, fabricating stories that she was elected by her peers to represent the school as Head Girl.'

I nearly spat out my tea. BB didn't seem the 'correct calibre' to represent any school as Head Girl.

'We were all hoodwinked into believing her academic career was textbook; super brainy and she had more qualifications than Professor Brian Cox.'

I sat wondering if we were actually talking about the same person.

'All her exam results were no less than an A, her A-Levels were a breeze and she easily secured a place at her first choice of University – Oxford of course.'

'Only the best for Bernie,' I sniggered.

I was fascinated by this story; this wasn't the BB I knew. The BB I knew didn't give the impression she was a super academic, but maybe I had got her entirely wrong. This couldn't be the same person! But I had witnessed that look between them in the playground.

'Each week during antenatal classes the group would joke that it was story time with Bernie. Her stories were amazing; her achievements were outstanding; and not a week went by without her winning an award locally or nationally. Every mother in the antenatal class wanted to be her. I wanted to be her; not only were her clothes, nails and hair immaculate, but her handbags were simply to die for. What an inspiration she was – hardworking, baby on the way, making her own money. I was impressed along with all the other mothers who simply didn't have the drive, energy, or inclination to do anything except watch re-runs of Bargain Hunt.'

I was now shaking my head at Melanie with a puzzled expression on my face. I was flabbergasted. The words inspiration and BB used in the same sentence?

'Then one evening my ex, Rob, decided out of the blue to take a night off from the gym and attend the class with me. We were late due to the road works on Buttercup Lane and we could have sworn the traffic lights were broken, as they appeared to take forever to change to green. During the car journey, I gabbled constantly to Rob about Bernie, singing her praises and all her amazing achievements. It wasn't negotiable; this woman was Wonder Woman.

After the delays on the road, we finally arrived and parked the car. Hurrying into the hall, we found the antenatal class already in full flow. All the mothers, now in their third trimester, were lying there like stranded whales, on their mats; with their puffy ankles and high blood pressure, just willing for the day that the labour pains would begin.

I spotted Bernie and with Rob following, waddled over. She had kindly placed a spare mat next to hers for me, as I had texted her that we were running late. He sat down on the mat and turned to shake her hand while I introduced them. I could only describe the look on his face as pure shock soon followed by a smirk.'

I was mesmerised by this story; I had no idea what was coming next.

"So this is the woman who is giving Lord Sugar a run for his money?" Melanie mimicked Rob's surprise.

'Bernie's reaction was shifty to say the least – her eyes widened, her face turned beetroot red and she looked as if she wanted the ground to open up and swallow her. Unbelievably, Rob recognised Bernie from many years earlier when he had been in the same class as her.

He told the group that not only did she leave school at sixteen without one single qualification; she was fondly known as the 'school bike – slapper extraordinaire'. So Bernie's cover was blown, and her deceit uncovered.'

I let out a huge hoot of laughter. This was more like the BB I had come to know over the past year.

'Rob went on to reveal she was from the Moorland estate, a notorious slum – drugs, prostitutes, you name it!'

I stared at Melanie in amazement; 'Surely this isn't correct? According to Bernie's profile on Facebook, her roots were in posh Tipland.'

Tipland was an up-market housing development inhabited by Premier league footballers and successful executives who drove the latest Jags and kept their helicopters on the helipads that marked the surrounding area.

'She is a Moorland's girl, through and through,' confirmed Melanie with a knowing look on her face.

'Really? Seriously?' A snort of laughter came out of my nose.

'Bernie is the mother of one child, a boy called Lonsdale but you'd know that already,' Melanie continued.

I was aware she only had one son but that was as far as my knowledge went. Other than her indiscretions on the morning of New Year's Day, I was only privy to her playground antics. I had no idea what her child was called, but seriously, Lonsdale – I couldn't see that name becoming the top of the list of popular baby names any day soon.

'Lonsdale is named after the boy's father; she only met him once, picked him up on a night out in the local sticky-floored nightspot. She didn't even know his name,' Melanie went on.

'Hang on, you just said he was named after the father, but she didn't know his name, how does that work?' I asked.

'According to another reliable source, one night, apparently, Bernie had been out with a few friends in the club, the jukebox was rocking and the beers were flowing and they partied until the early hours of the morning. A group of men were standing by the bar swigging back their pints. Bernie and her friends singled them out and invaded their space. She began to flirt with one man in particular, one that she was instantly attracted to. He was married – had a ring on his left hand – but she didn't care. All men were fair game as far as she was concerned, and if there was a wife she could, if need be, dispose of her at any opportunity. Bernie did what she does best; she enticed him into her lair bragging about her status, money and fast car.

He jumped on the bandwagon, which was actually more like the two-nine-five bus, back to her house, not a fast car in sight. But she was a sure thing, offering everything to him on a plate – as well as a flea-infested mattress, and a scented candle to mask the damp smell of the house. They shared a single night of lust and when she awoke in the morning, he had disappeared, never to be seen again. No note, no number, nothing.'

'How did the child become named after the father then?' I asked.

'The bloke left his skeggy, stained Lonsdale boxer shorts discarded on the bathroom floor. Nine months later, Lonsdale was born. I'm not sure if she ever tried to find the father. Maybe she went back to the nightclub to try and track him down, but as far as anyone knew he was long gone.'

I was now grinning from ear to ear.

'We left the antenatal class that night and Bernie never spoke to me again. She soon moved out of the area and must have relocated here, to Tattersfield, to spin her lies to a new set of gullible mothers.' Melanie finished off.

The cuppa with Melanie had entertained me to say the least. It was only the first morning back on the school run after the holidays and it was already proving a very interesting start to the new term. Who knew what other delights would be revealed by the end of the school year.

I looked down at my watch; an hour had already lapsed. I had been putting off the inevitable; I now had to return home and face Penelope, and ask her politely to leave. There was no way we could have another three bodies filling up space in the house. I knew that Penelope would be upset. It wasn't going to be easy for her to embark on the path of a single woman, but I had my own family to look after, and I needed to put them first. Melanie and I said our goodbyes after paying for the cuppas with the promise of a get-together very soon. I bonded well with Melanie; I really liked her, a very down-to-earth woman in my opinion. I had a feeling we were going to be great friends but in the meantime, I had to hurry home and evict Penelope before she transferred the deeds of my house into her name and took over the mortgage payments. I was clueless about squatters' rights and that's the way I wanted it to stay.

CHAPTER 7

On my return, Penelope was up and dressed and looking rather more human. Sitting in the armchair, feet up, hugging a mug of tea and scoffing my chocolates, she had made herself at home. She was absorbed in a re-run of the Jeremy Kyle show on the television.

This prompted me to have the conversation sooner rather than later about her immediate departure. There was no way I could tolerate other humans arguing with each other in my living room, whether they were on the telly or not. Some guest on the show started to hyperventilate, as her lies about her child's father had been uncovered. I wasn't very knowledgeable on biology matters at school but I was convinced that they wouldn't need to do a lie detector test to confirm that the man on the screen wasn't the biological father. The baby was white, he was of Chinese origin. Grabbing the remote quickly and clicking the standby button, I turned to face Penelope just in time to witness her stuffing the last of the strawberry creams into her mouth.

'We need to talk,' I stated.

I was rather taken back by my own tone, as it was somewhat direct. I couldn't pussyfoot around Penelope any more; she lived in a perfectly good house within walking distance up the lane.

'I know what you are going say,' she replied.

I was gobsmacked but happy that this was going to be easier than I ever imagined.

'I'll be off then,' she smiled.

I was shaking my head in disbelief, not quite believing the eviction was proving exceptionally stress free. Wow! There wasn't even a 'can we talk about this' conversation moment; no begging, absolutely nothing.

Penelope stood up abruptly, reminding me of a sulky toddler. Throwing the chocolate wrappers in the waste paper basket, she then proceeded to scoop the magazines up, which she laid in a neat pile on the coffee table, before plumping up the cushions on the sofa. She eventually left the room, clearly short of any further time-stalling tactics.

Two minutes later, she was back and stood in the living room sporting an expression that reminded me of the Cheshire cat featured in *Alice in Wonderland*. She nodded her head at the front door, and tugging on the lapels of her duffle coat and pulling them up around her ears, she dropped the bombshell.

'I've taken your front door key; I shan't be too long, there's a blustery wind out there now. I can definitely see myself back soon; it shouldn't take too long.' She placed the key on the table while wrapping her scarf around her neck.

Anxiety flooded through my veins and I was paralysed, frozen to the spot. Scanning the room I established this was not Wonderland and she was not Alice but there appeared to be a mad hatter amongst us. What did she just say? What shouldn't take too long? What did she mean?

'I don't understand Penelope,' I managed to stammer.

'It won't take me long; you can't imagine how relieved I am to be able to stay here with the children. I'd best fill a suitcase with clothes and hurry back before the school pick-up time,' she beamed cheerily.

Suddenly my mouth went very dry, two paths to my life flashed before my very eyes, the first one being, that I should find my inner kindness and let Penelope stay, and the second, that I too would be husbandless and bringing up four children on my own.

How could Penelope get this so wrong?

'No, No, No, Penelope, you have got this all wrong,' I said grabbing the key from the table. 'I'm sorry, but you have a perfectly good home to go back to; talk to Rupert, maybe he can find alternative accommodation but we just don't have the room.'

There, I'd said it. I reminded myself of my New Year promise – it was still intact – I wouldn't be a doormat. I couldn't believe how well I had taken control of the situation; I was very impressed with my little self. The realisation that I had put myself first after all last year's antics genuinely excited me.

Penelope was eyeballing me, as if she wanted to kill me; I knew she would be aware of the many years she would get for murder, so the odds were I was quite safe – I think.

Her face had already taken on the Oompa Loompa look. I thought she was about to have a massive toddler strop as steam appeared to rush out of her ears like a cartoon character. She leant forward and singled out the Turkish delight that was left in the box of chocolates on the coffee table, then stuffed it into her mouth. She unbuttoned her coat and plonked herself back in the armchair – my armchair. I detested Turkish delight; I was never going to eat them but that wasn't the point; they were *my* chocolates.

'What am I to do? I've left my husband; I am unemployed thanks to Camilla Noland and my children are now, technically, from a broken home,' she was beginning to get hysterical.

Who was she trying to kid? There was nothing broken about her home; it was less than half a mile up the road with running water and electricity.

Life could be worse; she could be hanging her dirty laundry out in public on the Jeremy Kyle Show.

There was no way, no way on this planet she could stay here. She had driven me insane with all her one-sided talking last year during our keep fit walking sessions, I had listened to her constant chatter about Little Jonny for months on end without ever getting a word in; my only escape was to return home and lock the door behind me.

The thought crossed my mind that the timing of this separation may suit Rupert down to the ground. The Farrier's flat had just become vacant now he had taken possession of his father's property. This could be a stroke of luck for Rupert, his own bachelor pad, close enough to visit his children, but far enough away from his wife to provide his own entertainment.

I was going to suggest that perhaps Penelope could move in with the Farrier. His house was definitely spacious with enough bedrooms, but I wasn't sure that was one of my better ideas, as for many months, Camilla had been bed-hopping with Rupert, and if anything more dodgy went on in that circle of people they may just be featured on the next Jeremy Kyle show.

The day was flying by and there were only a few hours until we had to brave the school pick up. In the meantime, I offered to drive Penelope home. This wasn't down to my caring nature, it was more to make certain she had left and wasn't coming back tonight, or any other night for that matter.

After gathering all her belongings and double-checking there was nothing left behind, she reluctantly climbed into the car. When I dropped Penelope back at her home, Rupert's bubble car was parked on the driveway. I wondered if he would be rushing out to purchase another boy racer if his marriage was now over. A car that would attract the women, just like the one he'd had that Penelope had made him trade in. I wished her luck as she grudgingly prised herself out of the car seat and slowly shuffled towards the front door. I shouted words of encouragement as she placed the key in the lock, then drove off quickly.

At school pick-up time, I trudged back through grey slush, as the snow had now begun to thaw. I passed the cliques that had gathered outside the school gate, gossiping about some poor sod as usual, and stood in my normal spot. Melanie was already there, keen to collect her child on her first day and anxious to hear how the day had gone. I was always lastminute.com, arriving as the bell rang out. That was always the best way though, as it left less time for tedious conversations.

Eva my eldest was first out of the door, waving two letters at me as she ran towards me. I really needed to start a career in gambling because it was a dead cert that one of the letters would be asking for money for something and no doubt, the other one was to inform the parents that on the first day there had already been an outbreak of nits. I was correct on both counts. The school never wasted any time asking for money. This time it was for a school trip, a trip that was less than five miles up the road and they wanted a voluntary contribution of ten pounds. We all knew voluntary doesn't mean voluntary in this case and it would have been cheaper if I'd dropped Eva at the destination myself.

Penelope arrived late, a little flustered which was understandable. Her living arrangements for the near future appeared to be under control. Rupert was moving into temporary accommodation into The Farrier's old flat. I was certainly relieved and I was sure Matt would be too.

I was about to introduce Penelope to Melanie but Melanie had been summoned by her child's teacher, probably for a quick update on how well she had coped on her first day at school.

CHAPTER 8

One week later, I had the joy of attending Frisky Pensioner's funeral. I had no intention of going until the Farrier asked me if I would accompany him. I wasn't sure I wanted to pay my respects to a man who on many occasions tried to snog the face off me and who had stalked me for the best part of a year. On the other hand, seeing him buried deep in the ground with no chance of escape might help me to sleep better at night. The Farrier's mother (Frisky Pensioner's wife) had disappeared off the face of the earth, allegedly having taken a leaf out of Shirley Valentine's book, to sun herself on a foreign beach somewhere, and had no idea that her randy husband was about to be entombed six feet under.

I agreed to go, not for my own sake but for that of the Farrier. We were becoming friends and the day ahead would no doubt be difficult for him. It was the end of an era. His wife, his father and his mother had all disappeared out of his life and he didn't seem to have any other family or friends he could rely on. To be honest, I didn't have any other commitments that day, Matilda and Daisy were at preschool and I wasn't working. My part-time job that I'd started last year when I first arrived in the village had unexpectedly ceased due to lack of funding in their budget.

Penelope was becoming a limpet again. Having initially been dumped for the wonderful Camilla Noland, now she'd done a runner, I had unfortunately been promoted back to the top spot as Penelope's number one best friend. The morning of the funeral I left the school playground very quickly, and rushed back home to grab a quick shower. The Farrier updated me with the funeral timing by text. The hearse would be leaving the house a little after ten, to start the procession.

I was all dressed and ready for the funeral with thirty minutes to spare when there was a knock on the door. I was hoping it would be the postman with my parcels that had gone astray during the Christmas period, but no such luck. I was amazed to find Penelope standing there, well not technically standing there; she was skipping. I don't mean she was skipping from leg to leg like a child skips; she was actually throwing a rope over her head and counting. I had that horrible sinking feeling that I was about to be roped into another mad keep fit challenge just like last year when she had manoeuvred me into climbing a mountain with her. Penelope must be Tesco's dream shopper at this time of year. In her matching shorts, T-shirt, and a white towelling head-band, she looked just like John McEnroe.

Watching her bounce up and down in front of me, I began to feel dizzy. It was worse than the motion sickness I had experienced on a ferry ride a couple of years ago when I thought I might take out shares in Joy-rider tables.

'What are you doing Penelope?'

'Isn't it obvious? We are in training again.'

I was sure I had heard the word 'we'. I stared at her; after last year's mountain climb there was no way I would be talked into any madder, ridiculous ideas. I didn't have time to argue with her.

'Why are you dressed in black? You look like you are about to attend a funeral,' she continued.

'I am. I'm accompanying the Farrier to his father's funeral in ten minutes,' I replied, not amused.

'Well, why the hell didn't you tell me?' She stopped skipping.

'Don't leave without me, I'll run home and change quickly.' And with that, she was gone, bounding up the path in freezing cold conditions in Tesco's bargain flannel fitness shorts.

I hadn't engaged in any sort of conversation with Penelope regarding Frisky Pensioner's funeral. There was no need, they hadn't been friends and I had no idea why she would even want to pay her last respects – or any respects come to that.

At that moment I received another update text from the Farrier; the hearse was about to leave.

Grabbing my coat and locking the front door behind me, I made my way down the path and headed towards the Farrier's house. Penelope must be the fastest dresser ever, because she was already hurrying back up the road, very hyper and shouting, 'wait for me!' She was dressed in a sort of tight-fitting yellow dress with a red blazer thrown over the top. There was only one thing that crossed my mind – a human rhubarb and custard. Don't get me wrong, I love clothes, but who wears yellow and red to a funeral unless it's for a departed cheerleader?

Tottering up the lane behind Penelope on the most ridiculous high heels ever, was BB. Even a clown in the local circus would have stilts lower than those heels. With the weight of her artificial boobs pulling her forward, on those heels, BB would be lucky if she spent any time upright today. Why was she here? To tout for more business among the assembled mourners? It would be like shooting fish in a barrel; there would be plenty of pensioners for her to befriend; those who would shortly be on their way to the pearly gates – those who would leave their small fortunes to the likes of her in exchange for one last night of passion. No doubt, she would be asking for payment up front, a cash advance from their life savings.

Unlike Penelope, she had the mourner attire down to a tee. She had draped a black veil over her face and her long black hair was smoothed down to the arch of her back. Her sunglasses were a hooker version of the type that wouldn't look out of place on Joan Collins and the dress; well she was coming very close to spilling out over the top of her dress. Anyone would have thought she was the widow, not the tart that had finished him off. I wondered whether this was one of many funerals she had attended of those she had helped to shuffle off this mortal coil; she looked as if she was a dab hand in the role of the grieving funeral guest.

Thankfully, the Farrier was coping well although he probably thought he was in the middle of a pantomime. All we needed now was Widow Twanky bringing up the rear shouting, 'he's behind you'. He didn't give the impression he was upset, but I suppose, as he had distanced himself from his father many years ago, he certainly wasn't going to start bawling crocodile tears now, not like some we knew. I glanced over at BB who was currently dabbing away a tear from the corner of her eye with a hanky – like I said – bloody pantomime.

In no time at all a crowd of people had gathered outside to pay their last respects; they fell silent when the hearse drew up alongside them outside FP's house. Then out of the corner of my eye, I noticed my neighbours, Don and Edna peering out of the upstairs window of their house after deciding to stay behind closed doors. I couldn't blame them. They had fallen out with the Frisky Pensioner forty odd years ago when Edna caught him spying through a man-made hole in the fence when she was sunbathing topless. At least Edna could now sunbathe topless in her own garden if she so desired.

Outside the gate, BB stood licking her lips in a seductive manner trying to catch the eye of the funeral director. When this didn't work, she started to wail; the same wailing sound she had made on the morning that Frisky Pensioner died, when she had dropped to her knees in the street with only the flea-ridden chinchilla to preserve her dignity. I looked round the crowd and wondered whether this was an outing from the local psychiatric hospital. The world was full of mad people and most of them appeared to be standing next to me in my lane. It gave a whole new meaning to the village people.

An unfamiliar car pulled up, and parked a little further up the road. A tall lanky man opened the car door and sauntered towards the funeral director at the front of the hearse. There were a few perplexed looks from the crowd, as they waited to discover who this man was.

'Who's that?' I whispered in the Farrier's ear, genuinely curious.

'Probably a long lost brother, or a love child of my father's, I'm sure there will be a few of them emerging from the woodwork hoping to claim his non-existent fortune,' he joked half-heartedly.

The onlookers were soon to be disappointed as he was simply a passer-by who noticed the hearse had a flat tyre. The body of Frisky Pensioner would have to stay where it was until they got the wheel changed. BB wailed more intensely as the elderly man kindly touched her arm and softly said, 'I am so sorry for your loss.' This woman was unbelievable; she wasn't even a relative of Frisky Pensioner.

My feet felt like blocks of ice from all the standing around. I began to shiver in the cold air so the Farrier kindly draped his arm around my shoulder and invited me back into the warmth of his house to wait while they fitted the spare wheel. Penelope followed us; she didn't wait for the Farrier to ask her in, and as soon as she was over the threshold she plonked herself down in an armchair. The Farrier disappeared upstairs mumbling that he needed to find a scarf.

Inside, the house had a musty aroma about it, and the walls were covered with old photographs of buildings and houses. The fireplace was high, maybe original; I couldn't tell as an ivy plant trailed down covering it and the brass ornaments adorning the hearth. The Farrier would have his work cut out trying to modernise the room to bring it into the twenty-first century. I wondered where Frisky Pensioner had died; I could be standing on the very spot. Shivering, I glanced out of the window to see the hearse balancing on a jack and two men struggling to change the tyre. Unfortunately for the dead Frisky Pensioner, his flowers had slid down the coffin when the front of the car was lifted off the ground and now lay squashed and piled up in a heap against the corner of the window. Penelope wandered into the kitchen to admire the buffet, where we were out of earshot of the Farrier. 'I'm only here for the buffet; I do love a good sausage roll and pork pie,' she claimed. 'Times are hard now that Rupert has left me; anything for a free feed.'

'Forgive me Penelope, you left him. Now put the foil back over those sausage rolls, they are for the wake!' I exclaimed.

The thought of eating a sausage roll at FP's wake turned my stomach; all I could imagine was a sausage and a roll with the delightful BB, and my appetite had suddenly disappeared.

The Farrier appeared at the kitchen door; awkwardly, Penelope quickly re-covered the sausage rolls with the tin foil.

'The cars are ready now. The tyre is fixed, but unfortunately, the flowers they look ... well ... dead just like my father.'

We followed him to the bottom of the path and noticed BB was still lurking on the edge of the curb. All of a sudden, it seemed to turn dark outside and I felt as if the temperature had dropped. It was as if there had just been an eclipse of the sun, I shivered, feeling as if someone had walked over my grave. It crossed my mind that maybe Frisky Pensioner had been refused entry into the good world up above, and I made a promise to myself, there and then, that I would never to participate in any form of ghost hunting or Ouija board antics in case he came back to haunt me. I hoped it wasn't too late to add another New Year's Resolution.

The rest of the mourners climbed into their vehicles; engines were running, doors slamming and the smoke from exhausts trailing behind as the procession started. BB was giving the idea she was the grief stricken widow – another person on track for an Oscar nomination. Sweeping her hand continuously across her forehead, she gave the impression she could faint at any moment. I was hoping she would – sooner rather than later – anything to stop that awful wailing.

The funeral director must have taken pity on her; for we watched him halt the hearse and flinging the door open, he waved his hand at her, gesturing for her to jump in and take a seat. She clambered in. The Farrier laughed and shook his head in disbelief; then he climbed into his car and invited me to join him. Penelope wasted no time at all and quickly jumped into the back and we drove away tailing the hearse.

CHAPTER 9

The funeral cortege halted outside the crematorium. I thought I would witness the Frisky Pensioner being buried in the ground today, but apparently, he had opted for a cremation.

It made no difference to me as long the ashes were scattered and he didn't perch on the Farrier's mantelpiece indefinitely. You do hear of people whose better halves sit there in their urn as large as life so to speak because the bereaved can't face the final separation. I once worked with a woman who placed her husband in pride of place on top of the fireplace. Then at mealtimes, she would place his ashes on the dining table, set his place with a knife and fork and pour a glass of water. Without fail, she'd always ask him how his day had been. The conversation must have become a little one-sided over time.

Everyone was seated in the wooden pews; the crematorium wasn't packed with people, but could be classified as a good turnout. I recognised half the pensioners from the post office queue on a Monday morning. The day they gather to collect their weekly benefit and carry out their mental roll call to determine whether or not their number had been depleted. They must have thought all their Christmases had come at once with a free feed so soon after the festivities.

I wasn't quite sure where to sit. I wanted to park myself quietly at the back, undetected, but knew the Farrier would need to be somewhere near the front. The Farrier had decided that

Rosie's relationship with her Grandfather wasn't a close one. In fact, she barely knew him after all communications between him and the Farrier had broken down, so she was safely tucked away behind her desk in the school classroom.

I was rather amused by the Reverend who appeared to have a lisp and sounded as if he had overdosed on helium; either that or he had been swigging more than holy water. Every time he spoke, he sprayed the occupants of the front row with his spit.

As I watched them take cover and dodge his frothy spray, I couldn't believe what I saw. There in the front row, in pride of place was BB. What the bloody hell was she doing taking up space in the places that were allocated to family members?

I also noticed a woman from the village called Elsie sitting with some of the neighbours. This woman didn't even attempt to whisper, and bellowed out that Iris Fletcher-Parker (Mrs Frisky Pensioner), the Farrier's mother, had finally come to her senses and had decamped, leaving the philanderer in the arms of a prostitute. I noticed a reporter from the local newspaper hovering nearby furiously scribbling on his notepad, picking up the trail of a story recounted by the vocal Elsie. Aside from the fact that her outburst echoed all around the vast space of the crematorium, she was also sitting directly behind BB who promptly turned round and stared straight at the woman – if looks could kill – well, we were in the right place if nothing else.

The Farrier ushered Penelope and me into a pew a little further back. After numerous prayers and hymns, I couldn't help sniggering to myself as 'You Raise Me Up' belted out from what looked like an 80s' style ghetto-blaster plugged in behind the prehistoric organ that had certainly seen better days. I thought this song was very apt as the Frisky Pensioner was most definitely attempting to raise himself up on the night of his death. All we needed now was an encore of 'Died in Your Arms.'

After a few more prayers and a reading, the spotlight lowered down onto the coffin lighting up the photograph of Mr Fletcher-Parker that was perched on top of the oak casket. Vera Lynn's 'We'll Meet Again' was next to play from the top ten funeral hits.

'Goodbye my love,' BB mouthed at the coffin. The heavy-duty crimson curtain of crushed velvet began to lower while the coffin slid forward out of sight. Was this woman for real? 'Goodbye my love?' This was no great love affair; she was simply the escort with benefits that he had hired to entertain himself on New Year's Eve. Unfortunately, for him, he ended up dead. BB was delusional but probably thought she was in with a chance to claim some sort of financial settlement. No doubt, she would sue the Farrier for Frisky Pensioner's fortune while she faked PTSD – post-traumatic sex disorder. Give her some credit though, if that wail was anything to go by she absolutely knew how to fake it – no question about that at all.

Much to my and the Farrier's amusement, it appeared the music was cued incorrectly, and all eyes were eagerly fixed on the Reverend, as he raced to the ghetto-blaster to quickly switch off 'Another One Bites the Dust,' muttering, 'I'm so sorry,' as he ran.

Once the coffin had disappeared completely behind the curtain there must have been some weird electrical current that interfered with every pensioner's hearing aid in the room as they all started to whistle in a very high-pitched tone.

The three of us filed out of the pew. I was relieved to be leaving the service. I was beginning to feel chilly and was looking forward to hugging a hot mug of tea. There were only so many cliché funeral songs and so much of BB that anyone could tolerate in one hour.

All of a sudden, Penelope halted. I bumped slap bang into the Farrier's back leaving a powdery foundation mark on the shoulder of his black jacket. I quickly tried to brush it off while glancing over it to see why we had unexpectedly stopped. Penelope was standing still and glaring at a woman who was blocking the aisle; the woman was staring back at her.

The Farrier looked up. 'Hi,' he managed to mumble even though he looked as if his mouth had suddenly become completely dry.

'Hi there, back,' the woman spoke warmly.

'Melanie Tate,' he breathed; his body radiated sudden heat.

'It's been far too long.'

'This is a lovely surprise but what on earth are you doing here?'

'I'm back, permanently,' she said gazing at him so intently that even I felt I could be hypnotised at any moment. One couldn't deny that these two were pleased to see each other.

'Out of all the funerals in all the land, you turn up at my father's,' he joked.

Melanie cocked her head to one side throwing out a cheeky smile, and they grabbed each other in a bear hug with the Farrier stealing a kiss on her cheek in the process and smoothing his hand over her hair.

'I can't believe you are here. It's been way too long,' he stated with real pleasure. Their eyes locked.

'You look well,' she whispered, and reluctantly pulled away.

I could see from Penelope's reaction and her raised eyebrows, that she was not in the least bit ecstatic about this reunion.

Swiftly turning towards the Farrier, her eyes now bulging with rage, she cleared her throat then demanded rather harshly, 'How do you know her?'

'Hi Rachel,' Melanie greeted me, ignoring Penelope completely.

'And how the bloody hell do you two know each other?' Penelope snarled. She seemed to be stifling some strong emotion, but unfortunately, began to turn purple. Sherlock Holmes wasn't needed to reveal there was something going on here, but I was having a real problem trying to fathom what it was all about. Well, if I couldn't beat them, I decided to join them in question time.

'How do you lot know each other?' I asked in turn.

However, no one was moving or answering any sort of questions.

The crematorium was nearly empty by now; the mourners were already on their way back to the house to be fed and watered. I noted BB had latched onto another ancient friend of Frisky Pensioner. Nevertheless, this man looked very different from him; he was tall and lean, with silvery grey hair; his suit looked tailor-made and his designer shoes were polished. He gave the impression he was a successful businessman. I overheard him saying that he couldn't believe he had met a movie star. I watched her link arms with her new friend, no doubt blagging herself a lift back to the warmth of the Farrier's abode.

Penelope still muttering under her breath, pushed past Melanie, flounced out of the crematorium, and made straight for the Farrier's car. The Farrier and Melanie seemed oblivious to her strop and were still gushing all over each other.

'I've missed you,' he whispered. 'So much.'

'Have you? Really?'

'You really don't need to ask me that ... I can't believe I have found you again.' His voice was now trembling.

'You didn't find me,' laughed Melanie. 'I'd run out of milk and nipped to the local post office, only to find the postmaster was closing up early. He was all flustered and rushing to attend the wake of a local pensioner. I was shocked when I learned it was your father. Curiosity got the better of me and before I knew it I'd jumped into my car, and came, not having a clue of what to do or say, or if you were even here. I am sorry about your father,' She added quickly.

'A lot has happened since the day I saw you last,' he said sadly.

The Farrier looked different; it was hard to describe. There was a glimmer of happiness in his eyes that I had never seen before. Unhesitatingly, he draped his arm around Melanie's shoulders. I stayed silent; I still wasn't up to speed on what the ins and the outs were, but I wondered if this was the same Melanie who the Farrier spoke about on New Year's Day, it didn't take a genius to know that this pair had a history – the sparks were flying – but where did Penelope fit into the equation?

I was beginning to feel ravenous. I found myself thinking that flaky-pastry sausage rolls were equivalent to the best sirloin steaks from Jamie Oliver's restaurant. We drifted towards the car. Penelope, who now looked like a sour rhubarb and custard, was slouched against the car door with her arms crossed in toddler-like fashion. Her behaviour wasn't lost on Melanie but this wasn't the time or the place to acknowledge Penelope's petulance.

'Come and join us back at the house, you will be more than welcome,' suggested the Farrier hopefully. Judging by the look on Penelope's face, she would make Melanie as welcome as a new mother attending a PTA meeting.

I'd thought about making my excuses once the wake was over. I was happy I had done my good deed for the day by accompanying the Farrier to the funeral, even though I felt like a trussed-up chicken in the dress I was wearing and I really needed to change out of my shoes and put some flats on my feet. However, things were starting to get interesting. Something had rattled Penelope's cage and I was intrigued to find out what that was.

CHAPTER 10

We drove back to the wake in complete silence. Melanie followed us in her car. The journey was agonisingly painful, as I was dying to ask questions, but judging by the look on Penelope's face, I didn't dare speak first.

Then, I decided enough was enough, and in a bold move, I blurted out, 'Well is someone, anyone going to enlighten me as to what is going on?'

The Farrier frowned, and glanced in his rear view mirror directly at Penelope; her eyes widened glaring back at him. I felt ridiculous now as the silence continued. I wondered how long they could keep up this childish behaviour. If I was reading the signs correctly, they both had issues and I wasn't sure they were actually connected to each other. I got the impression that neither of them had quite worked out how the other was connected to Melanie. We pulled up at the house and the wake was in full swing. It seemed the house had been invaded by the local retirement home; every pensioner within a ten-mile radius must have been there. There was an abundance of headscarves, blue rinses and grey angora knitted cardigans. Every woman over 70 years of age in the room wore thick tan tights, fur-lined zip-up shoes, cream polyester petticoats that hung lower than black skirts with elasticated waistbands. Glasses were clinking and cheap plonk flowing. Penelope was the first to swipe a glass off the silver tray placed by the front door to welcome new arrivals. I wasn't far behind her, followed by Melanie, who had parked her car and who was now standing beside us.

'Come on we'd better go through,' the Farrier suggested, reaching out and holding Melanie's hand whilst escorting her into the living room.

I lingered, standing inside the doorway to scan the room. I noticed BB was already in her element, a sausage roll in one hand, and booze in the other. She had disposed of her Joan Collins spectacles and her coat. Her eyes were furiously flitting around the room surveying the area, no doubt identifying who her next target would be; the man she picked up at the ceremony was nowhere in sight. He didn't realise how lucky he was, escaping with his life to live another day. BB seemed hell-bent on capturing a man today – any man to be precise. She grabbed another drink from a passing tray and swallowed the entire glass in two mouthfuls not even having time to taste whether it was red, white or water. She knew how to work a room all right and I noticed she had studied her prey well.

She handpicked a distinguished man from a small group that had gathered near the fireplace – the one wearing the Rolex watch; whom she had clocked parking his Bentley outside the front window on the lane.

BB sashayed over to him, the demon drink giving her courage. Obviously not understanding the concept of personal space, she interrupted the conversation and invaded his. Her voice was beginning to rise, and I realised she must be quite tipsy. She started to discuss her new movie career with the man wearing the expensive watch. He didn't seem to be listening to a word she was saying; but his eyes lingered on her black dress with the plunging neckline that left nothing to the imagination. They moved closer, laughing and whispering to each other, and he tilted his hips towards hers. It was more of a scene that one would witness in a nightclub, certainly not at a wake. If they got any closer, they may as well just drop to the floor and have sex. I saw him place a business card into her red-painted talons, which she accepted and pushed into her bra. She lifted one of her immaculately manicured fingernails and traced the rugged stubble across his jawline. He placed a hand firmly on her backside in a sleazebag way and together they disappeared out of the living room towards the stairs.BB probably knew this house like the back of her hand and was undoubtedly leading him to a vacant bedroom; perhaps she was hoping to drive off in his Bentley after hoodwinking him into believing she had some sort of movie career.

I noticed that Melanie and the Farrier had moved into the only vacant space in the corner of the kitchen. The buffet was declared open and the kitchen was busy with hungry mourners forming an orderly queue, waiting their turn. I could hear Melanie and the Farrier's conversation while I queued near them, and I leant against the units in the kitchen waiting for the pensioners to load up their plates first.

'I can't quite believe this happening,' I heard Melanie say.

I watched as she took the Farrier's hand and cupped both her hands around his. 'My heart is skipping beats never mind the butterflies that are fluttering around my stomach at the rate of knots. You haven't aged at all; you are just how I remembered you.' She glanced up at the Farrier, who smiled at her, eyes sparkling.

'It has been nine years, three months and two days to be precise since you disappeared out of my life. I thought you'd gone forever.' He gently replied.

Melanie gasped, 'I can't believe you counted the days.'

The Farrier continued to stare into Melanie's eyes. 'I can't take my eyes off you in case you disappear out of my life again as quickly as you have just reappeared.'

'I am back, permanently back, not a day has gone by that I didn't think about you. I dream, I dream I will be one day back in your arms, please tell me you still feel the same way.'

'Of course I feel it. It's unquestionably there and it will always be there.'

Piling sausage rolls and cheese sandwiches on to my plate, I saw the Farrier wrap his arms around Melanie and pull her in close to him. She didn't attempt to pull away. 'You still smell the same; your aftershave, it's the one I bought you before I left.'

'And why did you leave me Melanie Tate? One minute you were there and next gone, I don't understand.'

Melanie looked up, 'I had no choice, you chose Camilla and I couldn't hang around and watch you love someone else right before my very eyes.'

I noticed the Farrier pull away and place his hands on both her arms, 'I wasn't in a relationship with Camilla, that came about after you left. I was so distraught. What in heaven's name made you think that?'

'She did. She told me you were together.'

'What! Why didn't you come and ask me?'

'Maybe I was just young and stupid, but Camilla was also my friend at the yard, she had no reason to lie to me. I didn't want to put anyone in an awkward position and most of all I couldn't face being rejected by you.'

The full extent of his wife's deception must have suddenly dawned on the Farrier, for his face darkened. He tilted her chin towards his face, 'I promise I was never with Camilla until you left, I was a broken man. She picked up the pieces at the time. But you are here now and that is what all matters.' The Farrier pulled Melanie back in close again.

I walked out of the kitchen and left them to it. They already looked like a couple, so very at ease with each other.

I on the other hand was now stuck with a sour-faced Penelope who was, unquestionably, not in the best of moods. She collared me on the way out of the kitchen. Discreetly, I kept glancing at my watch, planning my escape, when Penelope opened her mouth.

'Melanie is not new to the village,' she told me, pulling out a chair, propped up by the patio windows, for me to sit on. 'Far from it,' she whispered, beginning to frown again. I had no idea why she felt the need to whisper; we were on our own as most of the mourners had now gathered around the kitchen table wildly spooning the fresh cream trifle into paper bowls as if it might suddenly be rationed.

I had thought this wake would be insufferably boring but on the contrary, it was keeping me very much entertained. I noticed BB hadn't yet re-entered the room; she was no doubt, having her cake and eating it – I hoped she didn't want any trifle.

'Once upon a time, Melanie was my best friend.'

This statement didn't take me by surprise. It seemed everyone in the village had been Penelope's best friend at one time or another; there was nothing unusual about the story so far.

I was suddenly distracted by BB sloping back down the stairs swinging her sling back shoes in her hand looking rather like a naughty teenager. Her long hair was ruffled, her make-up was smeared around her face, and there was a reddish rash above her top lip. Her low cut dress appeared lower cut than it did before she sneaked up the stairs with the distinguished man. Observing a white mark below her chest area I realised the label of the dress was sticking out, BB's dress was on back to front – probably an occupational hazard for her.

Smiling to myself, I leaned over to the small old-fashioned cocktail cabinet next to me, and picked up one of the small glasses. As I blew on it, a cloud of dust leapt into the air. The glasses looked as if they hadn't been used since the 1960s. I poured myself a drink and swigged back the potent spirit, which burnt my lips, while I continued to listen to Penelope. I watched another pensioner shuffling around the room offering leftover egg sandwiches to anyone with an empty plate. The alcohol from my sneaky tipple entered my bloodstream and instantly made me feel slightly lightheaded.

'Are you listening to me?' Penelope demanded.

I turned quickly to face her. 'Sorry, yes,' I apologised, 'I'm listening carry on.'

'I met Melanie at night college, years ago, I'd already had Little Jonny and felt my life was becoming so mundane, I carried out the same routine day in and day out so I decided to sign up to a night school course to expand my mind and embark of a new social life with like-minded people. This is how I met Melanie.'

'What course did you sign up for?' I enquired.

'Some sort of business studies course.' She replied.

I nodded my head and she continued.

'I was furious with myself; I'd missed the connecting bus to the college and was already terribly late for my first lecture. When I finally arrived, I stood outside the college feeling anxious and nearly turned round to go straight back home. I can remember staring up at the gigantic building in front of me with its colossal stone lions and railings that surrounded it.'

I wondered how much more of this story there was to hear. I glanced around the Farrier's living room, which was emptying; the swirly patterned carpet was a sea of white paper plates, and flakes of pastry, and every surface was covered with empty glasses abandoned by the mourners who had returned to comfort of their own tartan wingback chairs. Melanie and the Farrier were still in the kitchen with a few old pensioners patting him on the back, telling him they were sorry for his loss...

'I approached the battered green classroom door with caution, pulling down on the handle I juggled my new brightly coloured A4 files and pushed down on the door. I scanned the room quickly and was fully aware that the whole room of people were looking at me, watching my every move. I hurried over to the only vacant seat in the room and sat myself down next to a friendly, smiley person.'

'Melanie?' I asked.

'Yes, Melanie. She pulled a chair out for me to sit down and at that very moment all my files slipped out of my hand and went crashing on to the floor, I felt humiliated, my hands were trembling and everyone was still watching me. I can remember muttering an apology for the disruption whilst Melanie helped to pick up the scattered files.'

I could imagine fresh-faced Penelope turning crimson with embarrassment.

'Then the battered green classroom door swung open again, the leaflets pinned on to the tatty cork boards that were fixed to the equally shabby walls flapped in the ensuing draft. Everyone's eyes swivelled towards the door; they were no longer interested in my arrival, as the lecturer strolled in as large as life ...'

The Farrier's living room was becoming very warm and stuffy; my eyelids were beginning to droop. Desperately trying to stay awake, I began to fiddle with my bracelet. There just wasn't the opportunity to escape, well not anytime soon it would seem. Penelope continued with her story.

'The lecturer was a bloke named Rob who had a relationship with Melanie, but they split up when Dotty was born.'

'But Penelope how did you fall out with Melanie,' trying to cut to the chase.

'I'm just getting to that,' she answered annoyed,

'It was all down to Melanie's underhand ways that we fell out,' stated Penelope.

'I'd given birth to Annabel shortly after Dotty and we decided to share a small gathering at my house for their first birthday.'

Alarm bells were already starting to ring in my head. Shared kids' birthday parties should be avoided at all costs; that's a cardinal rule in the mother's handbook, as it will only end in disaster. The kids will be disappointed over the lack of parity between the two cakes and the parents will fall out from the constant one-upmanship over the party bag contents. Why some parents insist on shopping at Selfridge's for the giveaway gifts is beyond me; the whole lot can be sourced for a quid a head in Home Bargains.

'The party had been quite successful with no major hiccups until I counted the presents. Now either one child's mother hadn't the good grace to bring a present for Annabel, or Melanie had sneakily returned home with the stolen goods for Dotty.'

'I'm sure it's not Melanie's style to be pinching a one-year old's birthday presents,' I stated firmly.

'Well she must have, because I didn't have it. I contacted the mother of the child who we didn't receive a present from and she confirmed they had definitely brought one.'

'Why didn't you ask Melanie about it then?'

'I tried to, I sent her lots of texts demanding where the present was and she stopped replying, that's sign of a guilty conscience to me,' replied Penelope.

It was more likely that Melanie couldn't be bothered with Penelope's demands and drama and took herself away from the friendship, I thought to myself.

'Even though we were friends, once Dotty was born, there was always an underlying rivalry between us, more on Melanie's part, I hasten to add. After all I did for her when she became a single mother; she let me down, and fleeced me for a Fisherprice talking telephone.'

I stared straight at Penelope and shook my head in bewilderment. I had been listening to this tedious story out of politeness, only to have the climax revealed as a fall-out over a child's toy. Surely not, what was my life coming to? Nevertheless, what else did I expect? This was Penelope I was talking to.

Lifting my hands to my face in fake shock, I asked, 'Surely not over a talking telephone?' I stopped and took a breath waiting for Penelope to respond. She didn't disappoint me. I saw a flicker of annoyance flash across Penelope's face; quite clearly, she was still narked after all these years over the missing birthday present.

Just at that moment, Melanie appeared at our side. Penelope abruptly stopped speaking and turned a shade of crimson.

'Are you leaving?' I asked.

Melanie looked down at her watch. 'Yes, I need to pick Dotty up from school.'

'Oh, is that the time? Matt kindly worked from home this morning and has looked after Matilda and Daisy all day, but I'd better pick up Eva and Samuel too. Do you need to collect Little Jonny and Annabel, Penelope?'

'No, they are going to Rupert's for tea tonight; he is collecting them.'

'I'll come with you then Melanie,' I said, thankful for the chance to escape.

The Farrier appeared and stood behind Melanie. He touched her arm lightly. 'I need to mingle with the remaining guests and tidy up and I'll catch up with you soon.'

'Very soon I hope.' Melanie replied.

They smiled at each other and he began shaking the hands of a group of mourners who were leaving. Melanie and I walked towards the front door.

'I know it's only a short journey to school but do you fancy a lift?'

'That would be a yes in these heels, thank you!'

Melanie blasted up the heat to get the car warm. We were actually about twenty minutes early, but I'd rather be sitting here with Melanie then listening to Penelope, and also, it would give me plenty of time to question Melanie's relationship with Penelope.

CHAPTER 11

Sitting outside the school gates with the engine running to keep warm, I decided to ask Melanie how she knew Penelope. Even though I didn't know her particularly well I didn't feel as if I was prying because after all, without any encouragement, she had quite openly told me how she and BB had crossed paths.

Melanie beat me to it.

'Come on, you are dying to ask me how I know Penelope!' Melanie grinned.

We both laughed 'I am! I was just about to ask,' I replied.

Glancing down at her watch, 'how long have we got?'

'Long enough, now stop stalling,' I joked.

'I met her on a night school course,' Melanie began.

I nodded. That tallied with Penelope's story, so far so good.

'She was late for the first class and all the students were already sat down in the classroom, the only spare seat was next to me. I'm sure if Penelope was telling you this story she would have made it all about her.

I could tell by the pained expression on Melanie's face that there was more to this story than a missing present.

'It all began the minute the tutor walked in to the room. I can remember smiling to myself because Rob was so charismatic. Not only was he extremely good-looking with floppy blonde hair and a lopsided cheeky grin but he oozed fun. Penelope quickly spotted his wedding ring. I was fully aware I was ogling my new lecturer; I can remember watching his every move as he glided around the classroom handing out sheets of paper and textbooks. He was gorgeous.

Penelope and I became friends, I was single but she was with Rupert and had already given birth to Little Jonny. The classes were at night-time which was convenient for Penelope because Rupert would look after Little Jonny once he had finished work. Each week we would meet outside the college and go in to the classroom together. At break times, we behaved like giggling teenage girls hanging around the corridors sipping cans of coke, and usually discussing Rob. Penelope and I were becoming inseparable; it was a friendship that seemed to develop quickly. She was always asking me to go, here, there and everywhere with her, shopping, the cinema, or grabbing a bite to eat after the college course. To be honest, Penelope was doing me a favour by keeping me busy. I was suffering from a broken heart.'

'The Farrier?' I interrupted.

'Yes, how do you know that?'

'I overheard you in the kitchen.'

'Did you ever meet Camilla?' Melanie asked.

Raising my eyebrows I answered, 'She has crossed my path a few times, unfortunately.'

We both laughed.

'Camilla told me that they were a couple and I disappeared from the stables we were working at. I couldn't bear to see him with someone else and now it seems that wasn't quite the case.'

'I bet that was difficult for you?'

'It was, the Farrier belongs in my heart, he is the only man I ever carried a torch for; and then there was Rob.'

'The tutor?'

'Yes, the first lesson of the course we found out Rob was single after he introduced himself. I can still remember his words very clearly.'

'Please do not call me Sir or Mr Hardy. My name is Rob and I love fancy restaurants, appreciate a full-bodied glass of wine, strolls in the country and I play the odd game of football at the weekend in an attempt to maintain some level of fitness. I have one son and one wife, well soon to be ex-wife.' I can remember Penelope spinning round on her chair and declaring 'he's single he's bloody single!' Melanie mimicked.

'I hope you don't mind me asking but how did you two get together then?'

'Rob was very flirtatious in the classroom, but more so towards me with his cheeky winks and banter and after the third lesson, he suggested we met up in a nearby pub after the class had finished. We sat at a table in a dark corner of the pub, away from the hustle and bustle of the other drinkers so we could talk. We flirted; it was fun, and the memories of the Farrier were slipping away. Rob was a good catch, maybe too good to be true.'

A sudden sadness flooded across Melanie's face.

'Are you OK?'

'Yes, I've never told this story, but it's good to finally share it with someone.'

I gave her an encouraging smile to continue.

'I started to enjoy myself, realising for the first time that other men might actually find me attractive. I could count on one hand the number of dates I'd been on in the past years but all were disastrous and best forgotten. I lost my confidence and self-esteem was depleted when the Farrier took up with Camilla.

'Then we began to get closer. He would take me out more and more and I could safely say I was in an established relationship with Rob. I can remember when he whispered, 'I love you' for the first time. It melted my heart and at last, my mind and emotions were beginning to recover from the hurt and the pain caused by the Farrier. I began to fall in love with Rob. I let him in, but as time went on it appeared his words were nothing more than sweet nothings.'

Melanie was now visibly upset. She wiped away a tear that escaped and rolled down her cheek.

'My relationship with Rob seemed to deteriorate overnight. I knew Rob was a flirt. I had witnessed it for myself at the evening class, but panic started to set in when the topic of conversion began to include his colleague Laura all the time. I challenged him on numerous occasions but each time he would declare she was only a friend. He dropped her name into the conversation at every opportunity – far too much for my liking and alarm bells began to ring loud and clear.'

'What did you do?'

'He told me she was his rock, and that she had supported him during the breakdown of his marriage, but then it also transpired that the luscious Laura was also the best friend of his soon to be ex-wife. She was the same age, thin, but not what I would call attractive. She was also a single mother, and her child was the same age as Rob's son.'

I could guess what was coming next, but I was still none the wiser as to how Penelope and a child's toy fitted in to all this.

'My gut feeling, the pangs of anxiety, and that ghastly distressing feeling were festering deep down in the pit of my stomach. I knew that Rob and Laura were more than just friends, the 'just friends' routine didn't bode well for me. I suspected he was a player, and more than likely sleeping with both of us. By the end of the course, he had started to ignore me in class and Laura began popping in to the classroom more and more. Then I saw it, that look in his eyes, that grin, and there she was standing as bold as brass in front of the class tilting her head and smiling back softly with those doe eyes of hers. I am not a jealous person by any stretch of the imagination, quite the opposite, in fact, but he made me feel so insecure. Every time I tried to talk to him about it he was ingenious enough to make me doubt myself leaving me feeling stupid and inadequate.'

'He sounds like a very devious man to me.'

Melanie nodded.

'He would humiliate me with his constant chatter about Laura and would taunt me about what a good friend she was, and of course, that she didn't nag him. He was cruel and reduced me to tears on numerous occasions. I asked him to stop seeing Laura but Rob claimed that if I loved him I should trust him.

'It sounds to me that this was a no win situation, a stalemate.'

'Exactly. I asked myself to what lengths was I prepared to go to make Rob love me? The answer was simple, none. It was time to walk away but only after, I did one more thing.

'What did you do?

'I followed him one night from the college and he led me straight to the front door of Laura's house. I parked the car on the road opposite and I watched them embrace on the doorstep and disappear inside the house. Before I could even decide what to do, I found myself running up the path and hammering on the front door. Laura opened the door, and of course, Rob was still standing in the hallway because he had only just arrived. The look on his face said it all, as if he wanted to be anywhere else except standing there; he couldn't even make eye contact with me. I asked Laura outright if she sleeping with Rob. Before he could answer, she replied, yes and what did it have to do with me. I announced that I had been too. Rob was busted and he stormed to his car and drove away at high speed with no explanation leaving Laura and me standing on the step.

'But at least you found out the truth and you now know it wasn't all in your imagination,' I offered.

'Laura invited me in and told me that Rob's marriage breakdown was due to a one-night stand with her after he'd had a row with his wife. After that, they had continued to sleep together regularly. In a way, I was relieved. It was like the weight of my uncertainty had been miraculously lifted off my shoulders.

Rob was clearly a selfish man and had manipulated the situation with Laura. She told me their relationship had been kept secret due to Rob controlling her. He told her if the news escaped of their indiscretions before his divorce was finalised, their relationship would be over.

I could only assume that she too had been hypnotised by his charm and was prepared to do anything to keep him interested – playing the role of family friend, and ready to support him at a moment's notice in more ways than one. She was waiting in the wings and didn't mind how long it took. He took us both for a fool.

Rob was more concerned about saving his own reputation. He was very highly regarded within his family. His father was the local parish priest, and his mother belonged to every committee within miles; heaven forbid his good reputation should be tarnished in any way.

Laura had no inkling of his relationship with me; his excuses were believable; he was the model lecturer supporting students after hours with their course work, attending training courses, or marking essays. Well, what did she honestly expect? He'd already cheated on his wife with her best friend, I wasn't sure if that said more about him or the best friend, but why did she think it was going to be any different with her?'

Is this when you called it a day with Rob?'

'If only it had been that simple,' Melanie stated.

'Why what happened then?'

'I confided in Penelope about my decision to split up with Rob. I wasn't going to play his mind games anymore or even give him the benefit of the doubt. I wanted to take back control of my life. Don't get me wrong. Rob begged me to take him back. He came up with all the excuses under the sun, but I was sick of the constant lies, lack of trust and for the obvious fact I wasn't prepared to share him with another woman. Then within 48 hours the unthinkable happened.'

I held my breath, 'go on.'

'The two blue vertical lines appeared on the white stick and yes they were there, loud and proud screaming 'baby here'! Just as I'd made the decision to walk away from the relationship, I was pregnant with Rob's child. There was no other way to describe this situation other than a complete and utter disaster.'

'Dotty?'

'Yes, Dotty. At the same time, Penelope was also pregnant with Annabel.'

'Did you take him back?'

'He told me this would be the making of him; a child would keep him focused and provide a fresh start for us all as a family.'

'I'm assuming it didn't last very long?'

'No, my original instincts had been right; the relationship came to an abrupt end on the day Dotty was born. Rob, the lowlife that he is, was caught in the maternity ward toilet, partaking in his own kind of internal examination with another one of my friends who had come to visit me. Busted by Penelope, and not an excuse between them; well what could they say? That they were wetting the baby's head? I kicked him out of my life for good before I'd even heard the baby cry, or put my paper knickers back in place. What should have been one of the happiest days of my life came crashing down all around me.

'Is that why you fell out with Penelope?'

'What? Because she told me about the pair of them? No. Penelope showed solidarity towards me. She was great at first, but things became strained. I was a single mother, extremely tired, but with no one to share the midnight feeds with me, I had to do everything myself and I had hardly any money. However, I loved Dotty and wouldn't have it any other way. Penelope had Annabel, and it was she who suggested a joint first birthday party. We had a few mutual friends at the time – people from the antenatal classes etc.

As I lived quite a distance away, Penelope suggested we hold the gathering at her house. But the day of the party I was exhausted. I hadn't had much sleep the night before, because Dotty was coming down with something and had been restless all night. I barely kept my eyes open during the party and to be quite honest, I was relieved to return home. I placed Dotty in her cot and I must have drifted off to sleep on the top of my bed.

'When I awoke I checked my phone and I had received numerous messages from Penelope demanding where the present was that I stole. She stated if I valued the friendship, I would return it immediately. The texts went on and on and she was demanding that I return the present immediately. Then Dotty woke up a few hours later with blisters all over her body and the doctor confirmed she had chicken pox.'

'No wonder she didn't sleep much the night before.' I said.

'Yes exactly, and I was so tired that I couldn't be bothered with Penelope's drama and didn't text her back. She knew that for the past year I had found it extremely difficult to cope, and I would have thought she should have known be better than to think I would to pinch a present.

I just took myself away, and because Rob had controlled me for most of that relationship, I didn't need a friend who was just as demanding. I wanted peace and calm. I did check the presents and yes, I did have an extra toy, which I placed on Penelope's doorstep a week later, with a note explaining the mix-up but I didn't hear from her again.'

I shook my head in disbelief, it was typical of Penelope to tell me what Melanie had done, yet failed to tell me what she had done to make amends.

CHAPTER 12

After a couple of months of fending for herself and the two children, Penelope was feeling more positive about life. Rupert was supporting her financially and appearing on demand to babysit whenever he was summoned. Life had been tough for Penelope when they first split up; the rumours of her new single status were circulated among the mothers in the playground, and she had become the talk of the village. Swamped with fake concern and constant sympathetic hugs, all anyone really wanted to know was if Rupert had another woman. I helped her with some of the necessary more mundane tasks such as changing the car insurance and opening a new bank account; a trip to the benefit office was also needed now she was unemployed, thanks to Camilla's overnight bunk.

Overall, she was coping brilliantly; her social life was practically non-existent due to the lack of disposable cash, but her domestic chores were organised and accomplished on a daily basis leaving her modest detached house on the estate looking like a show home. Her daily routine was becoming entrenched.

Penelope accepted this was her life; well for the time being anyway. At this moment in time, the only love of her life was the new Dyson vacuum cleaner she'd managed to purchase before Rupert sneakily shut down the joint bank accounts without her consent.

She needed a change, she told me, but she wasn't sure what that change was, except that having fun was, without doubt, at the top of that list. Her stance in the playground had already been decided; she had at present relegated herself back to her original position of standing next to me. For most of the day, Penelope would communicate with nobody; her only company was the unfortunate human beings that were exposed as liars and cheats on the Jeremy Kyle Show. Occasionally, she allowed herself to be distracted by the veneer of happiness portrayed by her cyber-friends when she scrolled through their family photos posted on their social media sites. On the whole though, she was coping well and was standing by her own tough decision to break up the family unit and dispose of Rupert.

The morning of March 3rd will be etched in my mind forever. I placed the children into their school lines and dropped the other two for their morning at pre-school, and had a pleasant walk home up the winding lane, listening to the birds tweet and observing the daffodils that were dancing in the light breeze. My walks around the village were more enjoyable and stress-free now that my pensioner stalker was no longer popping out from behind hedgerows.

The list of jobs that needed completing today was endless, but on arriving back home I began my usual routine – flicking on the kettle and retrieving my china mug from the dishwasher and making myself a cup of tea.

At that very moment there was a knock on the door. I glanced at my watch wondering who on earth would be calling at this time of the morning; it was too early for the postman. Picking up my mug, I wandered towards the front door.

'Rachel, Rachel let me in, I have a plan.' Penelope stood breathless on the doorstep. Wiping her feet on the doormat and rubbing her hands together, she flounced straight past me into the living room, nearly knocking the mug straight out of my hand.

'Good morning Penelope, don't mind me,' I said, 'come in why don't you.'

'What are you doing?'

'Having a cup of tea. The mug in my hand may be a little bit of a giveaway.'

Penelope looked more dolled up than usual. Not a hair was out of place, and she was proudly wearing a new purple shade of lipstick – it had been a few months since I had seen her wearing any lipstick.

'I've decided I need to change my ways; it's time I began to enjoy life again so I'm going to take the bull by the horns, have more fun and let my hair down so to speak. It's time; I'm ready – I need to find a man.'

I sighed with relief at this announcement – there would be no input from me required! 'And you're just the woman to help me.'

Sure enough, my sigh of relief had been released way too soon. There was no way I was going to chase, follow, or stalk any potential husband for Penelope. Life had been so much simpler before I met her.

'Relax Rachel. I'm not going to ask you to go on any double dates or anything. Everything will be fine, I promise.'

I wasn't convinced. 'Hmm, can I have that in writing?' I replied, thinking that would make Matt feel a whole lot better about the situation when I informed him of the latest goings-on in the mad world of mothers. Sometimes I really envied Matt, going to work every day, communicating with normal, sensible people with no need to ever visit the dark side of a playground.

She leaned closer towards me from the armchair, her face serious. 'I know you're married but I've got the best plan ever; we are going speed-dating!'

Then there was silence. I felt the colour drain from my face.

'Rachel, are you OK? You have gone a funny colour, a whiter shade of white to be precise, can I get you anything?' Penelope asked with concern.

'A glass of whisky,' I instinctively replied, the standard response to the majority of Penelope's ideas.

I could see by the look on her face that Penelope was serious – deadly serious.

'Really Rachel, it's only quarter to ten in the morning.'

'If you are serious about speed-dating then yes, I'm serious about a whisky. I'm not sure if it has escaped your notice Penelope, but I'm married and I have four of those little people that are called children. I like being married and frankly, I'd like it to stay that way. You can't really expect me to pay money to meet and speak to blokes,' I patiently explained.

'Ditch or date to be more precise,' she grinned.

I was completely flabbergasted.

'Penelope, I cannot go speed dating with you,' I replied insistently.

'But you must.'

'No Penelope, it's a categorical NO.'

At that very moment the waterworks started.

'Please Rachel you must. You will make sure I am OK, I've lost all confidence since my split with Rupert and I'm just getting back on my feet, you are the only one I can trust with this.'

Retrieving a tissue from her pocket, she blew hard on her nose.

I could see from the look on her face it didn't matter what I said. I actually felt a pang of guilt; maybe I had been a little hasty; after all, Penelope had trusted me with her plan. Maybe she did need a sensible friend to help her out on this occasion. The Playground Mafia would more than likely end up ridiculing her, and one thing was for sure, I wouldn't be gossiping about it in the school playground or anywhere else for that matter, she could count on that.

'I can't wait,' I muttered sarcastically.

'Thank you, thank you,' she said, suddenly throwing her arms around my neck giving me a quick hug and rather rapidly forgetting her tears in the process.

As plans go, this was not one of Penelope's painful plans – it was an excruciating one.

I urged her to change her mind – in fact, I begged her to reconsider, but her mind was made up and there was no way I could talk her out of it. The next Thursday night – to my utter shame – we were going speed-dating.

That evening when Matt returned from work, I got the distinct impression he was not thrilled with Penelope's decision for me to support her with her ditch or date plan. I think the way he slammed down of his bag and stormed into the kitchen rather gave it away.

He was seething and did not pull any punches letting me know that this was not one of my better ideas

'You are doing what? Are you on a different calendar – or planet – to me? April Fool's day is still a month away.'

Willing the kettle to boil, I clinked the spoon in the mugs and after what seemed like a lifetime, the steam began rising out of the spout and it finally clicked off. I handed Matt a brew, which in his own words 'is nature's cure for everything'.

He sat down at the kitchen table opposite me. With a half-hearted and sarcastic laugh, he begged me to tell him I was winding him up. Stirring my tea nervously, I was livid with myself; why didn't I stick to my New Year's resolution and just say no?

In my defence though, I'm not sure Matt was fully grasping the situation. It wasn't as though I was going to find a red-hot date, was it? Did he really think that the likes of Brad Pitt and

Gary Barlow were hanging about in run-down village halls up and down the country or paying to chat-up women in the dusty back rooms of the nation's British Legions? Surely not.

Five minutes later, Matt reluctantly agreed. Unfortunately, on my part, the deal clincher was the promise of an early night. I was bloody livid with Penelope again. It wasn't even a dead goldfish's anniversary or a flippin' birthday and I had to put out. She owed me big time!

The following Thursday, I could hardly contain my excitement. There was a need for speed and I don't mean speed-dating – more along the lines of the narcotic type which could help me get through the evening. Penelope constantly drove me mad for most of the day, continually texting questions.

What time are we leaving?

What are you wearing?

Hair down or up?

Flats or heels?

I, on the other hand was not very enthusiastic about the whole situation and had already decided what my outfit would be; I would be wearing my dungarees and chicken-shit wellies. I was going with the firm intention of impressing noone. No make-up would grace my face and my hair would be scraped back and tied tightly in a ponytail.

Matt grudgingly kissed me on my cheek when it was time for me to leave. It wasn't as though I was actually going out on the pull – my attire didn't ooze sex appeal and I was stinking after cleaning out the chicken coops. I didn't even bother to shower. Penelope pulled up on the drive grinning from ear to ear. She looked like a demented Cheshire Cat. I climbed into the passenger side of the car being particularly careful not leave a trail of mud from my wellies.

Glancing across at Penelope I was astonished; she was the complete double of Bet Lynch. Not only had she dyed her hair a new peroxide blonde which was completely preposterous – her hair was naturally jet-black and those roots would be a bugger to keep under control – but she had pinned a beehive hairpiece to the top of her head. I wasn't aware there was a sixties theme for the speed-dating night but it definitely appeared that way. My eyes glanced downwards and stopped dead at the dangly gold fan earrings that hung from her earlobes. That was nothing in comparison to the gold spandex dress that clung to every bulge of her body. The outfit was completed with gold strappy high heels; she certainly had the gold theme going on tonight. I wasn't sure this was the appropriate dress code for a night of speed-dating but to be fair, she would look equally out of place in a salubrious Blackpool ballroom.

The scene was set; we were travelling to the dilapidated snooker hall a couple of miles down the road. Penelope thought this was an excellent venue, not too local but not too far and there was the double bonus of potentially meeting the man of her dreams while incurring minimal petrol expense!

In complete contrast, I was very sceptical; in my opinion, this was way too close to home. If there was a glut of hot single-tons living a few miles from our place, where were they? The only single person I had regularly observed was Roger the one-eyed alcoholic hobbling up the road on his wooden leg to the local pub; all he was missing was a parrot on his shoulder. This latest escapade had disaster written all over it.

The cost of this exclusive event was twenty pounds. I was more than a little miffed when I realised this didn't include any kind of refreshments but as a goodwill gesture the snooker hall was offering a reduced price on membership – that said it all really. To add insult to injury, we'd had to pay in advance by credit card which I assumed was the organiser's way of ensuring they had the cash upfront in case no one showed up. Penelope explained that prepayment was necessary to ensure that an equal number of people and the correct distribution of men and woman would attend because if all participants turned out to be women, it could be a little tricky if you weren't a lesbian. She had a fair point. Bloody hell, they had thought of everything.

A strict age policy was also applied to the event, which I found quite reassuring, as it would be just my luck that I'd attract another frisky pensioner stalker who was partial to chicken shit. As we drove into the car park, I couldn't believe my eyes. This was a revelation for me; these people took these events seriously! If I hadn't known better, I'd have thought I was about to stand on the red carpet at a glitzy film premiere. All the women were dressed to the nines, with myriad shades of lipstick, sparkly dresses and clutch bags shoved under their arms. And the men? Well the men all stood in line with their beer-stained T-shirts that barely covered their rotund bellies.

We were now forming a queue shuffling forward; I was even amazed that people queued to enter these sorts of places. The ultimate challenge of the evening was yet to materialise – finding Penelope a date – but to be fair, if any of the blokes in this line turned her down, they had a bloody cheek.

CHAPTER 13

There was no turning back now. Our names had been checked off and we had been gestured inside. The room was unbelievably shabby; I wasn't sure if the lighting was dimmed intentionally for a romantic ambiance or simply because they couldn't afford to replace the bulbs. A couple of toilets were situated in the corner of the room, a unisex toilet and one for the disabled, both with handmade paper signs stuck to the front of the painted-over cream doors. I made a mental note that it would be better to burst my bladder than to empty it. Matt had been fretting over absolutely nothing, never mind making any romantic involvements with pot-bellied, stinky men. His main worry should be the risk of me contracting a disease from the lavatories.

This experience was surreal; I almost felt as if I was going back to my youth; I reminisced about that loitering moment on the edge of the dance floor, fiddling with my hair in the nightclub praying someone, anyone, would pick me for one of the slow dances at the end of the night.

I bounced back to the real world when I received a tap on my shoulder. Swinging round, I came face-to-face with the gentleman standing behind me – a gentleman in the loosest sense of the word – wearing an eye-watering psychedelic shirt. Above the dodgy music that was being piped through a prehistoric speaker fitted above the potted plastic palm tree, I faintly heard him.

'Can you turn the heating up love, it's freezing in here?" he asked.

'I must apologise for my friend,' Penelope butted in, 'but she doesn't work here, she's come straight from the farm.'

'Loony farm to be more precise,' I muttered under my breath.

The bloody cheek of it! The so-called gentleman mistaking me for the caretaker, and the feeling of being underdressed started to prey on my conscience, but I suppose I did look more like Worzel Gummidge than Aunt Sally. My immediate mission was to convince Penelope to escape now while she could still totter in those heels with a little dignity in tow. I kindly offered to pay back her twenty pounds, which I thought, was extremely generous of me, but she blankly refused.

Then the room fell into complete silence. The event organiser appeared from behind the door marked 'Private'. The woman introduced herself as Marjorie. Proudly she announced to the wannabe daters that this was the fourth successful year she had run this event in the snooker hall premises on a weekly basis.

Everyone applauded. I on the other hand was bewildered.

People clearly measured success in numerous ways. I didn't see any accomplishment in turning up week after week. If all these people had been attending for four years, why didn't they have a date yet? Eyeing the area carefully, I quickly found my answer. More than half of them – well if the truth be known most of them – resembled zoo animals the way they grunted, snorted, and scratched.

Marjorie placed her long talons on the whistle draped around her neck and brought it up to her mouth. With one sharp gust of air, she blew hard. The applause stopped.

'Right, are we ready? Do we all know the drill?' she enquired. 'Collect your pen and paper from the hatch … men sit on the right and women on the left. Place a tick by any names you wish to date, a cross by those you want to ditch and I will email any compatible matches later on this evening so dates can be arranged.'

Who was Marjorie trying to kid? My guess was she hadn't fired up her laptop – if she had one – for the last four years and had never successfully fixed up any couple on a date in this room. She was no Cilla Black. Shooting Penelope uncomfortable stares, I collected my piece of paper and biro from the hatch. Penelope was already seated at a table with her head down, intently studying the line-up of names of potential suitors. I spotted a vacant table near the emergency exit, which would be handy, if I needed to do a runner. After reluctantly plonking my backside on the chair, I clasped the biro and meticulously placed a cross by every name on the list just so there was no confusion: I didn't want a date.

Marjorie blew the whistle again and we were off.

In a round-robin rotation style, we were allowed four minutes with each potential love interest. I glanced around the room and did the mental arithmetic so fast Carol Vorderman would have been proud of me. Twelve blokes, four minutes each, this could potentially be the worst forty-eight minutes of my life.

My mind was racing; even if I were single, I would never want to meet a bloke through speed-dating, especially this format. My guess was the majority of those taking part had more baggage than Penelope had during last year's mountain climb. I'm sure I was about to hear the words 'my wife doesn't understand me,' but then I reconsidered; there was no way on this planet any sane woman would have married any of these men in the first place.

The first bloke that squeezed into the seat in front of me was a sight for sore eyes. His podgy red face exhibited the most amazing hairy mole that appeared to have a personality all of its own.

Marjorie blew the whistle again.

'Your four minutes start now,' she bellowed.

'I'm Dwayne,' he announced, gruffly. Instantly, I moved my chair backwards trying to escape the halitosis fumes.

'Rachel,' I managed.

Then he grunted. Leaning closer over the table, he continuously stared at me. His mouth opened again, so I braced myself for the next verbal masterpiece.

'Your eyes are like spanners, every time you look at me my nuts go tighter and tighter.'

I shook my head in disbelief. My initial reaction was to slap him, but common sense prevailed; I didn't want any part of my body coming into contact with his.

Marjorie blew the whistle. 'Your time is up. Please remember to mark down on your list whether you'd like to ditch or date.'

I couldn't believe it when Dwayne placed a tick next to my name with the word 'chaleng' written next to it. I could only assume that meant I was a challenge; I'm not sure if that was a compliment or not. I suppose he must have had some education at some point in his life, how else would he have known the 'ch' sound.

The women stayed in their seats while the men moved around and found new prey.

I looked over at Penelope; she had a wide grin on her face. She gave me a thumbs up. We'd see if she still felt the same after her encounter with Dwayne, who had now slid onto the seat opposite her.

Marjorie blew the whistle again. Another four minutes of hell was upon me.

The species opposite me spoke first without hesitation. 'I'm Wayne," he grunted.

Déjà vu hit me like a slap in the face. Throwing my head up to inspect the person in front of me, there was no mistaking – Wayne was Dwayne's brother. I wasn't capable of speaking but my mouth fell open regardless and my jaw hit the table.

'I'm Wayne," he grunted again.

In exactly the same routine as his brother, whom I didn't doubt for one moment had the same mother and father (who were possibly brother and sister), he began leaning closer over the table whilst continuously staring at me.

He leant over and whispered, 'I'm no weather man ... but I reckon you'll get a few inches tonight.'

I made a pact with myself; if I ever became single again I would stay that way until the day I died.

Marjorie blew her whistle again. 'Your four minutes are up, date or ditch – make your choice now,' she hollered'

Wayne leant forward again. 'I'm Wayne, you didn't said your name.'

'Erm, Penelope. My name is Penelope,' I replied.

Clutching his biro he placed a tick next to Penelope's name with the word 'def' in the margin. Puzzled by this I was tempted to enquire if he had written this because he thought I was deaf on account of me remaining silent for the four minutes or because Penelope was definite date material.

Thankfully, before I plucked up the courage to ask, the blokes swapped seats again. Lucky me.

I scanned the list of names on the sheet in front of me and was relieved to have survived eight minutes with Dwayne and Wayne. The excitement was becoming too much, I wondered what the next male specimen to park themselves at my table would be like. I didn't have to wait long to find out.

Marjorie blew the whistle again.

That was enough, I couldn't take any more. I stood up abruptly, scraping my chair across the floor and stomped over to Penelope who appeared to be listening intently to Wayne's chatter.

I held out my hand and demanded, 'Give me the car keys now.'

'Rachel you don't need the car keys, it's not that type of event. All you need to do is place a tick or a cross against the names on the list,' Penelope giggled.

'I know it's not that type of event, I'm not stupid,' I retorted. 'I've had enough.' I thrust my hand towards her again and pointed to her bag where the car keys were stored. 'I'll wait for you in the car.'

'Are you sure you want to leave?' Penelope looked surprised.

I didn't dignify her question with a reply, just a furious glare. Obligingly she bent down to retrieve her bag from the floor. Wayne's eyes followed her; and he copped a look of what was potentially hidden beneath the gold spandex dress.

Hurrying out of the snooker hall, I overheard Wayne talking to the bloke on the next table indicating he thought that his conversations had gone well so far that evening. Was he serious?

CHAPTER 14

I climbed into the car and locked the doors, feeling relieved that I was now in a man-free environment. I guessed I would be waiting a little over half an hour for Penelope to return if her endurance skills were better than mine. It was freezing and all I had for company was an Alexander O'Neill CD – Mr Smooth himself – but on the plus side, I suppose that was better than spending another minute in the snooker hall.

Forty minutes later, the wannabe daters started to filter out from the snooker hall. High-fiving each other as they left the building, they were obviously celebrating a successful night.

Ten minutes later, I was still waiting for Penelope to materialise. Even Marjorie had left the building clutching the list of daters tightly as if it were the golden ticket to Willy Wonka's Chocolate Factory, and no doubt chalking up another successful night in her mind.

I was beginning to get cold and a little agitated so I made the brave decision to re-enter the snooker hall in search of the absent Penelope. It did cross my mind that maybe she had copped off and sneaked out the back door of the building but then I remembered the calibre of the males we had observed. Surely, Penelope had drawn the same conclusion I had and ditched all the potential dates?

Inside the snooker hall, the lights were now off and it was in complete darkness. Penelope was nowhere to be seen. I remembered the light switch was situated near the blue door marked private that I had observed on the way in. I carefully manoeuvred my way over to it, being careful not to trip over any tables or chairs on the way.

I successfully reached the light switch without bruising my leg and flicked it on. The fluorescent tubes started flickering and popping to life, bathing the area in artificial light once more. I surveyed the area a number of times but there was no sign of Penelope anywhere in the room. How very peculiar, I thought, where the hell had she disappeared to? Never mind a ditch or date event; this could very well progress into a murder mystery evening. I had suffered enough. I removed the car keys from my pocket, and decided there was nothing else to do except to head home.

I flicked the lights off again and ventured back outside. I could feel the temperature had dropped; it was only the beginning of March and even though there were signs that spring was approaching, it was still very chilly late at night. Shivering and glancing around the car park, I spotted another parked car. Alarm bells started to ring and I wondered if Penelope had been kidnapped or worse.

I hurried back towards the building in a panic, and with little regard for my own safety, acrobatically dodged the tables and chairs like a middle-aged version of Wonder Woman and flicked the lights on again. Still no sign of Penelope, where on earth could she be? Suddenly I had a brainwave, I could just phone her! I reached into my pocket for my mobile, dialled Penelope's number and waited nervously.

Over the hum of the bar chillers, I heard the faint sound of a phone ringing – not just any phone but Penelope's phone. I would recognise that ringtone anywhere. It was the distinct sound of the Weather Girls' 'It's Raining Men' I had heard it many a time.

I listened carefully, homing in on the direction of the sound. It had to be Penelope's phone and surely, Penelope's phone was with Penelope although she was taking her time answering. The ring led me to the painted cream doors that concealed the toilets, which thankfully, I had managed to avoid for the entire evening.

By the time, I reached the door the ringing sound had stopped so I placed my ear close to the surface of the door, being particularly careful not to make any type of contact. There was not a sound to be heard so I dialled Penelope's number again. I heard her phone ring again loud and clear, 'It's Raining Men,' blaring out from behind the door of the disabled toilet.

Penelope clearly needed my help; maybe the poor woman had collapsed, or was hurt in some way. I looked down and noticed the lock was broken so I grabbed the handle and threw the door open. My heart was nearly jumping out of my body and I was feeling genuinely guilty that I had abandoned her and left her to fend for herself. What sort of friend must I be?

My jaw hit the floor as the Weather Girls belted out 'Hallelujah!' and my eyes observed the sight in front of me.

He was definitely not tall, blonde, and lean as the song goes. He had a Jonny Vegas look about him and was wearing the same psychedelic shirt I had the misfortune of being confronted with earlier, which immediately dazzled me. When my eyes eventually refocussed, I could see Penelope's gold spandex dress was hitched up over her hips and she was bent over the washbasin. Mr Vegas was holding his shirt under his double chin, which flapped in time to the thrusting movement I was witnessing.

From Penelope's moaning, I gathered that the real name of the Jonny Vegas look-alike was Clive. At least she had enquired as to his name – he began shrieking, 'You have reached your destination.'

A mortified Penelope squinting into the mirror hanging on the bog wall in front of her finally noticed me standing there.

Losing her footing – probably due to exhaustion from her shenanigans – she fell to her knees. Vegas must have thought his luck was in and shouted gleefully, 'Yeah baby!'

Banging – no pun intended – her head on the cracked washbasin Penelope instinctively reached for the long, white cord hanging from the ceiling in an attempt to steady her fall. A shrill alarm echoed through the snooker hall and red lights began flashing inside the disabled toilet. She had inadvertently activated the rescue alarm.

Mr Vegas, now realising they had company, released his shirt from his chin, pulled his beige trousers over his boxer shorts and fled the disabled toilet, knocking me over in his hurry to escape.

Penelope scrambled to her feet muttering, 'I'll see you in the car.' I turned around hastily and headed away, allowing her to maintain a little dignity.

She emerged slowly and tottered down the snooker hall steps, eventually removing her heals to expedite her progress to the car. Penelope made her way towards the driver's side of the car. I had removed the Alexander O'Neill from the CD player, and was already sitting behind the wheel with the engine running. I flashed the headlights at her to open the passenger door. Once she was safely sitting inside, I put the car into gear and pulled out of the car park. Neither of us spoke; we drove home in complete silence. I vowed never to return to any snooker hall ever again in this lifetime.

Penelope's plan was to become a sexy saucy seductress; the only thing she accomplished was a dirty bang with a Jonny Vegas lookalike in the 'disabled' toilet in the snooker hall. As plans go, I considered the speed-dating experience one epic failure.

CHAPTER 15

After the insane speed-dating debacle, decided I didn't need any more of Penelope's madcap ideas or anyone else's for that matter, and I kept myself to myself as much as I possibly could. Some mornings, I was glad to escape out of the house for a brisk walk, with the dog in tow, stumbling across an idyllic countryside path up the lane and over the fields for some fresh country air.

Life was beginning to settle down. Penelope too kept her distance, which probably had more to do with the embarrassment of the situation. I, on the other hand, was glad, and I never wanted to witness Penelope in that dress ever again.

The house rang with Matt's laughter the night I arrived home after speed-dating. I'd rather never visualise that moment again. Needless to say, no emails from Marjory seeking to fix me up on a successful date pinged in my inbox that night or any other.

Melanie was becoming a regular visitor to the Farrier next door. The realisation that Camilla had duped both of them with her games all those years ago saddened both the Farrier and Melanie; they'd missed many happy years together. Melanie and my friendship was blossoming. Every morning we stood chatting together in the school playground, and she would often walk with me when I dropped Matilda and Daisy at pre-school. On many occasions, we would grab a cuppa after the morning school run. I really liked Melanie; there were no hidden agendas with her. I could be myself and we weren't in competition over the children, and to be honest, we barely talked about them. She was a different kettle of fish from Penelope. We were certainly on the same wavelength.

One morning after returning home from walking the dog, Melanie rapped on the door to share her wonderful news. Opening the door, she was standing before me with a beaming smile that spread from ear to ear.

'Are you sleeping with the Farrier?' I asked.

'Who said that?' she replied, laughing.

'You just did, when you didn't say no! Busted!' I laughed.

There was only one way to celebrate – a slice of Victoria Sponge and a cup of tea. Oh, and I wanted to hear all the details!

The marvellous news didn't end there; the Farrier was determined not to waste any more time being without Melanie and after careful consideration and approval from his daughter Rosie, both invited Melanie and Dotty to move into their home with them. They were going to be one happy family.

'Jeez, that was quick but don't get me wrong I am really pleased for you.'

'I know,' replied Melanie 'but we have just picked up where we left off all those years ago and if you know that you want to spend the rest of your life with someone, why not? We don't need to ask our parents' permission.'

'Well in the Farrier's case that would be difficult, his father is dead and goodness knows where Iris Fletcher-Parker is.' I joked.

'We are going to be neighbours!'

'I'll drink to that,' chinking my cuppa against Melanie's mug.

After all these years, Melanie's feelings towards the Farrier had never disappeared; he was 'the one,' the man she wanted to grow old with. I was overjoyed for both of them, I was a sucker for a love story, and they made a lovely couple.

Clearly, Penelope wasn't thrilled for Melanie when I bumped into her at the end of the lane on the afternoon school run. I thought it was general chitchat sharing such delightful news.

Storming off towards the playground, she left me for dust and I shook my head in disbelief. I struggled with the logic behind it all; Penelope was clearly jealous for whatever reason. Perhaps she was afraid that Melanie might become an even closer friend of mine. To me it was insane; Penelope falling out over a toy – was that really worth it? Melanie's view on it all revealed it was a genuine slip-up – I hadn't doubted that for a second – just an extra present scooped up in haste with all the others.

Penelope, for some reason, considered Melanie a rival; someone she must struggle against for my attention. Even though at times it was quite amusing, at others it was tiresome and frankly, I was getting a little fed up with dancing to Penelope's tune. In fact, those dancing shoes were long disposed of in the recycle bin when I made my New Year's resolution. The speed-dating was a slight blip. However, I was back on track.

Oh the joy of it all, on my very arrival at the playground there appeared to be a minor dilemma. Penelope and Melanie were standing on either side of the patch of playground where I always stood. Their arms were folded and both were ignoring each other. I, as usual, was piggy-in-the-bloody-middle.

Positioning myself between the two women, I spoke, 'Before either of you huff or puff or say anything I feel you ladies need to recapture your sanity. Are the pair of you never ever going to speak again because of a child's birthday present?' There I'd said it; taking my life into my own hands I'd put it out there when it was absolutely nothing to do with me. Silently they stared at each other. To be quite honest, this wasn't Melanie's doing and I felt a little awkward for putting her on the spot, but since we had to stand here every day, even if they had no intention of becoming best buddies, it would make for a more comfortable atmosphere if they at least acknowledged each other. Scrutinising Penelope's expression, I couldn't predict which way this was going to end up.

Thankfully, Melanie chiselled through the tension, and held out her hand. We waited hoping Penelope would reach out and grasp the olive branch being offered. Luckily, for all of us, Penelope swallowed her pride and did just that.

Saved by the school bell, the children came running out chattering excitedly about their school day.

'Mum, we had my favourite lunch today,' Eva excitedly told us all.

'Erm ... Let me guess, it wouldn't be spaghetti bolognese by any chance would it?' I grinned.

'How do you know that?' asked Samuel seriously.

'I think the tomato sauce smeared around Eva's face and spilt down her polo shirt was a dead giveaway,' Melanie joined in, giggling.

Eva looked down at her shirt and burst out laughing.

'Mum, I have a letter for you here,' Little Jonny handed the letter to Penelope.

'Here's Dotty!' Melanie stated as we watched her skip towards us.

'Have you had a good day at school?' Melanie asked Dotty.

'I loved literacy today we had to write about poem about something life changing.'

'Ooh what did you write about Dotty?' I asked.

'My poem was all about changing school and making new friends.'

'That's lovely.'

Penelope interrupted the chatter of the children. 'Have you seen this?' she asked thrusting the letter towards us.

We all quickly perused the letter headed up in bold black with the title, THE PTA NEEDS YOUR HELP.

'What do you think of this?' Penelope enquired.

'What do I think of what?' I answered. In the pit of my stomach, I hoped I was wrong that Penelope wasn't going to suggest we all jolly along together and join the Petty Tedious Army.

'I think we should unite and enlist our help.'

I think it's best when Penelope doesn't think at all.

Melanie began smirking behind Penelope's back. 'Penelope, this has your name written all over it, you are a fantastic people person with great communication skills and anyone who is anyone will totally respect you. Not only that, just think; there will be many advantages to this role; you would even secure front row seats at all school productions in the future,' Melanie stated.

It seemed that only I noted the sarcasm in her tone.

'I completely get what you mean,' Penelope responded smiling.

I, on the other hand, thought this was a disastrous suggestion.

'What about you, Rachel?' Melanie guffawed.

I shook my head. 'There's no rush for me, my primary school sentence has a few years left to run, plenty of time,' I replied with equal sarcasm, and I grinned at Melanie.

Watching Penelope saunter off the playground, I knew that by seven tonight my phone would ping with a text message telling me that Penelope was going to be the newest PTA representative. I wasn't disappointed. At exactly seven o'clock, while juggling with Matilda and Daisy and trying to get them ready for bed, I heard my phone ping over the over the theme tune to Emmerdale that was blaring out from the television in the living room.

* * *

Oo-er! The very next morning, saw Penelope in the playground dressed up to the nines, and looking very smart. Wearing my usual attire that entailed wellies and scruffy mud-splattered jeans, I was grubbier than usual. I had been fighting with an escaped chicken that decided the grass looked greener in the garden next door. It then flew into the brutal jaws of the neighbouring dog. Wrestling with the dog, I finally released the hen from its mouth.

'Goodness, where are you going to?' Melanie asked Penelope.

My gut instinct told me I didn't need to enquire what Penelope was up to; this outfit oozed her new PTA status.

Melanie and I exchange a knowing glance.

'I'd like to formally introduce myself as the new chairperson of the PTA,' Penelope said, stretching out her hand.

Reaching forward to cup her hand, Melanie said 'Nice one.'

'Congratulations! That will be nice for you,' I chipped in.

'It was a gruelling application process, interviews with Bridget, the head teacher, discussions with the previous chairperson, not to mention the grilling I received from the governors.' Penelope gloated.

'Hark at Penelope now on first-name terms with the headmistress, anyone would think she was the new prime minister!' whispered Melanie.

I knew Penelope was prone to exaggeration but I let her run with it and have her moment. We had only received the letter the previous evening and three hours later she'd texted me to say her application had been successful; any sane person would surmise from that it was more likely no one had been daft enough to apply for the role.

Excited to be assigned her first mission on her very first day, Bridget the headmistress formally allocated her the task of organising a uniform sale.

'What an excellent idea, rummaging through other people's old clothes,' Melanie said sarcastically.

Penelope explained to us she had one week to design a leaflet to be distributed amongst the children notifying them of the sale. The idea behind it all was to benefit those families that might struggle to purchase uniform at costly prices; this way, any second-hand uniforms in good condition could be sold on, for next to nothing. Overall, I thought it was a superb idea. Various items of uniform, which were no longer worn, were still hanging in our wardrobes with their labels intact. It would give me the chance not only to have a clear-out, but also to help some other families from the school.

There was nothing too taxing about Penelope's first mission. Firstly the designing of the leaflet, followed by setting a date, then the washing and ironing of the donated uniforms, and lastly hanging them on little rails in the hall ready for mums to purchase.

Changing my mind, I considered this would provide Penelope with something to focus on. Keeping busy was a positive move forward; she was still unemployed and small tasks would keep her mind off Rupert's latest antics.

It was rumoured that Rupert was coping fairly well with his new life; this really didn't surprise any of us, because his life was exactly the same now as it had been when he was living with Penelope. The only difference was that he had acquired a bachelor pad and entertained his women without the need to sneak around. Let's face it, he must have thought all his Christmases had come at once. A string of women were often witnessed leaving his pad at various hours of the day and night.

Penelope was aware of the rumours circulating in the village regarding Rupert's women, but she chose to stay strong and hold her head up high. I was beginning to admire her determination

to stick to her guns. She threw herself into the PTA wholeheart-
edly. Her high-heeled shoes were resurrected from the deep dark
depths of her wardrobe (all except the hooker gold ones from
the speed-dating fiasco – which were certainly best forgotten);
power suits were pressed and worn with pride, which led to an
all-new, very confident Penelope.

Penelope took her role seriously — she flitted in and out
of the school office mingling with the teachers and assistants
at every opportunity. Her new position had given her a sense
of standing within the school circle. She was now somebody.
Any excuse to use the photocopier or acquire stationery gave her
the opportunity to poke her head into the children's classrooms,
ensuring Little Jonny was securing his lead at the top of the
reading scheme display board. I was all for this new importance,
it gave me the opportunity to spend some quality time with
myself.

My influx of unoccupied time, now with the children attending school and pre-school, led me to thinking. Walking the
dog each day over the fields supplied me with ample time to
myself, but I'd noticed something recently. Not only were my
jeans becoming tighter, but also orange peel type dimples were
beginning to appear on the top of my arms – not an attractive
look. It was true, that becoming content with life only meant
one thing, the pounds were starting to pile back on.

I'd noticed it was becoming the norm to pour myself a glass
or two of wine in the early evening while preparing the children's tea. These were empty calories to say the least that needed
to be disposed of immediately, but sometimes a small tonic was
just what I needed during the children's meal times when they
refused to eat or were squabbling amongst themselves.

Finally admitting to myself that I needed to take back some
control, my mind began racing with keep-fit ideas. I wasn't the

type of woman to feel comfortable spending time at the gym, competing against other men and women drenched with sweat. Wearing the latest sports gear, exhibiting the latest headphones in a driven environment, and taking out a yearly membership that in all likelihood would be wasted after a couple of visits, wasn't for me. Diet products were equally as dreadful: chalky milkshakes, chocolate looking bars that tasted of cardboard; anyone with an ounce of common sense knows the only sensible way to lose weight is to put less in and move more.

Deciding that walking was no longer keeping me toned or providing me with a mental challenge, my mind was made up; I was going to start running. Every runner I noticed was not only fit but also thin. Magazine articles highlighted stories from women who became addicted once the running bug took its hold.

In all honesty, I had no idea where this thought emerged from; it was a laughable plan, really. I detested running and I couldn't do it very well. I was the kid at school that did everything in her power to skive the cross-country races, nipping behind the bushes and walking up the lane to the nearest friend's house to enjoy a can of coke. Then, smearing ourselves with mud and splashing in puddles, we'd sneakily re-join the race on the bend where the teachers didn't have the manpower to supervise, and sprint over the finish line; but I was still always last.

Yet despite this, my mind was made up, there was nothing like the here and now so I went to retrieve my old battered trainers from the overcrowded shoe boxes in the utility room. Throwing on a T-shirt and pair of shorts and hiding the front door key under the broken plant pot, I headed off, attempting

to co-ordinate my arms and legs in broad daylight, looking
more like a demented drunk spider than Mo Farah.

Clasping my water bottle, my heart was pounding, sweat
poured off my forehead as I'd never experienced before. I
wasn't sure I'd even clocked up 400 metres; I was going to
die, and fighting for my breath, I soon halted. Bending over
clutching the pain that crippled my side, I concluded I'd spent
longer getting changed for the outing than actually running.
Turning around, I headed home, which actually wasn't very
far at all.

CHAPTER 16

Determined not be beaten, I decided I had gone about this running lark all wrong. Throwing myself into strenuous exercise like this was simply idiotic; I'd obviously been hanging around with Penelope way too long as this was the type of madcap idea she would normally be responsible for. Putting my best foot forward – I wasn't quite sure which was my best foot – and coming up with plan B, I decided the best thing to do was to up the ante at a reasonable pace.

Plan B: After dark, I would attempt to run again. Outlining the route in my mind, nothing too strenuous of course, I prepared myself to half walk and half jog to the telephone box approximately a mile up the lane, which was located on the corner outside the local shop, then return home walking.

Once all the children were fed, washed and ready for bed, I placed my old battered trainers on my feet once more. Matt was curled up on the settee with the dog, looking comfy, 'I'll see you in five minutes,' he said smirking. 'If it's any longer, I know you will have nipped into the local for a pint.'

'Cheeky,' I laughed, winking back.

Wandering out into the cold night air my second attempt was underway. I'd show Matt; this time next year I would be running marathons. Setting my new running app, which I'd downloaded that afternoon, I was off. This time I was not sprinting like a rabbit being chased by a fox, but taking deep breaths and finding a rhythm that started to suit my clumsy co-ordination. Slow and steady wins the race. I was jogging, albeit slowly, but faster than walking – just. Fighting against the voices in my head that were screaming for me to stop, I created myself targets, pushing my legs to the next tree, the next bus-stop. I was ambushed by a gaggle of women on the main road through the village, who overtook me at great speed, dressed in bright pink trainers and tight black running leggings. I was amused by the wearing of sun visors, I wasn't sure of the purpose of those at this time of night. I recognised the women; they were mothers from the same school, obviously the running clique.

Before I knew it, I was leaning against the phone box fighting for breath; nevertheless, I'd done it. I was enormously proud of myself.

I turned round to head back home slowly – I actually had trouble putting one foot in front of the other if I'm truly honest – yet I was delighted with my achievement. I spotted a figure in the distance walking rapidly towards me. I recognised Penelope who was approaching me faster than a high-speed train, and I immediately noticed her tear-stained face.

'Are you OK?' I asked her.

Penelope, looking up, appeared startled; she was obviously not expecting to bump into me, never mind dressed in old shorts and T-shirt and fighting for breath.

'Whatever has happened?' I asked.

Penelope was having difficulty communicating through the sniffles, but she waved her tissue in the direction of her house and we walked over together. Taking the house keys from her hand, I unlocked the door. Flicking on the light switch, I helped her to remove her coat, hung it on the peg, and ushered her into the living room. Grabbing a box of tissues, I thrust them into her hand and headed towards her kitchen to make a cuppa.

I fumbled for the light switch, and then stopped dead in the kitchen doorway and stared. The sight was unbelievable: mountains and mountains of clothes in mammoth piles were heaped on the table, drooped over the chairs and dangled from the curtain rails. After finally tracking the kettle down under all the clothes, I removed the mugs from the cupboard and dropping the teabags into them, I stared around the room.

Recognising the sea of red and black garments scattered around the room, I saw that Penelope really had her work cut out for the uniform sale. There was tons of the stuff; she could never manage all this on her own and she had clearly buckled under the strain. Picking up various items near the kettle and inspecting them, I saw they were in dire condition. The pile on the table were in the best condition with the price tags still attached. In fact, all the clothes on the table still had the labels attached. Hopefully Penelope would remember to remove them before the uniform sale.

Placing a mug of tea in Penelope's hand, I realised Matt would be wondering where the hell I was after leaving the house nearly an hour ago. Quickly taking my phone out of my bum-bag – which I acknowledge is not a good look, after observing the running clique mums – I sent him a informing him I was with Penelope.

Meanwhile, Penelope's tears began to flow faster and she was plucking the tissues out of the box at a rate of knots, she was certainly devastated.

'I'm going to have to reacquaint myself with Rupert, and take him back; we need to be a family again,' she wailed.

I didn't understand; she was coping fantastically on her own; less manic than usual and was appearing a lot more chilled about life. OK, so it had taken her a few months to adjust to single life and organise her finances but the toughest times were hopefully behind her now.

'We need to be a family again, and the sooner the better. It's Little Jonny, the separation, split whatever you want to call it, is having a massive effect on him,' she sobbed.

My heart truly went out to her. Her tears were genuinely out of concern for her children. I hadn't realised the children had been affected so much, and was quite saddened that as a friend, I hadn't detected they were struggling. I'd let her down. Leaping from the chair and throwing my arms around her, she continued to sob into the dark depths of my sweaty armpit.

Gently releasing her, I apologised for not spotting any signs. As far as I could remember, Little Jonny had been bounding to school quite happily from the times I had witnessed in the mornings and bouncing out just as happy at the end of the school day. How did I get this all so wrong?

'It was today, the shock when I saw it, I felt sick to the pit of my stomach,' she carried on.

All kinds of thoughts were racing through my mind; what could she have possibly witnessed? There and then I made up my mind to support them through counselling or whatever it took to help Little Jonny and Annabel deal with the trauma of coming from a broken family.

'I was paralysed in the doorway I couldn't move, and not believing my eyes I took a closer look. My eyes weren't deceiving me, It was there in a fluorescent pink circle: Miles has overtaken him on the leadership board. Little Jonny is no longer the best reader in the class,' Penelope cried.

The look on my face must have said it all. Penelope was pounding the streets wailing, all because Miles in the same class as Little Jonny had overtaken him on the reader scheme. I was speechless, utterly speechless.

'I've neglected him, it's my entire fault, I decided to put myself first and dispose of Rupert not giving it a second thought on how it would affect Little Jonny's education.'

Penelope was unbelievably distraught and I sincerely didn't like to witness her in this state, but it was just a reading book. All children develop at different rates in their own time. Little Jonny was probably enjoying himself a fraction more now he has been released from the gruelling schedule of workbooks, reading and spelling due to Penelope's readjustment to her circumstances.

There was nothing more I could do. In all sincerity, I was utterly perplexed by the situation. School work with the children was never really high on my priority list; my general opinion being the little ones spend hours at school and when they return to the comfort of their own home they need to relax, play games and have a laugh. Respecting that we are all different, I gave Penelope a quick hug and told her to get an early night, tomorrow was the uniform sale day and judging by all the piles of clothes in the kitchen she would have her work cut out transporting and hanging them all up before nine o'clock in the morning.

Matt was convinced my detour from my exercise regime had been straight to the bar of the local pub, and not to Penelope's.

CHAPTER 17

The day of the uniform sale was upon us; the hall would be opened up to the mothers at 9:30 a.m. for the purchase of items. Penelope wasn't present in her usual spot next to mine on the morning school run. Time was getting on and I was just about to enquire where she was, when Melanie noticed her hanging out of the headmistress's office shouting coo-ee and waving wildly at the pair of us, ensuring every other mother in the playground noticed her too, of course.

She was really taking her role seriously, especially as she had descended on the headmistress at this time in the morning; Melanie joked that she bet the headmistress regretted off-loading the job on to Penelope now. Waving back at Penelope I wandered across to the window that she was hanging out of; she seemed in very high spirits compared to how she'd been the night before. I asked if she required my help to hang all those clothes up and organise the sale, but she assured me it was all under control.

Melanie and I decided to hang around the playground after the children had filtered into their classrooms, to give Penelope some moral support. She must have been up at the crack of dawn transporting all those clothes to school, preparing price tags, and hanging them up onto the clothes rails. There were other mothers circulating in the playground waiting for the doors to open, but not many that I recognised any more, maybe they were newer mothers from the years below. Glancing around the playground, it suddenly dawned on me I hadn't seen BB for a while

The lovely school secretary opened up the side door to the school hall sharp at 9.30 a.m. The school building was nothing remarkable; in fact, it was very unimpressive. It was home to approximately 120 children based in six classes. It was a very spacious building, all on one level, with a large hall that doubled up as a dining room at lunchtime and was used by the after school clubs for activities. In addition, there was one large field, a netball court and a bandstand – still to be used – bought by the Petty Tedious Army after numerous fundraising efforts.

Melanie and I were standing back in amazement   as we witnessed a frenzy once the doors were opened; for a moment, we thought Gary Barlow must be in the building as the mothers, re-enacting a scene from Black Friday, pushed into each other, tripping and falling as they tried to squeeze through the door. The school secretary was lucky to have escaped with her life. Melanie and I headed in slowly; neither of us was in any rush to fight our way through the hysterical mothers trying to bag a bargain and I was in no hurry to purchase back any of the clothes I had donated. Once inside the hall the previous five minutes seemed like a dream, everyone was calm, no one was pushing, and in fact, they were all standing in an orderly fashion looking mystified.

The hall appeared strangely quiet, which led me to stare in Penelope's direction. She was standing behind a table with an aluminium tin – probably full of loose change – her homemade name badge with the words PTA chairperson was being worn with pride, and I honestly felt like saluting her, or placing one leg behind the other and giving a quick curtesy.

Melanie was nudging me in the back, bending forward to whisper in my ear, 'Where are all the clothes, I can only see one rail; I thought you'd told me Penelope's kitchen was overrun with uniforms?'

Glancing from the back of the queue, straining my neck to see, Melanie was correct there were no clothes except one rail with a handful of jumpers and polo shirts with the odd skirt and pair of trousers thrown in for good measure. The mothers began muttering amongst themselves, 'Is this it? Where are all the clothes? What a waste of time!'

Soon enough, we witnessed the mothers who had fought hard to elbow their way to the front of the queue, now turning away, disappointed, scuttle back to their household chores, rattling their loose change with not a carrier bag to swing between them. Apart from Penelope, the only two people that were left in the vast vacant hall were Melanie and me.

Dumbfounded by the lack of clothing, I wasn't sure that Penelope's first mission set by Bridget the headmistress had been a resounding success. Penelope, appearing embarrassed by the whole scenario, began to unhang the few items that were dangling on the rail and to drop them back into carrier bags. We were just about to question Penelope on the whereabouts of the clothing when Bridget appeared at the doorway to supervise the sale. There was only one thing for it; I wasn't going to be summoned to the headmistress's office at the age of thirty-five. Retreating quickly out of the school hall, Melanie and I left Penelope explaining to Bridget where it had all gone wrong.

We were both feeling a little parched and at a loose end so decided to drive into town to treat ourselves to one of the delicious pastries that were sold by the quaint little coffee shop located in the corner of the church square.

Luckily, we managed to find ourselves a table situated in the window, and sank into the comfy chairs. We sat waiting for the waitress and watched the hustle and bustle of the town pass us by. Our chat turned to Penelope and the disastrous clothes sale. I just didn't understand it, swearing blind to Melanie that her kitchen had been jam-packed, full to the brim with uniforms – piles and piles of the garments cluttering up her kitchen – where had it all disappeared to? The only explanation we could come up with was that between the time I left Penelope's house last night and the early hours of the morning, she had been working extremely hard to secure sales of the items before the actual event started. Which would ensure that she wouldn't be giving up hours of her time in the morning; hats off to her for using her own initiative if this was the case.

With Penelope, still our topic of conversation, Melanie began quizzing me over our upcoming holiday arrangements. In fact, for the past few months I had been successful in blocking the very thought of this holiday out of my mind. To be honest I had no idea what was going to happen; the holiday had been booked during Rupert and Penelope's anniversary meal last year. At the time, they pressed that final button on the laptop to confirm they were spending their holiday at our house in Spain with no proper discussion. Matt and I felt conned and that our holiday had been hijacked. Over the past couple of months, walking on eggshells, I had managed not mention the holiday in front of Penelope, and wished that Matt, the kids, and I could slip away during the May half term unnoticed. We were longing for the situation to just disappear, but time was ticking on and the holiday was creeping nearer and nearer. Matt and I had discussed the awful scenario of Penelope still wanting to come on her own with the kids, but being as useless as we are, neither of us had managed to come up with a plan of action.

Melanie thought it was highly amusing, chuckling into her teacup; she could just visualise Rupert lording it around the pool strutting his stuff swinging his beer bottle and wearing his black speedos with the white drawstrings dangling.

It was not an image I was chuckling at, believe me. Spending a fortnight with Penelope, Rupert, Little Jonny and Annabel was something I didn't find amusing at all, but with Rupert currently out of the picture, it would be just my luck that I would end up babysitting Penelope and her kids for a fortnight on my holiday in my house.

Melanie was still giggling over the image of Rupert in his speedos, when I looked out of the window and there was Penelope striding straight past us. Looking as if she were on a mission, she didn't notice us and pushed her way through the double doors of Marks and Spencer. She was clutching three black bin bags that looked as if they were about to burst open all over the floor. Leaping up and leaving our money on the table, Melanie and I followed her into Marks and Spencer's; we were intrigued by the contents of the bulging bags.

Almost immediately, we spotted her standing in the queue for refunds. With each second that passed, she edged forward towards the counter dragging the black bin bags behind her along the floor. As she made her way to the front of the queue, Melanie and I were in fits of giggles, like a couple of school girls. Hiding behind a humongous artificial potted plant placed on a pillar, we began pushing each other out from behind it. An elderly couple wandering past, tut-tutted, not impressed by our childish behaviour, it was obviously a crime to have fun now we had hit our middle years.

Penelope heaved the bags on to the top of the refund counter, she turned them upside down and the contents spilled out. Melanie and I were speechless as we witnessed the items that fell out in front of the shop assistant.

The missing uniforms – pinafores, trousers, and polo shirts aplenty lay out on the refund counter. The uniforms I had donated from my wardrobes, still with the price labels intact were being handed over the counter in exchange for a refund.

'She is unbelievable, what a cheek! Please tell me she has not been filtering off all the pristine uniforms and cashing in on them for her own gain? We donated that uniform for the less fortunate families and the new chairperson of the PTA, it seems is abusing her newly appointed position!' Melanie whispered in amazement.

I had to admit the scene we were witnessing did suggest just that, but surely, Penelope wouldn't stoop so low? 'What are we going to do?' I asked. Scanning the refund desk, I saw the next two bin- bags of clothes being turned out onto the counter; the shop assistant looking flustered by the volume before she carried on zapping the labels with her price gun then folding the refunded clothes neatly into piles. The cash till with its constant pinging reminded me of the slot machines ringing out in the arcades of seaside towns as the amount of money was still increasing automatically on the cash register.

Scrutinising the numbers that were lighting up on the display of the till, we were flabbergasted; it was already confirming the sum of the refund was a whopping one hundred and seventy pounds, not at all bad for a morning's work.

Our giggling girl mood rapidly evaporated; Melanie's mood, I sensed, was now one of anger and mine was of disappointment, not because I was judging Penelope for her actions, but because there were genuine families genuinely struggling to make ends meet at the school, and the uniform sale would have made a huge difference to them.

Melanie took it upon herself to approach Penelope. I stood rooted to the spot behind my pot plant. Melanie tapped Penelope firmly on the shoulder. Penelope turned around looking startled.

I was fixed to the spot still hiding behind the artificial plant in the pot. Not knowing what to do, I contemplated just waiting there until Melanie had confronted Penelope. I didn't want Penelope to feel as if we were ganging up on her and judging by the look on Melanie's face she was really gunning for a pound of flesh.

However, the decision was made for me, as just at that moment, I was pushed from behind, and my knees buckling underneath me, I grabbed onto the potted plant, and there was an almighty crash. My face bounced off the plant and then the pot, which then smashed into hundreds of little pieces shattering all over the floor. I was face down, sprawled out on the floor looking a complete idiot. A woman hauled me up apologising profusely. She was the owner of a double buggy with two jam-smeared faces belonging to two small people who were both laughing at my misfortune. Bending down to retrieve a dropped beaker the woman hadn't noticed me or the plant and had pushed the buggy right into the back of my legs, bringing me down to the ground like a professional rugby player. In all the kerfuffle I momentarily forgot about Penelope and Melanie.

'What are you doing down there?' I heard Melanie's voice from behind the store manager who had rapidly appeared and was sweeping up the broken pieces of pot muttering like a mad man. Being dragged to my feet and brushed down hurt my pride more than my clothes. Melanie was standing in front of me fanning herself with a wad of notes, nearly two hundred pounds to be precise.

'What the hell happened? I was just about to come over when that mother ran me over!' I said.

'It was exactly what we had suspected; we caught Penelope red-handed abusing her position as PTA chairperson.'

'Surely not?' I still wanted to give Penelope the benefit of the doubt.

'She crumbled when I tapped her on her shoulder and apologised profusely for siphoning off the uniforms, and then she begged me not to report her to Bridget.'

I was genuinely shocked. I thought to myself that maybe Penelope was finding it financially difficult due to the split with Rupert, desperate times sometimes equalled desperate measures, or more than likely, knowing Penelope's obsession with Little Jonny's reading ability, it was possible she was going to use the money to fund a tutor.

'I demanded the cash and she handed it over. She was probably too embarrassed she had been caught to put up a fight.'

'Where is Penelope now?' I asked.

'She flounced out the shop in tears.' Melanie confirmed.

CHAPTER 18

The first few days at the beginning of May proved to be a difficult time for Penelope. A full enquiry took place after her escapade of attempting to steal the money from the donated school uniforms and the headmistress called the boys in blue. Bridget, the headmistress, ousted Penelope from the PTA; her title was removed, and her chairperson badge returned. She was the only mother I knew to be sacked from the Petty Tedious Army (PTA). According to Penelope, the headmistress had taken pity on her circumstances and dropped the criminal charges, due to the fact that all the money had been returned. She took no further action on the understanding that Penelope had no involvement in school activities ever again. Unfortunately, matters were made worse for her when she became the victim of playground gossip led by Botox Bernie who not only seemed to take great pleasure in anyone's misfortune, but also had a very short memory of her own misdemeanours.

I felt a bit sorry for Penelope; she'd had a rough run of it lately, so I decided to visit her one evening knowing that she would be feeling mortified and pretty miserable.

Arriving outside Penelope's house, I was in two minds whether to knock on the door. Observing that Rupert's car was already parked on the driveway, I parked mine, and then touched the bonnet of his car. It felt cold, so by my calculations it would appear he had been inside the house for some time. I stood on the gravel driveway, wondering whether Penelope would be grateful for the interruption, when the front door was suddenly flung open. Penelope had already spotted me from the kitchen window and was standing in the doorway smiling, signalling for me to hurry on in. Considering the trauma of the last few days, she was looking very relaxed and happy. It didn't look as if her sacking from the prestigious PTA was having any effect on her whatsoever.

Following Penelope into the living room, I saw that Rupert was indeed there sprawled out on the couch, which was actually a sight I had never, ever wanted to witness again, but at least this time, his clothes were intact. He looked very much at home, which also surprised me.

'Sit down,' said Penelope grinning, and ushering me towards the armchair in the corner of the room. 'We have some fantastic news.'

Waiting in anticipation, I was hoping the fantastic news wasn't the fact that Little Jonny had regained his place on the top of the reading leader board. Watching Penelope whilst she plonked herself next to Rupert on the couch, she began touching his knee like a giddy school girl, and he too was grinning from ear to ear.

'We are back together: ta da!' she revealed.

What? Surely, my ears were deceiving me. Actually, I was now gutted the news wasn't the fact that Little Jonny had regained his lead at the top of the reading board. They were back together; how and why had this happened?

'Not only are we back together, we can still enjoy our family holidays together in your villa in Spain in a couple of weeks' time. How exciting is that!' Penelope prattled on.

Feeling as if a high-speed train had hit me, I attempted to speak but no noise came out.

'We ought to go shopping for holiday clothes and organise the travel arrangements,' she continued.

Completely gobsmacked I managed, 'well that's just great news, and Matt will be pleased.' I'm afraid there wasn't much enthusiasm in my voice.

Part of me thought they had rekindled their relationship just to spite me. I wouldn't put it past either of them to have concocted a pact to rub along nicely together for the next few weeks so I could feature on the next television show 'Holidays from hell'.

I was also a little surprised Rupert had agreed to this sudden unexpected reunion, for a particular reason that I couldn't mention right at that wonderful moment in time. But I was remembering the numerous occasions recently, well more than numerous to be precise, that I had seen the posh car with its private number plate parked outside Rupert's bachelor pad. Penelope of course had been unaware of his regular lunchtime dates, and in my opinion, more than likely engineered the whole situation for Rupert's return. I could visualise Penelope begging him to come back home over an early morning phone call explaining the sorry demise of Little Jonny's education, Rupert would have agreed his return to ensure his son gained the stability he needed to reclaim his lead at the top of the reading scheme, or maybe it was just for an easy life.

Over the years, I'd heard of numerous explanations as to why separated couples salvage their marriages; to my knowledge, not one couple had ever rekindled their love over their children's reading books. Rupert was about to secure the best of both worlds; the sly cunning fox convincing Penelope he should still maintain his flat for the time being, until they were both one hundred percent sure the living arrangements would be permanent. I, of course, knew of the real reason he was willing to pay out the extra money on rent each month, to keep his bachelor pad for longer.

Remembering my manners, I offered my congratulations to them both. Penelope lunged forward flinging her arms around me and giving me a tight squeeze.

'I'm so, so happy,' she gushed, 'can you believe it? We are still coming on holiday with you all!'

No, I couldn't bloody believe it. Gritting my teeth I managed to say, 'How wonderful, I'll hurry home and let Matt and the children know the fantastic news immediately.'

Feeling very deflated, I certainly wasn't looking forward to returning home and sharing their joyous news with Matt. To be honest it was no skin off my nose whether they wanted to live under the same roof again, but the thought crossed my mind to offer a lump sum of money to support Little Jonny's education by way of a tutor, therefore helping him regain his lead on the reading scheme. Rupert and Penelope could stay separated, and for my own selfish reasons, it would prevent the trauma of the Kensingtons sharing our family holiday.

As I unlocked our front door, I was panicking as to how I was going to break the news to Matt. I pushed open the front door and he was sitting on the bottom stair with his head in his hands. He looked so sad, I panicked even more – had something happened to one of the children?

'Whatever is the matter?' I asked frantically.

'I know everything,' he replied flatly. 'There's no need to try and cover it up.'

Apparently, Rupert had texted Matt once I had left, to tell him they were coming on holiday with us. No wonder Matt was sitting with his head buried in his hands. Both of us had honestly thought, well maybe hoped, they would have cancelled the holiday and neither of us in a million years ever anticipated they would give their marriage another try. There was absolutely nothing we could do. We did joke about telling them straight that they weren't invited to share our holiday however, neither of us had the nerve.

Therefore, that was that. In two weeks' time, we were going on holiday with the Kensingtons.

The next day I was woken up to a very early morning text message, with the suggestion from Penelope that today would be a good day to go shopping for holiday clothes. Rolling over in the bed, I didn't answer; I didn't know what to answer, as far as I was concerned no day would be a good day to go holiday clothes shopping with Penelope. I wished the holiday would disappear. I'd even suggested to Melanie that she and the Farrier could have our flights as a gift, but after thanking me for my kind offer she informed me she would rather stick pins in her eyes than share a villa with Penelope. I knew exactly how she felt. There was only one thing for it; I needed to find some positivity in the situation. It couldn't be that bad. Apart from the school uniform blip, Penelope had given the impression she was coping without the trials and tribulations of Rupert's antics and it wasn't as though we were going to spend all day every day together on the holiday, was it? There would be times when we would go our separate ways and do our own things. That was most days according to Matt.

Still lying in bed and willing myself to move, I received another text from Penelope; if nothing else she was persistent. Reading the text I realised I had no choice; whatever else I had planned for the day would simply have to wait.

She was collecting me after dropping the children at school and I'd dropped the younger two at preschool; at least on the positive side it would all be over very soon. Just as the text suggested, Penelope was raring to go, beeping and revving the car engine right on cue outside my house just after nine fifteen. In comparison to my excitement levels, she was off the scale ... bordering on delirious. The constant chatter of the holiday was all I had the pleasure of listening to on the entire journey to the shops. Glancing down at my phone trying to block out her relentless chatter I smiled, as I read a text, with a winky face attached, from Melanie. '*Are you there yet?*' Somehow, I knew I was in for a long day.

Penelope, being eager about the holiday, had spent her time the previous evening surfing the web, researching the area surrounding our property in Spain. Not only was she zealous, she was bordering on obsessive, continuing into a long spiel regarding the itinerary she'd already planned.

The only factor that had been discussed between Matt and I, was to avoid any day trips and meals out with the Kensingtons where possible. Maybe we were being a little harsh, but I'd read many articles in magazines on the topic of holidaying with friends and quite predictably, they usually ended in a complete disaster.

In addition, Matt and I are simply not itinerary people; our plans on holiday usually involves waking up whenever the mood took all of us and deciding as a family what we felt like doing each day.

I was beginning to feel a little anxious. After driving into the car park space at the shopping centre, Penelope bent down to retrieve a rolled up piece of paper from her handbag. Handing it to me, I opened up the paper. Gulping, instantly sweating and not believing my eyes, I couldn't believe Penelope had even gone to the trouble, but there was my holiday mapped out in ink before my very eyes.

Penelope had taken it upon herself to create a neat square table with days of the week typed across the top in Arial font, with certain restaurants provisionally booked in for the night-time entertainment. The days were plotted with trips to the zoo, water parks and of course, the beach.

I knew I needed to act quickly, and start talking. I loved my holidays, Matt loved his holidays. He worked hard and the whole family appreciated this was his time to unwind, have fun with the children and not to be dictated to by a couple who had technically gatecrashed our holiday. The Kensingtons hadn't even offered to pay a bean towards the villa. In my mind, they were definitely taking advantage.

I had to say something. 'Penelope, thank you so much for thinking about us and involving us in your plans. I can see you've spent so much time putting together this holiday time-table of events but we've been holidaying in our villa for the last ten years. If I'm going to be honest with you, we just get up each day and go wherever the mood takes the children, and us but your itinerary will be excellent for you, Rupert and the kids. The more activities and visits you cram in the better, I don't want you wasting your holiday waiting around for us; you go and do your own thing.'

There I'd said it. I couldn't believe I'd been so brave, usually I was all for an easy life but there was no way I was traipsing around any type of zoo visits with the Kensingtons whilst Penelope continually tested Little Jonny's knowledge of all of the exotic animals. I was with Melanie on this one; I'd rather stick pins in my eyes.

Penelope appeared a little deflated. Biting her bottom lip, I could see the cogs were turning over, digesting what I'd just said.

I began wandering around the shops, closely followed by Penelope. The shops were laden with pretty, brightly coloured

holiday clothes. I didn't need to purchase much today, perhaps a
new bikini and a couple of lightweight maxi dresses. We had numerous items of holiday clothes already stored in the wardrobes
in our house in Spain so we always travelled light.

Penelope still seemed very subdued. Surely the fact we didn't
want to spend every waking minute of the holiday in their pockets couldn't have thrown her off balance this much. Trying to
gee her along, I began pulling clothes off the hangers, holding
them up to my body and asking her opinion on each item. I
tried my best to make her smile but it was glaringly obvious her
mood had changed and that she wasn't enjoying her day out at
all anymore.

Changing tack, I suggested we grab a cup of coffee in one of
the department store restaurants. Perhaps she felt a little light-
headed and a quick drink and bite to eat would maybe do the
trick. Arriving at the cafe and grabbing a brown plastic tray, I
placed a couple of coffee mugs on top alongside a couple of
sticky buns. Penelope wandered off to the toilet leaving me to
pay for the drinks.

Securing the only vacant table, I begin sipping my drink,
waiting for Penelope's return. Looking around I observed two
yummy mummies dripping in designer clothes with a young
child strapped into the latest exclusive buggy parked next to
the table. They were sitting there with their perfectly manicured
nails sipping their cappuccinos whilst discussing the upcoming
birthday of a boy named Seb.

Seated at the table next to them was a man wearing a pin-
striped suit, his jacket unfastened, sinking his teeth into a bacon butty that oozed brown sauce and dripped onto his plate
below. He then slurped his tea and tapped on his laptop as if
the financial world depended on it. Ten minutes had passed,
and there was still no sign of Penelope. Not wanting to be rude,

but I'd waited long enough, I tucked into my sticky bun. Penelope's coffee, by now, would be barely luke warm and certainly freezing cold if she didn't hurry back soon. Finally, after nearly twenty minutes, I spotted her making her way back towards me at the table.

'Is everything OK?' I enquired. 'You've been ages.'

'Actually no, I'm feeling a little dizzy and I have one of my headaches coming on; do you mind if we drink up quickly and go back home?'

I was a little taken aback; this shopping trip was all her idea, but to be honest I didn't really mind. I didn't have anything to drink up quick, having already demolished my sticky bun and coffee, I was ready to go. There were plenty of household jobs I could be getting on with before the afternoon school run.

'While you sit there and drink your coffee, I'm going to nip quickly back to the shop next door. I really fancied that pink striped bikini I saw earlier, so I'll just be two minutes; you wait here.'

Penelope only managed a nod while I rushed next door to make the only purchase of today's shopping trip.

That was that; our holiday shopping outing brought to an abrupt end. Penelope was extremely quiet on the whole of our return journey, she dropped me back home, and with a quick wave of the hand, she was gone. Maybe she was just hormonal or about to come down with a bug; whichever it was, an afternoon nap was maybe the tonic needed to recharge her batteries.

CHAPTER 19

It was the night before the holiday and all four children were bathed, hair washed, wearing their PJs, and ready for an early night. Each one of them was excited; willing that tomorrow would come sooner. Tomorrow our holiday would start, the holiday with the Kensingtons. The children seemed unperturbed, yet Matt and I were both anxious; we could only hope the next two weeks were not going to be as bad as we anticipated. The children's clothes were set out in little piles at the foot of the bed ready for the morning. I packed a small rucksack for each of them filled with books, games and colouring pens for the flight. Next to their rucksacks lay a small wheelie case each with the minimal amount of clothes; just a new swimsuit each, change of clothes in case of any spillages on the flight and a cap and sunglasses. I didn't envy any families at the airport with tired crying children trying to manoeuvre suitcases around winding belted areas, running over people's feet and forever hurling them back upright once toppled over due to the excessive weight. We were lucky we didn't need any luggage except our hand luggage on the short flight to our second home.

We settled down on the sofa with a bottle of wine once all the children were sound asleep in their beds. I lay my legs over Matt's knees while he poured us a couple of glasses. Thoughts were running through my head, I really needed this holiday, since I'd began my running regime I'd begun to feel a little drained and tired really quickly. Putting it down to the excess calories I was burning no matter what the next two weeks had in store for us, I was determined to rest and enjoy myself with my family. Matt and I clinked our glasses 'Here's to a happy holiday,' I laughed.

'I think there's only one thing we can do over the next two weeks and that's to try and make the best of the situation,' I said.

'Maybe we are misjudging the Kensingtons, for all we know they may the best holiday companions one could hope for,' grinned Matt.

'Do you really believe that?'

'Of course I don't!'

We both laughed then, and took a sip of our wine.

'We will need buckets of patience.'

'I know, but let's hope they surprise us and the next two weeks run smoothly.'

'Yes, fingers crossed. What could possibly go wrong?' I joked.

We both raised our eyebrows at each other and then cuddled down on the sofa.

'Well, let's hope they have done the right thing in getting back together for the sake of the children and lets pray to God Little Jonny doesn't disappoint them and he secures his place at Oxford,' Matt laughed.

The landline rang; Matt placed his wine glass on the table and reached out to pick up the receiver. After saying hello, he began mouthing at me like a demented fish, pointing at the telephone informing me it was Penelope. Smirking and pulling daft faces at him I detected the change of tone in his voice and his serious face began to emerge, 'I'm sorry Penelope it didn't cross my mind to tell you, but it won't matter, it's only for a couple of hours max if that. It's nothing to worry about, we will all be at the other end before we know it, sunning ourselves with a beer in hand,' he said, apologetically.

'We don't need to leave that early; we will meet you in the departures lounge and send you a message as soon as we arrive,' Matt continued, obviously replying to whatever Penelope was throwing at him.

Matt hung up and the first trauma of the holiday was upon us.

It hadn't been an intentional move, but Matt had already gone ahead and booked our seats on the plane using the on-line check-in. This had actually worked out in our favour, as it would mean that we wouldn't be sitting next to the Kensingtons on the plane. It had been an oversight on Matt's part but we were very pleased with the outcome. According to Matt, Penelope had called to confirm the time we all needed to leave in convoy for the airport. Matt was a last minute type of guy, a guy that would be late for his own funeral; he wouldn't hang around anywhere unless he truly needed to and airports were certainly not his thing – a pet hate of his to be more precise. By checking us in online, he had secured us another two hours in bed; we didn't need to arrive at the airport until one hour before take-off. Unfortunately, for the Kensingtons, they would have to be at the airport three hours before departure and then sit and wait in the departures lounge with next to nothing to do.

Matt genuinely had not realized the implications, but as on-line check-in was now shut there was nothing that could be done, the Kensingtons would be allocated their seats on arrival.

The following morning we awoke feeling much better for the extra hours. I already had a text from Penelope, sent at 4 a.m. I could not understand why she would be texting at such a ridiculous time in the morning, but it soon became clear. Penelope had begun panicking over the seating arrangements on the plane, coaxing Rupert to wake up even earlier than necessary, and ordered him to arrive at the check-in two hours ahead of their three-hour check-in time.

This was absolutely bonkers; why would anyone want to be sitting and waiting around in an airport when they could be still enjoying the comfort of their own home. Penelope's plan was to be first in the queue; she would be first all right, and she would be standing there waiting before the check-in attendants were even out of their own beds.

The method to her madness, and it was certainly madness, was that if they were the first family to arrive out of those that hadn't taken the opportunity to confirm their seats online, it might be a possible to have their seats allocated in a row near to us, if not adjacent to ours. I bet Rupert was not screeching for joy at this ridiculous scenario. For the time that we would be in the air, did it really matter if we were on opposite ends of the plane?

Once the children were washed, dressed and finished eating their breakfast, we were ready and raring to go. They were so excited to be returning to their Spanish home and Matt and I were especially looking forward to relaxing in the sunshine.

Passports – Check

Tickets – Check

Car Hire paperwork – Check

We were ready. We clambered into the car. Matt fired up the engine, and with squeals of delight from the children, we were off! We hoped by the time we arrived, the Kensingtons would have had their seats allocated and the situation resolved.

Inside the terminal building, we saw that our flight was in less than an hour's time, which by my reckoning gave us plenty of time to grab a quick drink and for one more toilet stop before setting off on our holiday.

We found the check-in counter and Eva, Samuel, Matilda and Daisy all screeching with joy, ran towards the queuing holidaymakers. We joined the back of the queue, which was extremely long – actually, so long that Matt made a comment that something must be up as it wasn't usually this busy with less than an hour to go before boarding.

The children promptly squatted on the brown floor tiles and chattering among themselves, began playing a game of Ispy. As we turned to face the queue directly in front of us, Matt and I suddenly became aware that the sea of people in front were staring straight back at us. There were only a two words that could describe every face that was glaring at us – FED UP. Mothers were soothing whimpering children, babies' nappies were being changed in the long line of people before us and we heard numerous tuts that seemed to be directed at us.

Two airport officials were walking towards us, and a strong feeling of dread suddenly came over me. Guessing this might have something to do with Penelope and Rupert; I prayed we wouldn't need a good lawyer. 'Are you the Young family?' one of the officials asked Matt.

'Yes we are, is everything OK?' Matt gulped.

'Nothing at all to worry about Sir, but we would be grateful if you could follow us please,' replied the second official.

Guiding us forward with the children following directly behind, we were escorted to the front of the queue.

Immediately, we spotted Penelope squatting on the floor next to three open suitcases while sipping from a bottle of water. Standing next to her was Rupert, looking anxious and constantly checking his watch.

Quickly counting their suitcases, eight in total, Matt and I raised our eyebrows at each other. It all seemed very excessive for a two-week trip to Spain. Next to Penelope were piles and piles of clothes laid out on the floor – more clothes than in my entire wardrobe. One whole suitcase was bursting to the brim with shoes – flip-flops, sandals, pumps, trainers, walking shoes – every type of shoe you could possibly imagine. Even the gold high heels from the speed-dating incident were crammed into the suitcase.

We could hear Rupert's flustered voice, 'Penelope, I am not paying in excess of two hundred pounds to take these suitcases with us. When are you ever going to wear all this stuff? We would need a container to ship this lot to Spain; it's ridiculous!'

Little Jonny and Annabel were perched on top of another couple of cases sharing out a packet of chocolate hobnob biscuits, which was obviously a ploy to keep them quiet.

'What is in this suitcase?' Rupert continued, wrenching at the zip and the clasp. The suitcase snapped open, and about 20 bottles of water spilled out. 'What the bloody hell do you need all this for?' Rupert shouted at her.

'Because we have never been to Spain and the water may taste different,' she shouted back.

Luckily, for Rupert, we arrived on the scene before he was arrested for causing bodily harm to his wife.

Penelope, scrambling to close the lid, quickly spoke, 'we are relieved to see you; it feels like we have been here hours.'

'We have been here bloody hours,' Rupert bawled back.

'What's going on?' I asked

Penelope told us that if all the suitcases were going to make it on to the plane, then they would need to pay an extra two hundred pounds. Rupert informed Penelope that this was just not going to happen. The two officials who were still standing

beside us looked bewildered by the whole situation and Little
Jonny and Annabel, who had scoffed all the chocolate hobnobs,
were beginning to get a little agitated.

'Mum,' Annabel said, her voice quivering. 'Mum ... '

'Will you be quiet,' Penelope shouted back at her.

Seeing someone needed to take control of the situation, one
of the officials took Rupert to one side. Handing him a pen
and a form, he explained to Rupert that he could either pay
the excess amount or he could complete the form and the airport would store the cases for the remainder of the holiday at a
smaller charge.

Rupert pointed to four of the eight cases that were to go with
them. The check-in attendant looking relieved, hurled the cases
onto the conveyor belt, tagged them and sent them down the
chute before Penelope could argue or Rupert change his mind.
Rupert filled in the form, muttering under his breath.

'Mum, MUM!' Annabel cried.

'For God's sake Annabel, stop whining whatever is the *matter*?' Penelope shouted back. Having stuffed her face with fizzy
coke and numerous chocolate hobnob biscuits, Annabel was
turning a shade of green, and I mean a very ominous shade of
green. Moving quickly – mother's instinct – I hustled Matt and
the children out of the firing line. Annabel standing up in front
of Penelope opened her mouth wide and threw up all over her
mother. The vomit oozed down Penelope's flowery Boden summer dress; and settled in the sides of her yellow canvas pumps.
Penelope was absolutely fuming.

'I feel sick,' Annabel declared.

If Penelope and Rupert hadn't managed to secure everyone's
attention before, I could categorically confirm that most travel-
lers' heads in the airport were now towards us.

Dripping in puke, Penelope was about to blow a gasket. Rapidly steering Annabel out of sight and into the toilets, I left Matt standing dumbfounded with the rest of the children, Rupert, the airport official, and a sick-covered Penelope.

Taking cover in the clean, white clinical airport toilets, I cleaned down Annabel using the baby wipes that were tucked away in the side pocket of my handbag. I wiped her mouth and washed her hands, by which time she was feeling better. Glancing at my watch, time was ticking away; we still had to check in and I needed to buy drinks and magazines before boarding the plane.

Grabbing Annabel's hand, we rushed back to the desk where everyone was still standing. Gaping at Penelope I was mesmerised. Changed out of her puke covered holiday clothes she was standing in front of us in the gold spandex dress and killer heels that she'd worn for the speed-dating episode. Oh, the humiliation for poor Rupert!

Matt, trying to conceal his laughter – not very well I might add – began whispering to me.

After I'd left with Annabel in search of the toilets, Penelope had insisted on opening the cases that the official was about to wheel off to be stored for the fortnight. However, the only outfit she could muster together was the lovely gold number.

At last, we could check-in ourselves. All the children were being very well behaved considering all the commotion that had surrounded them in the previous hour. Matt, handing over our tickets and passports to the patient operator, explained that our seats had already been allocated online. The check-in assistant behind the desk scrutinised our passports and tickets, and began to tap furiously on the keyboard in front of her. Looking troubled, she peered up from the computer screen. 'There has been a request for your seats to be moved Sir,' she said to Matt.

'I think you may find there has been a mistake, a computer error maybe? We have categorically not requested to move seats; we secured the front row with the extra leg room, all booked in online,' Matt responded calmly.

'Hang on, there is note that has been logged onto the system,' the assistant explained. 'A lady called Penelope Kensington telephoned this morning to request that your seats be repositioned next to theirs due to the families travelling together, is that correct Sir?'

I could only imagine what Matt was thinking. Fuming, he swivelled around and stared directly at Penelope, waiting for her to explain.

Penelope, fidgeting before us on her hooker heels and spandex dress, looked like no lady to me. Reaching into her handbag, she pulled out a huge pair of dark sunglasses, placed them on her head and pulled them down over her eyes. Now she looked like a hooker who was possibly seeking to hide two black eyes. Stuttering, she tried to explain herself, embarrassed that the note logged onto the computer system, particularly after she had insisted to the airline assistant not to make a record of her name, had uncovered her plan.

Matt looked at his watch impatiently, as if to suggest we didn't have all day to wait for her explanation. I was too livid to speak to her; how presumptuous and underhand was that to change our seats without checking with us first? The cheek of the woman!

Managing to keep control of the situation, I turned back to the woman at the desk and spoke calmly but directly, 'That is not correct. We will be keeping our original seats, thank you.'

Rupert was clearly taken aback, not knowing where to look or what to do. He inhaled deeply then whispered behind us,

'I'm really sorry, so sorry, I don't know what to say, I didn't know anything about this.'

The check-in assistant gathered all the passports back together and handed them over the counter to Matt. The frequent flyer loyalty card caught her eye as it dropped onto the counter. She picked it up immediately.

'Sir, does this card belong to you? Why didn't you say, Sir? This card entitles you and your family to premium economy; on behalf of the airline, we would be delighted to upgrade your ticket; you'll get extensive legroom, champagne, free drinks, and individual television screens.'

The children let out excited screams while Matt thanked the long-suffering check-in assistant. Clutching our upgraded boarding passes as if our lives depended on them, we spun round to view Penelope's bruised jaw bouncing off the floor in complete astonishment.

I couldn't wait to be seated at opposite ends of the plane for our two hour flight, and to stretch out my legs before me while sipping champagne; this was the life. We certainly needed the time to recover and recharge our batteries from all the drama Penelope had thrown our way in the last hour.

Rushing through security there was now very little time to grab a drink or make a last toilet stop. Penelope, sulky and mortified at being rumbled, tottered reluctantly behind me.

Rushing into WH Smith, I snatched a basket and threw in a couple of bottles of water, bags of crisps and the latest celebrity magazines. Little Jonny and Annabel were hot on Penelope's heels and halted dutifully right in front of the pick 'n' mix.

After filling her own basket with magazines, chocolate and drinks, Penelope succumbed to their demands. 'What would we do without kids?' she laughed trying to clear the air after passing each of them a red striped paper bag to load up to the top with sugary treats.

'Actually, without kids I would be sunning myself on a beach in Barbados with a beer in my hand,' I replied – and not about to embark on a holiday with the Kensington family, I thought, letting her into the queue in front of me. I checked my watch. We only had minutes to spare; we needed to get our bums on those seats in less than two minutes.

Penelope placed her basket next to the till. 'Throw me in a packet of fags and one of those scratch cards for good measure,' she said pointing at the roll of cards behind the plastic Perspex at the side of the till.

Tearing off a scratch card and grabbing a packet of fags the shop assistant placed the bulging carrier bag on top of the counter, and held out his hand. The bill came to twenty-five pounds. Which was when Penelope suddenly realised that Rupert, who had been minding her handbag while she nipped off to change her vomit-stained clothes, had already gone on ahead and boarded the plane with her handbag in tow. She had no means to pay for the items.

Handing over fifty pounds in cash to the waiting cashier, which was enough to cover both our purchases, I requested he tear me off a scratch card too. Then suddenly, we heard the final call over the tannoy, requesting all passengers on flight 290 to make their way to gate 14 immediately. As we hurried to the departure gate, I handed Penelope her scratch card and fags along with the receipt for her goods. Hopefully, she would remember to pay me back some time soon.

Oh my! The premium economy seating was the bomb; maybe that wasn't a statement I should have voiced aloud on a plane but there was no other word for it. Eva, Samuel and Matilda sat patiently waiting for the captain to fire up the engines for take-off so they could plug themselves into their individual television screens, munch on their freebies and enjoy a film of their choice. Matt sat Daisy on his knee and looped her baby seatbelt through his. He was smiling from ear to ear. I settled into my seat and stretched out my legs in the vast space before me.

The smiley airhostess was preparing the cabin for take-off, greeting her passengers while checking all seat belts were securely fastened and closing the overhead lockers.

Reaching down to retrieve my magazines, I realised I still had Penelope's carrier bag of goodies, which I had taken off her so she wouldn't break her neck running for the plane on those killer heels. I unclicked my seatbelt and quickly made my way up through the curtained-off area in search of Penelope. I heard her before I saw her; she was sounding a little stressed. 'Annabel will you sit down and be quiet! I won't tell you again, Rachel has your sweets and they won't let me through to her cabin. Little Jonny you cannot sit by the window, that is not your seat; I don't want to hear another word from you either, sit down in your proper seat, now.'

'But I want a window seat,' Little Jonny persisted.

'Here they are!' I said, all for family harmony, and hoping to diffuse the situation. I pulled out the red stripy paper bags full of sweets and handing them quickly to Little Jonny and Annabel. 'And Penelope, here are your magazines and the rest of your stuff.' I handed the carrier bag over to her.

I was called back to my seat, and Penelope, staring in disgust at an exceptionally unattractive couple sitting nearby, forgot her manners and failed to thank me for re-uniting her with her goodies – goodies she hadn't even paid for. I was relieved to be leaving cattle class and went quickly back to Matt. I was looking forward to my glass of champagne.

CHAPTER 20

The next two hours were not only peaceful but joyful; exhausted from the last couple of hours my feet were well and truly up. – Relaxing, sipping flutes of the fizzy stuff and reading the magazines before me, I was the lucky one. Matt and Daisy had drifted off to sleep. Matt didn't have any alcohol during the flight because I had already designated him driver at the other end. Eva, Samuel and Matilda were passing the time watching a film.

Doesn't time fly when you are having fun! Before we knew it we had landed, had trundled through passport control – staggered in my case – and now were waiting by the car hire desk for Penelope and Rupert join us. Everyone was in good spirits; the children were chilled, Matt was refreshed and I was a little tipsy from drinking champagne mid-morning – but I was on my holidays and something told me that only alcohol was going to help me survive this holiday.

The Kensingtons lugging their cases behind them, and heading towards us, didn't look chilled at all.

'Good flight?' Matt asked, innocently.

Penelope and Rupert both glared at him.

Rescuing the situation, I took control. 'Let's get the car, collect the keys, and before we know it we will be settled at the villa sunning ourselves. Do you have your paperwork handy Rupert?'

Penelope and Rupert, changing their glare to a puzzled stare, replied at the same time, 'What do you mean?'

'Your car hire car voucher, Rupert, and you will need your driving licence as well.' I said.

Hesitantly Penelope replied, 'we don't know what you mean; we haven't booked a car, we just thought we would share yours.'

Sobering up immediately, it was now Matt's and my turn to stare at each other. I knew exactly what he was thinking and he knew exactly what I was thinking. With a family of six, of us how could they even think it was possible to share our car? What were we going to do – strap them to the roof? We would need to hire a bus! Judging by the thunderous look on Matt's face, he wasn't by any stretch of the imagination amused. I knew what was coming next, the feeling flooding the pit of my stomach – that gut feeling that was always right.

'Neither of us has brought our driving licenses, Penelope stated meekly, now nervously shuffling from one killer heel to the other.

'They have got to be joking,' I muttered under my breath to Matt.

Matt and I had been well and truly stitched up like a pair of kippers. Not only were we providing a free holiday for the Kensingtons, but now they expected Matt to be their taxi driver for the fortnight as well which could only mean one thing – we were going nowhere without them.

Matt, keeping his cool by the skin of his teeth, handed over the voucher along with his driving license to the woman swinging on her chair behind the desk. Carefully explaining the situation, he enquired to whether it was possible we could upgrade our vehicle to accommodate both families. The woman who was not Spanish and was called Jenny according her name badge, pulled down her spectacles, perched them on the end of her nose and looked at us.

After a few taps on the keyboard she said, 'You are very fortunate Sir, we don't normally supply ten-seat vehicles, but our manager has one, and your booking coincides with his two-week holiday. He's a bit of a surf dude and travelled to Hawaii to surf only this morning to catch some waves. He's left his vehicle in the pound and for an extra £200 we can upgrade you and your party for your two-week holiday.' She thrust the card machine towards Matt, and we both moved aside automatically thinking Rupert would kindly offer to pay. How wrong could we get? Rupert wasn't forthcoming at all. He had suddenly became more interested in fiddling with his sunglasses and was clearly not about to stick his hand in his pocket.

A disgruntled Matt produced his credit card from his wallet and plunged it into the card machine.

Keys in hand, we trailed outside into the car park. The heat from the sun beating down hit us instantly and lifted everyone's mood. Scanning the number on the key ring, we began to search the car park to identify our vehicle.

'Here it is, here it is,' came the cries from the excited children.

Gazing at the sight in front of us we could only imagine the car hire woman must have allocated us the wrong vehicle. There parked before us was not a car but an oversized van; not just any van, but a florescent blue, green and orange van with psychedelic flowers painted on the wheel trims. All that was missing was the bold orange type that read 'The Mystery Machine'.

'I am not getting into that thing,' said Penelope indignantly.

She had an absolute cheek; they hadn't even offered to pay for any transportation.

Pulling on the door handles, the kids revealed the equally as bright interior. The van was kitted out with orange leather seats, one could only assume they weren't real leather but there were ten of them all the same. It appeared there was no room for any of the luggage; the cases needed to be strapped onto the silver metal brackets welded to the top of the roof. Once the blokes secured the cases on the roof rack, Rupert winched Penelope into the van and we were all off on our thirty- minute journey to the villa.

There's no place like home, there's no place like home were the thoughts filtering through my mind as Matt pulled the car on to the drive of our property. I loved it there; it was so tranquil – a place of pure relaxation. The villa, perched on top of a hill with a beautiful pink clematis clambering up over the stone walls, faced the inviting azure waters of the Mediterranean.

As soon as Matt switched off the engine, the children were out and running around outside the villa. I unstrapped Daisy, who was still dozing, from her car seat and carried her.

The view was breathtakingly beautiful. However, when I turned round to close the van doors, Penelope, giving the impression she was hacked off, rudely began whispering in Rupert's ear. He seemed uncomfortable and shot her a 'wind your neck in' kind of look.

'How the heck have you afforded this?' were the first words to leave Penelope's mouth. There was no 'Oh my, what a beautiful house' or 'Wow, look at that fantastic view. I couldn't believe her reaction and it was a question that wasn't going to be answered. Penelope was jealous, quite simply jealous. Matt raised his eyebrows at me, and came up with the best suggestion yet. 'Let's nip to the shops, load up with food, ice-cream' – which got numerous amounts of cheers from the kids – 'and beer for the evening and then we can sit and relax around the pool.'

That sounded like an excellent plan to me and once the Kensington's suitcases were deposited in the hallway, I strapped Daisy back in her seat, and we all clambered into the van – all except Penelope that is.

'Do you mind if I stay here? I'm feeling slightly nauseous and a little tired from the journey, I could benefit from a lie down. Rupert are you OK to go and take the children?' she said, swooping her hand up to forehead like an actress that was about to faint.

What could poor Rupert say? He too had been up since some stupid o'clock due to Penelope's obsession with the seating arrangements; he wanted nothing more than to place his feet in his flip-flops and sink a beer.

All the children were beginning to flag a little now; they too were tired and hungry and so was I. Every muscle in my body was tired and I made a mental note to nip to the doctor on my return to check my iron levels.

Hurrying along in the supermarket, we soon had two trolleys loaded up with food and drink for the next couple of days. At the checkout, Rupert's behaviour turned a little strange. After emptying the contents of the trolley onto the conveyor belt, he artfully moved away from the shopping, and stood completely out of the way. I knew exactly what he was up to. Narked, I whispered sarcastically to Matt, 'The *I've forgotten my wallet* routine springs to mind.'

I started to compile a list of items the Kensington's had not paid for: the holiday itself, goodies at the airport, car hire and now the bloody weekly shop; where was it going to end?

Rupert went in search of a toilet just as the cashier rang up the final total and only appeared again after it had all been packed into carrier bags and loaded into the van.

Everyone was certainly ready for lunch when we returned. We each grabbed a bag from the van trundling back until all the shopping had been placed on top of the table in the kitchen.

Matt, tapped me on my shoulder and nodded his head in the direction of the pool. Not believing my eyes, I thought Joan Collins must have rented the villa off us for the fortnight; there was Penelope not only wearing an oversized floppy hat, linen sundress, and huge designer sunglasses, but also she was dripping in jewellery, sunning herself on my sunbed while us mere mortals traipsed around purchasing and preparing food for the day.

It was only a few hours into the holiday and already I was feeling frazzled.

I carved up the freshly baked bread and laid the table with numerous cheeses, pickles and cold meats. Placing a jug of water onto the table, I went into my bedroom to freshen up, only to find that Penelope had already secured our very own bedroom. Indignantly shouting to Matt to come here, who appeared next to me in no time at all and we gazed at the sight in the room. Considering Penelope hadn't felt at all well, she'd certainly been busy emptying all her suitcases and replacing my clothes with hers in the master bedroom. The en-suite bathroom was laid out with all her lotions and potions and her sexy new nightie lay out on top of the bed.

'She is taking the piss,' I huffed.

It wasn't in the slightest Matt's fault but I was more than livid now. The villa wasn't even short of space, there were numerous double bedrooms along the hallway – six to be precise – all with crisp white fresh Egyptian cotton sheets on the beds, and all with their own assigned bathrooms. But no, she had nabbed our room with its view over the sea.

I found the room that Penelope had dumped all our clothes in, and scooping up all the garments she had tossed on the bed, I stamped my way back down the hallway, juggling with the clothes in my arms, and kicked MY bedroom door open with my foot. I was just about to fling the clothes on top of the bed and remove Penelope's clothes from my wardrobe, when I couldn't believe my eyes. This was no Sleeping Beauty or Snow White, I wanted to growl like the bear in Goldilocks, 'who's that sleeping in my bed,' as resting under my covers with her eyes firmly shut lay Penelope, who skipping lunch, had taken herself off for an afternoon siesta in my bed.

Matt was quick on my heels ushering me out of the room before my hands found my way around Penelope's neck. Kindly taking some of the clothes out of my hands and placing them back onto the guest bed, he gave me a hearty cuddle, and then placing a cool bottle of beer in my hand, he persuaded me to join him at the pool. I swigged my beer, took some deep breaths, changed into my new bikini, and went out to join Matt. Scraping the sunbed along the tiles I swivelled it to face of the sun, relieved that Penelope was nowhere in sight. The pool was alive with splashing excited children enjoying the water. Daisy lay kicking her legs with various toys inside a playpen that Matt had set up in the shade.

Then a shadow cast over my sunbed. I slid my sunglasses to the top of my head, and squinted in the sunshine. Transfixed I gazed at by the sight in front of me, like a scene out of James Bond, he was swaggering up to the deep blue water's edge. Rupert Bond was wearing nothing but a pair of budgie smugglers. His skin-tight speedos left nothing to the imagination, his dark hairy legs looked more like a scene from King Kong but there was nothing King or Kong about Rupert and he was certainly no Daniel Craig. Noticing he didn't have a six pack, more like cheap beer from an off-licence, he'd certainly let his physique slide whilst he had shared cosy lunch- time rendezvous with the woman with the posh car. An eyebrow raised once again, I exchanged glances with Matt who was keeping a watchful eye on the children.

I jigged my sunglasses back over my eyes, sank down into the comfortable cushions of the sunbed, and drifted off to sleep in no time at all.

CHAPTER 21

I was woken up by the reappearance of Joan Collins, fresh from her slumbers, sashaying around the poolside. Aware of her presence, I opened one eye. I could feel Matt's gaze upon me. He was staring intently at me with a look of horror on his face and willing me not to look in Penelope's direction.

There I was, lying on my sun bed wearing my lovely, new pink-striped bikini and there was Penelope parading around the swimming pool in her lovely, new pink-striped bikini – exactly the same bloody lovely pink-striped bikini as mine. I bolted upright on my sun bed and Penelope paused in front of me; I no longer needed to squint; her body completely blocked out my sunlight. Placing her hands on her hips and one foot in front of the other, she said, 'Ta-da! What do you think? I loved the bikini you purchased on our shopping trip so when I got home, I went straight on the internet and ordered one,' Penelope was genuinely pleased that we were on holiday wearing exactly the same bikini.

The only words that escaped from my lips were unrepeatable and the only words Matt could understand were 'shoot me now'.

So far the first day of the holiday was going extremely well; I hadn't been arrested for murder – yet – though there was still time, nor had I chucked Penelope out onto the streets. Needing time out I got up and without saying a word, marched back inside the villa, and headed straight for the fridge. There was only one thing to do at times like this – eat chocolate. Opening the fridge door and reaching inside to the tray at the top of the fridge, I felt around for the chocolate bar I'd secretly stashed, the one I'd purchased from the supermarket earlier on. I was in need of chocolate, that and alcohol were the only two things that were going to help me survive this holiday. Frantically searching and standing on the tip of my toes, I felt around again, but the chocolate bar had disappeared. It was gone, no longer in the top tray of the door. Mystified, I could feel I was about to erupt when I noticed the empty silver foil wrapper screwed up in a ball and tossed aside on the kitchen worktop next to Penelope's handbag.

It was one thing to take advantage of my good nature and fleece me for a free holiday, it was another to parade around my villa in a bikini identical to mine, but it was inexcusable to steal any woman's chocolate. I could see the headline now 'Death by Chocolate.' I flounced back outside. Penelope was no longer posturing around the pool but was snoozing on her towel on my sunbed in her identical bikini.

'She'll be uncoupling my foot from her backside if she doesn't stop,' I mouthed furiously at Matt.

Matt came to the rescue, he snatched another beer from the ice bucket and forcing it into my hand, did the gentlemanly thing by placing my towel on his sunbed whilst he dive-bombed into the pool to entertain the kids for the next half hour. Rupert on his sunbed didn't move a muscle; properly exhausted from his early morning start, his eyes were firmly closed; his black hairy legs were milk bottle white from the factor fifty sun cream he'd smeared all over them. I lay fuming on Matt's sunbed as I went through the list of Penelope's offences. I could not believe the audacity of the woman.

On a positive note, the children were having a whale of a time playing games with Matt, and jumping in and out of the pool. Their chatter and excited laughter was absolutely infectious and delightful to hear. Deciding to pour myself a gin and tonic I wandered back into the kitchen; it was nearly tea-time and the children would soon be tired and hungry. Removing all the splendid breads and cold meats from the fridge, I set about making a salad to accompany them. After laying the table outside on the patio, I pushed up the stripy umbrellas to shield the food from the sun. Placing the delicious looking foods onto the table, I called to everyone to dry themselves off and to come and eat.

Without so much as a thank-you for preparing the tea, Penelope pushed her sunglasses to the top of her head and mumbled something about going back inside for a moment, then disappeared indoors. It was no easy feat preparing meals and drinks for ten people and it was the second time today that I'd done it. The children clambered out of the water and dried themselves down with the pile of towels I'd left by the table near the pool. The sun was warm on my skin and as I sipped my gin and tonic and looked out over the sea I began to feel a little more relaxed, and hoped things would be a little easier tomorrow once Penelope and Rupert had enjoyed a decent night's sleep – in my bed.

All seated at the table and Daisy strapped in her high chair, we waited for Penelope to re-appear. Rupert poured ice-cold water for everyone. I heard the bedroom door open onto the balcony above and I watched Penelope, who had changed, flitting around above us. As she flicked her towel over the balcony, I was quite surprised she hadn't rung the maid's bell to summon me to hang it out to dry – as I was doing everything else around here at the moment. In the next instant, I observed what looked like a stripy bird soar through the early evening air. A little peeved that even the birds were the spitting image of my latest bikini, the 'bird' came flying towards the table of food, and a second later, it landed right on top of the newly tossed salad. We all flinched and the children squealed. Rupert, plucking the stripy creature from the plum tomatoes, exposed the nearly extinct stripy bird as Penelope's bikini briefs that had been wrapped up in her towel.

I was instantly put off the salad that I'd carefully sliced and blended together with the finest olive oil. Penelope came down and casually retrieved her briefs from Rupert's hand.

With day one of the holiday nearly over and one bottle of gin entirely empty, I knew this was going to be the longest two weeks of my life.

CHAPTER 22

I lay wide-awake and listening to the waves lapping on to the sandy shore; there didn't seem a cat in hell's chance of my falling asleep anytime soon. Matt was snoring gently beside me whilst I lay awake, completely exhausted, staring at the ceiling.

My thoughts turned to Penelope. It was a strange friendship to say the least. Fay was my real friend. She had been my best friend since I was 19 years old. We met when I worked for the civil service, and she was someone who I didn't have to text nonstop; even when we hadn't talked for a while, we would just reconnect as if we'd never been apart. With Penelope, it was different. We had been thrown together by the constraints of the school playground, and I had been handpicked to be her friend, partly due to my newness, but probably more because she had fallen out with numerous mothers before me.

However, it was all getting too much for me. After tea, Penelope had waltzed away from the table and curled up in a comfy chair with some magazines that I had paid for, leaving me with all the washing-up. In fact, for the last twenty-four hours, Penelope had been undermining me even in my own house. I wasn't here to wait on Penelope hand and foot and I was beginning to feel very much taken for granted. Suddenly, I heard footsteps pattering towards the kitchen I turned my head towards the door and listened more intently.

It was possibly one of the children who had woken up thirsty and had decided to grab a drink from the fridge. I heard the fridge door open and the faint humming sound from the light inside; someone was rummaging around. After a few minutes, the door was shut and the footsteps went down the hallway to the living room. I heard a faint sniffle then realised I could hear someone crying. Slowly pulling back the sheets, so as not to disturb Matt, I slipped my feet into my slippers and glided my arms into my dressing gown, fastening it tight around my body. As I made my way to the living room, I saw the outline of a person huddled on a chair. Penelope was perched on the edge of the seat hugging her knees tightly and softly crying to herself.

She was startled by my appearance when I handed her a couple of tissues from the box on a nearby table. Dabbing her eyes she thanked me.

Whatever could be the matter with her?

'I've made a terrible mistake, absolutely terrible,' Penelope whimpered.

I didn't want to push her for an explanation, as I knew of numerous mistakes she had made in the last twenty-four hours but none of them warranted this sort warrant this type of reaction. Penelope nodded in the direction of the table, where I saw a white, oblong cardboard box, which I would recognize anywhere. I was speechless.

'How long have you known?" I spoke softly.

'I don't know,' she replied, 'but I am about to find out. Deep down I already know the results;   the nausea kicked in nearly two weeks ago and the tiredness is beginning to be unbearable.'

What could I say?

'There's no time like the present,' Penelope stood up reluctantly.

She took the box from my hand, and went into the bathroom, leaving the door a little ajar. There was no uncertainty these days; if that blue line appeared Little Jonny and Annabel would be blessed with a baby brother or sister. Even I felt sick waiting on the other side of the bathroom door; but I couldn't possibly be pregnant. Last Christmas I'd been very astute, Matt thought I'd arranged a wonderful weekend away for two at a posh hotel in the country; he was disappointed to find that I'd booked him in for an afternoon for one person at Go-nads, the snip 'n' clip clinic. He was in and out in a jiffy and the rates were very reasonable to say the least. I could see Penelope looking at her reflection in the mirror then she placed the test next to the basin and closed the door.

I remembered the moment when I was waiting to discover whether I was pregnant with Daisy. Pulling down my knickers I'd held the white plastic wand underneath me while I peed. Usually, this would be the longest two minutes of any woman's life, but in my case, it hadn't been. There had been no need to hold the wand up to the light, there had been no need to wait two minutes, there had been no mistaking the dark blue line that was screaming 'pregnant' right back at me. I can remember Matt whooping with delight when I announced the news. I wasn't sure Penelope would be whooping, I wasn't sure what Penelope wanted, did she want to be pregnant?

'I feel sick.' I heard Penelope whimper.

Hearing her sobs from the other side of the door, I gathered they were not sobs of relief.

'Can I come in?' I whispered.

She opened the door clasping the white wand that was sporting a line that was too bold and blue to even think there was any kind of mistake. Judging by the look on her face the only mistake she had made was allowing herself to be in this situation in the first place.

She perched on the edge of the bath, tears streaming down her face while she clutched the-no-question-about it-I-am-pregnant stick.

'I'm useless absolutely useless,' she sobbed in my arms.

'Don't be daft; it's not the end of the world. This could be the making of you and Rupert. It may be the most wonderful news for you all, new beginnings for you and your family,' I replied, hugging her.

But I was quite surprised that Penelope was pregnant; she'd certainly kept it very quiet that she and Rupert were back sleeping together. I wasn't even sure what Rupert was playing at, as I knew for a fact he was still entertaining the woman with the posh car most lunch times. I hope that this might just be the news that would kick him up his backside and jolt him back into family life.

'I don't think so, this is a disaster. My world is about to be smashed into smithereens.'

'What what do you mean? Rupert may surprise you; this could be a fresh start for you all.'

'I know the exact time of conception and Rupert wasn't there.'

My jaw crashed to the ground. I wasn't expecting that bombshell.

'The location was the disabled toilet of the snooker hall – Clive.' Her moment of madness on the night of her speed-dating escapade. Wrong time – wrong man.

I remembered Clive, the Jonny Vegas look-alike, and winced. I brought my hands up to cup my face.

'Shit!' I said, unhelpfully.

I had to admit it was definitely a setback. What had Penelope been thinking? Who rides bareback with a stranger these days and who rides bare back with a Jonny Vegas look alike?

There was nothing more that could be done that night. With the pregnancy confirmed, Penelope needed to make a few decisions and at this moment in time, I was glad I wasn't the one in her stripy bikini. Luckily, for her, she could use the two-week holiday to take time out from her normal routine and establish a plan of action.

I didn't have any advice for her, but I knew I would just have to be around to pick up the pieces whatever happened, and knowing my luck I would be the one left holding the baby.

I knew Penelope was scared, but her mind would be in overdrive I could see the cogs were turning and that perhaps she was considering passing the baby off as Rupert's. I could feel it in my waters.

Looking out of the bathroom window, I noticed the sun beginning to rise in the distance. Its reflection on to the sea below gave a sense of calmness. Savouring the moment, I glanced at my watch. It was now nearly 5 a.m., and in just a couple of hours the children would be wide-awake, full of energy looking forward to the day ahead. I rubbed my hands over my eyes realising I too needed to gain a little sleep. I was feeling so drained; maybe I could catch a couple of hours sleep on the sunbed tomorrow. Removing the test from Penelope's hand, I disposed of the white wand – wishing I could wave a magic one – back into its packaging and slipped it into the pocket of my dressing gown.

Giving Penelope another hug, I suggested she try to get a couple of hours sleep at least.

I returned to bed, waves of tiredness came flooded through my body as I climbed back in.

'Where have you been?' Matt spoke softly. 'You've been gone ages.'

'Nothing to worry about, I just couldn't sleep. It must be this mattress, I'm not used to it, go back to sleep, it's only early.'

Instantly, Matt drifted off to sleep, and I lay awake. What an eventful couple of hours it had been. Penelope would need to make a few decisions fast. Rupert would be constantly under her feet for the next two weeks, and he wasn't daft. What if he was clever enough to piece together the change in her behaviour – the lack of alcohol, her tiredness, not to mention the morning sickness that could be a dead giveaway?

CHAPTER 23

When I woke up, bright sunshine was shining through the curtains, and I could hear the chatter of the children from the pool outside. Glancing at my watch on the bedside table, I saw it was nearly midday. Gosh, I must have been tired! Matt must have sneaked out of bed to entertain the children, letting me sleep in after my restless night. I wondered if Penelope was awake yet or hiding out beneath her covers.

Feeling wide awake and refreshed after a few extra hours I jumped quickly into the shower; there was only one thing on today's agenda: lying on the sunbed and catching a few rays while the children played. This plan would also suit Penelope; I wasn't sure if she would be up for a day trip with the sickness that she was suffering at the moment.

Everyone was seated outside around the patio table. Matt was busying himself bringing plates of sandwiches and bowls of crisps from the kitchen. Penelope, looking a little green around the gills, sipped a glass of iced water, while Rupert chattered away to the kids and handed out the sandwiches.

Matt looked as if he was in a foul mood, and barely looking at me he uttered, 'are you joining us for lunch?'

It wasn't like him to be in a such a bad mood, but perhaps preparing a meal for ten had taken its toll. 'Are you OK?' I enquired, but only got a stare and a grunt in return. I decided to leave it alone until everyone had dispersed from the table.

Penelope managed a 'Good afternoon.' She looked dreadful, but I suppose with no sleep and a lot on her mind, she wasn't going to look blooming any time soon.

Returning from the kitchen, one last time, Matt, with a face like thunder banged the glasses down before sitting down at the table. I knew something or someone had riled him, but I thought he needed to be thankful for small mercies. At least he didn't have the same speedos as Rupert. Penelope bit into a sandwich, but appeared to be holding onto her stomach contents. I could tell she wasn't going to have a craving for cheese and pickle sandwiches in the near future. The only craving in Penelope's case would be not to be pregnant at all. Nibbling on a bread stick, her complexion gradually changed back to a normal skin colouring. Making her excuses, Penelope left the table muttering she didn't feel very hungry and returning to the best sunbed, she drew her sunglasses over her eyes and within minutes was sound asleep. The first few months of pregnancy are always exhausting, but it would be even more so for her, while she considered what the hell to do about Rupert.

Once the children were refuelled, they went back to their games in the pool. I was actually quite amazed how there hadn't been any major hiccups or falling out; they all just seemed to be having fun. Unlike Matt who looked as if he was going to erupt; not only was he ignoring me, I noticed he seemed to be a little short with Rupert as well. Maybe he was feeling tired after being up for a few hours longer than me, so I suggested he go and have a snooze in the sun next to Penelope, while I cleared the plates off the table.

I watched Matt try to settle on the sunbed, but he was extremely fidgety and couldn't settle; he did indeed appear to be awfully tense. I was beginning to wonder if something had already happened this morning before I awoke and he hadn't been able to vent his frustrations in front of Penelope and Rupert, if it had been anything at all to do with them.

Clambering out of the pool, the children grabbed at the pile of towels that were drying over the chairs in the midday sun. Wanting a change of scenery and an escape from the burning hot sun of the early afternoon, they all decided to scoop chocolate ice cream from the freezer into plastic bowls and settled down to watch a DVD.

Without the children, it was especially peaceful around the pool; there was not a cloud in the sky and we could hear the waves were lapping up onto the beach below.

Rupert resembled a snowman, lying on his sunbed smothered from head to toe in factor fifty sun block and still dressed in his black speedos. Unperturbed, he was flicking through a car magazine.

Leaning forward to pick up the magazine that had fallen beneath Penelope's sunbed, I nearly jumped out of my skin, when Matt, slammed his hand down on the sunbed, swung round, and feet firmly on the floor, faced Rupert and me. Rupert and I stared at him and waited to hear what was bothering him.

Matt's eyes were piercing, dark and dangerous; I knew this wasn't about taking advantage this morning and sneaking a few extra hours sleep whilst he rallied around after the children.

'How long? How long?' Matt demanded.

How long was what? How long was a piece of string? I was flummoxed by his outburst. What the heck was he on about? Judging by the look on Rupert's face, he was none the wiser either. Both of us stared back at Matt, and waited for some sort of explanation. His whole body was now shaking with anger.

Trying to smooth the situation over and calm Matt's temper, 'look mate,' were the first words that escaped Rupert's mouth, but Matt responded with fury, not letting him finish his sentence.

'Do not "look mate me" – how long?'

Almost immediately, Rupert, believing he had been rumbled, began to apologise.

'Yes OK, we admit it,' Rupert continued. 'We are really sorry.'

'I knew it, I knew it! Sorry you've been busted more like,' Matt shouted at him. 'And what have *you* got to say for yourself?' Matt snarled at me.

I was stunned, flabbergasted. I thought Matt might have somehow been banged his head in the middle of the night and the concussion had completely changed his personality – well you do hear about these strange instances – I was completely baffled. Penelope was still asleep on the sunbed in the middle of World War 3, very oblivious to the row that was erupting around her.

'We will pay,' Rupert continued.

'Too right you will pay,' Matt spat back.

'How much do you want?' Rupert replied.

'I can't believe the cheek of you Kensington, you are offering me money?'

Feeling as if I was watching a table tennis match, my head was flitting back and forth between Matt and Rupert. I was still none the wiser as to what the bloody hell was going on.

'We have taken advantage of your good nature,' Rupert stated.

'You don't say,' Matt replied angrily.

So that was it. Rupert was feeling like a right fool, embarrassed to say the least. Matt had clearly realized that Rupert and Penelope did not intend to make any financial contribution towards the holiday.

'You were coming anyway,' Rupert claimed, overstepping the mark.

Matt was taken aback by this revelation and so was I. It was apparent Penelope and Rupert had concocted a plan to take advantage of our good nature. The tight-fisted couple had planned this free family holiday!

'I'm not on about you cadging a free holiday off us, eating our food and drinking our beer, I want to know how long have you been sleeping with my wife.'

There was deadly silence all around us.

Penelope took this exact moment to wake and sat bolt upright on the sunbed. Sitting up she removed her sunglasses and stared at me, then Rupert. 'You two! You two have been sleeping together?' she cried out incredulously, jabbing her finger in my direction.

This was ridiculous; where the bloody hell had Matt got this preposterous idea from? I'd been accused of some things in my life but there was no way in this lifetime or in any other lifetime, I would share an intimate moment with Rupert Kensington.

'You can't deny it,' Matt cried.

I stared at Matt open-mouthed, 'I bloody can and I will,' I yelled back, no longer calm. 'What the bloody hell has got into you?'

'Well, we all know what has got into you,' Penelope growled snidely.

She had a bloody cheek, lying there on my sunbed, knocked up with her Jonny Vegas's offspring.

My stomach was in knots, not knowing what had put this insane idea into Matt's head.

Stretching his arm under the towel on his sunbed, he pulled out a box. The box ... the one that contained Penelope's positive wand.

Throwing the pregnancy test directly at me he accused, 'how could you? You are not only sleeping with Rupert but you are pregnant with his baby! We both know it can't be mine!'

Then realisation hit me; Matt must have discovered the test in my dressing-gown pocket this morning while I was still sleeping. Putting two and two together, Matt's brain must have gone into complete overdrive, and made five. The funny thing was I had actually been feeling so tired recently, that I knew if Matt hadn't been snipped, I would actually be thinking I was pregnant.

'You're pregnant?' repeated the amazed Rupert.

'No Shit, Sherlock, by you!' screamed Matt.

This was insane. I glared at Penelope, urging her to do the decent thing and own up to the pregnancy test being hers. My hopes were dashed immediately though, as scrabbling to her feet as if she were in utter shock, she leant over my sunbed, raised her hand and slapped me hard right across my face. Wincing with the pain, I nearly returned the favour, but knowing she was pregnant, I simply glowered at her.

'I can't believe you have been sleeping with my husband,' she screamed, and stormed off to her bedroom – my bedroom.

CHAPTER 24

I couldn't believe the lengths to which Penelope would go to keep her predicament a secret. What was she going to do in another seven months' time when Baby Vegas decided to make its appearance in the big wide world?

Rupert stormed out of the villa to take a walk alone on the beach.

Thankfully, the children were still fully engrossed in the DVD that they were watching. I nursed my throbbing face. I was still stunned by the previous few minutes. Matt and I sat in silence staring at each other. I was fuming. He was waiting for me to explain myself and I was waiting for him to apologise.

There was only one thing for it. I realised Penelope was covering her own back, playing the victim but I had to remember she was also pregnant and confused about what the hell she was going to do. Her slapping me was to buy herself more time before her secret was discovered. I wasn't interested in blowing her predicament, I was more interested in proving to Matt I had never had an affair with Rupert Kensington and that I certainly wasn't carrying his baby or anyone else's baby for that matter.

I ordered Matt to follow me in a 'don't mess me with me' type of voice; he reluctantly stood up and we moved in to the kitchen. Snatching up my bag and grabbing the keys to the ridiculous Scooby Doo van, I informed the children we wouldn't be too long, saying Penelope was resting in the bedroom if they needed anything.

Forcing Matt to climb behind the wheel, I instructed him to drive to the nearby village. Muttering under his breath, he warned me if he were to come face-to-face with the man who had impregnated his wife, he wouldn't be responsible for his actions. I let him prattle on huffing and puffing for the time being because in less than fifteen minutes, he would be feeling like a fool when I proved to him that no way on this earth was I pregnant.

Pointing to the parking space at the side of the road, I directed him to pull over.

I pushed him into the Chemist, and alerted the shop assistant by pointing to the pregnancy tests that were stacked up on the shelf behind the counter. I didn't have any idea what the Spanish word was, so playing a game of charades I acted out the scene, stuffing my handbag under my T-shirt, and pretending to rock a baby in my arms. The shop assistant reached for the test and placed it on the counter. 'Do you want one of these,' he politely enquired.

'You could have said you spoke English,' I replied slightly irritated.

'You never asked,' came his flippant reply as he rung up the total on a prehistoric till.

Handing over the cash, I seized the test and marched quickly out of the shop with Matt hot on my heels. Heading down the busy Spanish high street towards the beach, I knew of some old stone public toilets situated on the shore. Normally I wouldn't choose to frequent any type of public toilets, but today it was needs must.

Opening the door to the ladies,' the stench that hit us was horrific; it smelt worse than an abattoir and looking around, it appeared worse things than animals had been slaughtered in here.

'I can't go into a ladies toilet,' Matt insisted

'You can and you will,' I told him, pushing him inside the cubicle. It didn't surprise me there was no toilet paper, not even the tracing paper kind and it would have been ludicrous to expect a working lock on the door. I ordered Matt to stand with his back against the door while I peed, he looked terrified. How times had changed, I thought, my mind flashing back to our early dating days when I would place toilet paper in the bottom of the pan to disguise the sound of me tinkling. Now I was demanding that he watched me – there was nothing kinky about this situation at all – believe me.

Removing the white plastic wand from the box, I squatted over the seat. There was no way I would lower myself to sit on the cracked wooden seat. I may not be pregnant but I wasn't up for contracting any sort of deadly disease from the gruesome conditions.

The warm stream flowed on to the stick. Removing a tissue from my pocket when I had finished, I wiped myself dry. Gasping for breath, the stench inside the lavatory was stifling, we hurried back outside where we were thankful to be hit by wafts of fresh sea air. Matt had remained silent the whole time we were inside the ladies' toilets; I wasn't sure whether he was traumatised about the state of hygiene in these types of places or fretting about the results that were about to be uncovered.

Perching on the wooden bench scribbled with graffiti overlooking the calm blue sea – no doubt a bench where a few unwanted pregnancies had been created – I pressed the test into Matt's hand. 'Look at it,' I insisted. 'Look at it!'

Staring down at the test, Matt's relief was instant. The test showed positively that I was not pregnant. There was no blue

line, not even a hint of one, absolutely nothing. I didn't doubt
it for a moment – as safe a bet as I could have placed. I was not
pregnant.

Matt looked battered and completely worn out.

'I don't understand; the test was in your pocket; you disappeared for most of the night; why would you have a positive
pregnancy test, if it's not yours? Who does it belong to?'

Penelope had played her part well; it never crossed Matt's
mind that the test could belong to Penelope after her Oscar
winning performance. Playing an absolute blinder, her smack-
ing me across the face insinuated my affair with Rupert was real.

I had two choices. My first option was to protect Penelope,
keeping her secret until she was ready to inform the world and
the second, well the second would mean I put my marriage first
and divulge Penelope's secret to Matt – putting his mind at rest.

Earnestly looking at me, he was waiting for an answer and
I couldn't blame him; Matt deserved the answers, but Penel-
ope's secret wasn't mine to tell. She had landed me in a huge
predicament. If I revealed Penelope was pregnant and disclosed
Rupert was not the biological father, it would be out there, and
I wouldn't be able take it back.

I began carefully, with a smile. Gazing at Matt I spoke softly,
'I need you to trust me on this one, I have not been having an
affair with Rupert Kensington and I have proved I am not the
one pregnant. I will share what I can with you as soon as I can.'

Matt didn't look happy; he wasn't in the least bit happy, but
he knew I would tell him when I was able to. I wasn't delighted
either. I wanted to spill Penelope's secret and blow her amateur
dramatics performance wide open – she would not be receiving
a standing ovation from any of us.

We climbed back into the van and drove back to the villa.
Matt was a lot more relaxed. He hadn't discovered all the an-

swers in the last twenty minutes, but one thing was for sure, he knew his wife was not expecting Rupert Kensington's child or having an affair with him. My plan was simple. I was going to give Penelope an ultimatum – either she told Matt the truth, or I would.

All was quiet when we returned to the villa. The children were still sitting in exactly the same spot and did not appear to have moved a muscle. Penelope was hiding out in her bedroom, probably concocting a plan of what to do next. Rupert was sprawled out on the sunbed by the pool; he wasn't reading or sleeping, just looking up into the bright sky.

Matt went outside, reluctant to face Rupert, but he needed to apologise. They both needed to apologise; Rupert for knowingly trying to fleece us for a free holiday and Matt for accusing him of having an affair – I wasn't sure which was worse.

Handing Rupert a beer Matt spoke, 'I'm really sorry mate, I got it all wrong, Rachel isn't the one pregnant. I should have never have accused you.' Holding out his hand, Rupert didn't hesitate and shook it. 'I've been a prat too; it was Penelope's idea to take advantage of the holiday and I should have put my hand in my pocket and paid up in the first place. I really haven't been having an affair with your wife.'

'I know that now.'

They clinked their beer bottles together. 'Who did the pregnancy test belong to then?' Rupert innocently enquired.

'I've no idea,' Matt sincerely replied.

CHAPTER 25

Penelope was lying on top of the bedcover when I walked into her room. It was far from polite to enter without knocking, but frankly, I was still rattled and the sting on my cheek reminded me of just how devious she was. Sitting up, she eyeballed me. Not knowing what to expect, she remained quiet. I sat on the edge of the bed and looked her straight in the eyes.

My heart was thumping and I exhaled sharply. 'Last night we discovered you were pregnant. I have invited you into my home to join my family on our holiday. When I say invited, actually if I remember correctly there was no real discussion, you booked the flights and gate-crashed our holiday when you found out we owned another home. To top it all off, you have decided to pay for nothing; not once have you offered to pay for food, the car or even contribute towards the villa. You have dumped my clothes in another room and evicted me out of my own bedroom.

Everything has to be on your terms and I am sick of it. I am stepping away from your drama. This is your circus and these are your monkeys. I would have supported you in your predicament, but time after time, you have taken advantage of me. The last straw came today, when I had to prove to my husband that I am not the one pregnant. I have not shared your news with either Rupert or Matt, but I suggest you get up off your sorry backside and go and own up to the hell that you have put me and my husband through this morning, because if you don't, I will.'

There I'd said it; I couldn't believe I had been so bold and not a quiver could be detected in my voice even though I was shaking inside. Without giving Penelope the opportunity to respond, I rose from the bed and walked straight to the kitchen to pour myself a very well deserved gin and tonic leaving behind a stunned Penelope.

'Is everything OK?' Matt asked me.

'Yes, I'm just going to nip to the bedroom and change into my bikini; I'm longing for a dip in the pool. I haven't even been near the water yet, and thank you for keeping an eye on the children, I haven't even spent enough time with them either.'

Returning to my bedroom – the guest room – I changed out of my clothes and into my swimwear. I thought I may have gone a little too far with Penelope. But not relaying the full facts of the situation to Matt was making me uncomfortable, and I was pleased I'd finally confronted Penelope and given her the opportunity to own up.

Tipping my junk-filled handbag onto the bed, I was tried to locate the sugar-pink nail varnish I knew I had tossed somewhere into the deep, dark depths of the handbag before heading off to the airport. A quick swim to cool myself down, painting of my nails and a read of the new Angela Marsons paperback I'd purchased was now the order of the remaining hours of the day.

I found the nail varnish, and began to scooping all the odds and ends back into my handbag, making a mental note to have a good sort out very soon. There were numerous receipts that I no longer needed; screwing them up into a ball, I successfully hurled them into the waste paper basket, shouting, 'get in.'

Noticing the scratch card that I'd purchased just before the sprint to the plane, I took a penny that had been lying in the bottom of my bag, and scratched off the silver foil. Smiling to myself, I reminisced about the time I'd won a tenner on a similar scratch card years ago and thought it was Christmas. Using that tenner I purchased a £9.99 bottle of Pinot, thinking I was the bees knees; I'd never purchased a bottle that expensive before. Flicking away all the speckles of black silvery dust, I was stunned; looking twice at the card, there appeared to be three matching numbers staring back at me. Things were looking up! I was not pregnant, and I was fifty quid better off than I was a few minutes ago. Smiling to myself and placing the card on the bedside table I turned to see Matt opening the bedroom door.

'What are you up to? You have been ages?'

'I've been changing and I've just had a quick sort out of my handbag while looking for my nail vanish, but look over on the bedside table, I was just coming out to tell you. That scratch card, the one I purchased at the airport, we have won fifty quid!'

'Excellent!' Matt exclaimed, wandering over to the table. 'We must remember to cash it in and not chuck it out,' he commented while retrieving the card from the bedside table and studying it.

Matt gasped and dropped on to the bed. 'Rachel, it doesn't say fifty pounds! Rachel come here quick, look! We have won fifty *thousand* pounds, Oh my! I can't believe it; we need to guard this with our lives!'

Taking the card from Matt's hand, I looked at it more carefully. We grinned at each other. He was correct; it was fifty thousand pounds! I thought that would be a fair few £9.99 bottles of wine I could purchase with that little lot. Matt, picked me up like a giddy schoolboy and whizzed me round in circles in excitement, 'I can't believe it! You little beauty!'

'It's probably best we don't leave it lying around in case we misplace it or it gets lost.' He took his wallet from his jeans 'I'll put it here for   safekeeping and we can cash it in when we return to England,' Matt suggested.

We moseyed back outside to the pool; our earlier upset replaced with excitement and laughter. The sun was beating down and if nothing else, I was determined to relax for the remainder of the afternoon. The children had organised themselves into teams, and were playing pool in the games room and Daisy was in her playpen.

I threw my book and towel on top of my sunbed, and jumped into the pool's inviting water. I swam a few lengths before climbing out and settling myself in the sun. Matt, who hadn't stopped smiling since the discovery of the lottery win, cracked open a beer and with an almighty 'cheers,' swigged it back. Rupert, as usual was also catching some rays; but with the misunderstanding from the morning madness cleared up and put behind us, the atmosphere was without a doubt less tense.

Penelope had not been seen since my little visit to her bedroom. I hoped I had given her food for thought while she was pondering her next move. I did sincerely empathise with her circumstances; no woman would want to be faced with the situation that she had created for herself, but I was not having anyone, and certainly not Penelope, cause trouble within my family unit.

With my feet up and my G&T resting on the table at my side, I started to read my new book. Matt was searching the internet on his iPad and Rupert was flicking through the pages of an English newspaper. All was peaceful and restful; even the gulls that usually circled overhead had flown elsewhere.

Hearing a sniffle I turned my head, thinking it was perhaps one of the children. They were getting on particularly well, but no doubt, an argument would soon erupt among them. But there wasn't a child in sight, just Penelope who was standing over all of us dabbing a tissue at the tears that were flowing from her bloodshot eyes. Rupert shifted over on his sunbed and she balanced on the end.

How could she possibly tell everyone about the baby? She knew she needed to do it now, before I confided in Matt because if that happened it would only be a matter of time before Rupert found out. Surely, it was now or never for Penelope, I thought. If she left it much longer, her clothes would be clinging tighter to her belly and people would soon guess.

Penelope snivelled, but said, bravely, 'The pregnancy test belongs to me,'

Matt was the first one to look up and process this announcement. The thought had never crossed his mind that the test could belong to Penelope. Rupert stared at her, and then said, 'Don't be silly Penelope, your test? How can it possibly be your test? Forgive me for a silly question, but don't you have to have sex to become pregnant these days?'

Now it was my turn to gawp at Penelope, and I suddenly realised the extent of her dilemma. Whatever their reasons for getting back together – a free holiday or to support Little Jonny – she would not be able to pass Rupert off as the father of her child.

What more could Penelope say, I was the only other person who knew who the biological father was, and the image of him and Penelope in that toilet for the disabled was one that would haunt me forever. Obviously, Rupert needed answers; he demanded answers.

'What do you take me for? How far gone are you?' he asked, furiously

'Approximately ten weeks,' she replied.

Rupert's mind seemed to be in overdrive, and speaking before he had put his brain in gear he said, 'well you still have plenty of time to get rid of it then, don't you.'

I would have quite liked to watch the drama unfold however, this was Matt's and my cue to leave. This conversation was none of our business; throwing Matt 'the look,' I nodded my head towards the patio doors. As much as he was dying to uncover the identity of the baby's father, he took my lead and followed me quickly in to the villa.

Just as I was about to slide the patio doors shut to give the pair of them more privacy, I overheard Penelope say, 'I've made up my mind; I'm going to keep the baby.'

Rupert looked stunned, and dropped his head in his hands.

'Spill the beans then,' Matt insisted the moment we were out of earshot. 'Who is the father? Is it a father from school – one of the petty tedious army husbands?' He winked, giving me a sly smile.

I knew the identity of the father would be revealed eventually, and there was no doubt about it, the vicious tongues of the playground mafia would most definitely be wagging when they discovered Rupert was not the biological father.

I hesitated, but against my better judgement I continued, 'Penelope has told me the baby was conceived in March.'

Matt tipped his head to one side, willing me to continue.

'Believe me, he wasn't a handsome man, he wasn't the type of person that carries a business card, more like a bloke that carries a menu from the local kebab shop.'

'Sounds like you shared the moment with her,' Matt joked.

I pretended to be insulted.

'So come on then, the truth, the whole truth and nothing but the truth,' Matt persisted inquisitively.

'Penelope shagged a bloke in the toilets at that speed dating night. It was just a one-night stand and he wasn't the type of bloke she could see herself with in the future.'

Matt's eyes widened. 'Wow,' he said, shaking his head and scratching his chin. 'What a mess.'

We exchanged looks. The boiling kettle interrupted the moment. Matt pouring two mugs of tea, and continued 'What do you think she is going to do?'

'Well, judging by what I heard when I slid the doors shut a moment ago, she told Rupert she was keeping the baby. Looks like Rupert will have a few decisions to make; he can either throw himself into the role of becoming a father again, or disappear back to his flat to enjoy a single life again – I know which my money is on.'

'Shush, they are on their way in,' Matt whispered.

Penelope was looking flustered and fidgety, her eyes burning with tears. However, Rupert appeared otherwise, quite calm in fact.

'I'll keep this short.' He announced. 'We will not take up anymore of your precious holiday; Penelope has made her decision to keep the baby.' Rupert sucked in his breath and continued. 'We had decided to give our marriage another chance for the children's sake but now things have changed. It's not exactly what I had in mind to bring up another man's child.'

Rupert had resolved the dilemma himself; he was going to return to his bachelor pad leaving Penelope holding the baby – but who could blame him – it wasn't his baby to hold.

'We will get our stuff together and if you would be kind enough to arrange a taxi to take us to the airport in about an hour's time, we will sit there until the airline is able to reschedule our flights home.

Penelope was about to butt in, but Rupert cut her dead with a sharp glance, 'don't you even think of suggesting staying behind with the children to spoil their holiday any further;

you need to leave these people in peace. Go and pack your cases.'

Matt and I were left looking at each other as they disappeared into the bedroom.

'Can you believe that? Day two of our holiday and we can now enjoy the rest of our two weeks in peace as a family. It's like winning the lottery!' Matt joked.

'We didn't even tell them about our lottery win,' I laughed.

'It is probably best not to rub any more salt into Rupert's wounds and I won't be telling a soul until the money is safely deposited into our bank account.'

CHAPTER 26

The remainder of the holiday was blissful – but the two weeks of pure relaxation was over. As we touched back down on the tarmacked English soil, I wondered what had happened in the village during our time away and whether the news of Penelope's pregnancy had spread. I was looking forward to catching up with Melanie and no doubt, she couldn't wait to grill me about all that had occurred on holiday. Of course, by now, she would be fully aware that Penelope's holiday had been cut short.

On the way back from the airport, we collected the dog, and purchased a few essentials from the local shop and finally arrived back at home. Once everyone had piled out of the car, I took a step back to get the full effect of our house. 'Home sweet home,' I smiled.

We had only been gone for two weeks but it seemed like a lifetime. I was curious to find out what had happened to the Kensingtons, but Matt had convinced me to steer clear. If Penelope wanted to resume the friendship on our return, she would no doubt soon be in touch.

Matt was right, did I really need a friend like her in my life? Penelope had always blown hot and cold; every time she needed bailing out of trouble, I was the one to be roped into the situation. Her antics in Spain could have caused massive trouble between Matt and me and even though I wouldn't wish her circumstances on anyone, her behaviour had been inexcusable. It was time to put my husband and children first.

Matt was about to put the key in the lock when an eager Melanie shot up the drive quicker than the Playground Mafia fighting for a seat at the Christmas school production.

'Hurry up and put that kettle on, I've been watching out for you all morning.'

'Hi Melanie, how are you!' I responded sarcastically. 'Really, I never would have guessed!'

'Are you OK Rach? You look shattered. It looks like you need a holiday!' Melanie joked.

'Cheeky mare!' I responded, but made another mental note to book a doctor's appointment to check out my iron levels.

Opening the door wide, Melanie stepped inside.

Matt walked past and ruffled my hair; he winked at me, 'you two enjoy your cuppa. I'm just going to nip upstairs and telephone the number on the reverse of the scratch card to see what we do about claiming the money.'

'Ooh, what money?' Melanie asked.

'I will reveal all in a moment, now get those teabags in the mugs, I'm parched.'

Matt disappeared upstairs clutching his wallet and the children settled down to watch a movie.

'Come on then Rachel, what on earth happened? Penelope was clocked in the local supermarket three days after you all left for sunnier climes.'

'Where do I start?'

'At the very beginning.'

'This may take a while.'

'I'm all ears.'

When I had finished telling her about the Kensington's shenanigans – from the outgoing journey to Penelope's pregnancy, Melanie looked utterly shocked. .

'The nerve of that woman! To terminate a friendship over a box of chocolates is one thing, but what she has put you through is another – it's unbelievable! You are a very patient woman Rachel Young, very patient.'

Raising my eyebrows at Melanie I replied, 'yes it is all a little unbelievable.'

Melanie clapped her hands in delight. 'Well come on then, you have missed out the only bit of information I want to know; who is the father? Is it someone's husband from school?'

My description of Penelope's speed-dating escapade with the Jonny Vegas look-alike had Melanie doubled over, with tears of laughter rolling down her face. 'Rachel Young, I can't believe you kept this quiet; why didn't you tell me you'd gone speed-dating with Penelope?'

'Probably because it is something I would rather forget, and I knew I'd get this reaction,' I replied, sticking my tongue out at Melanie.

'Oh gosh, make yourself useful will you, and pass me one of those tissues. I've never belly laughed so much in my life. So, I'm curious, is she still in contact with this bloke then?'

'Not to my knowledge, I'm not even sure she knows anything about him.'

'It's hilarious, such class, and you caught them at it?'

'Yes Melanie, now leave it there; it's a vision I would rather forget,' I stated.

That was what was missing from my life, a friend who made me feel at ease, someone I could laugh with. I was hoping Melanie was going to stay around for a while; she and the Farrier seemed settled and happy and school was definitely more bearable now I had an ally on the same wave- length.

Melanie and I were still laughing when Samuel opened the door to the kitchen. 'Mum, Penelope's here,' he said, as she strode behind him straight into the kitchen.

Penelope's timing was unfortunate. I gave Melanie a warning look to say nothing and disappear quickly. However, there was no way Melanie was going anywhere. As far as she was concerned, this was an opportunity not to be missed. I saw the mischievous glint in her eye. Standing up and waltzing over to the kettle she asked, 'anyone for another cup of tea?'

I wasn't sure that a cup of tea was going to make this situation any more bearable, but then sometimes life did seem better when hugging a mug of tea.

'Did you have a lovely holiday?' Melanie asked Penelope.

I didn't meet Penelope's eye, but from past experience I knew she would be scowling.

Now it was my turn to scowl at Melanie.

Melanie grinned back at me.

Penelope had already gained an awful lot of weight, but she didn't in the least look blooming, in fact she looked like she had overdosed on chocolate followed by a whirl on the waltzers. She looked positively sick. A change of subject was quickly needed.

All of a sudden, Matt burst through the kitchen door.

'Steady on Matt, you nearly took the door off the hinges,' I said.

Matt bounded over to where I was sat and cupped my cheeks in his hand, then planted a huge smacker right on my lips.

'Never mind the door, we could purchase a thousand doors, it's all ours! After confirming the serial number on the back of the card they double-checked our bank account details and fifty thousand pounds has now been deposited into our account. I can't believe it; it was as easy as that!'

My natural response was to bring my finger up to my lips. It wasn't the type of news I wanted to share with Penelope but they had already clocked my action.

'What's going on?' Melanie asked

'Wifey here, my gorgeous, lucky wife has picked a winner! She's only gone and purchased a scratch card that won us a whopping fifty thousand pounds!'

Now it was Melanie and Penelope's turn to stare at me.

'Who'd have thought? What are the flipping chances of that?' I screeched ecstatically. Jumping to my feet, I flung my arms around Matt's neck, squeezing him tight.

'Do you mean the scratch card that we bought at the airport?' Penelope was looking hostile and I began to sense some sort of animosity.

'Yes, that would be the very one.'

I don't know why, but I began to panic. What was with the unpleasant tone to her voice? Wouldn't any friend be genuinely delighted for you; join in your celebrations?

'Wow! That is absolutely brilliant!' shrieked Melanie. 'The most I have ever won was a fiver and I don't think I even cashed it in.

'You kept that quiet on holiday, when were you thinking of telling me?' sniped Penelope.

'There was an awful lot going on, if you remember,' I replied curtly.

I know the symptoms of pregnancy are moodiness and irritability – I wasn't sure what Penelope's excuse was before the pregnancy – but there was no need to be so tetchy with me.

'How do you know that card wasn't mine?' Penelope questioned.

'What the heck are you getting at Penelope?'

'How do you know that when you passed the card to me at the airport that you didn't hand me the wrong card? I bought the first card that was ripped from the roll; how can you be one hundred percent certain that you didn't hand me the wrong card? Half of that money is potentially mine.'

Matt and I exchanged a frantic stare and Melanie had no idea where to look. Fury was rising up inside my body. Luckily, for Penelope, she was pregnant. Remain cool and professional at all times, were the thoughts running through my head.

There was only one-way to tackle this situation – the death stare. I felt wretched; my body was trembling, my heart thumping, and my blood was pulsing in my neck.

Staring Penelope straight in the eyes I spoke. 'I'm not sure what court of law you are thinking of dragging me through with your petty attempt to steal half of our money, but I think you may find you will be laughed out of any solicitor's office. No money was exchanged for your ticket Penelope. You didn't pay me for your scratch card, holiday, car or food. Go on Miss Marple, do your worst, prove it.'

Penelope began to squirm.

Melanie, shaking her head in disbelief started to clap, a slow clap.

Matt strode to the kitchen door and held it open, 'I think you should leave Penelope, I think you should leave NOW.' There was a different quality to Matt's voice, he meant business and Penelope knew it.

'You've not heard the last of this,' she screamed as she stomped past Matt and slammed the front door behind her.

Right at that second, I knew I could never be friends with Penelope again.

'Well you've outdone me, Young. A child's toy is nothing compared with fifty thousand pounds!'

Rolling my eyes, I looked at Matt, 'Jesus! I need a drink. Is it too early?'

CHAPTER 27

This year, it seemed as if the days and weeks were flying by and already another Friday was upon us. Every night I'd taken the same route running to the telephone box, pushing my legs a little further and faster each time. With my headphones plugged in and listening to the tunes that still needed to be updated on my iPod, I was beginning to feel like an established runner. Saturday morning I was up and out early, 6 a.m. to be precise. Matt, thinking I was completely crazy, rolled over in bed and hid beneath the warm duvet. Saturday was the only free day without any children's activities and I was determined to keep my running regime going over the weekend. I was pushing my body more and more, and my body ached, but with my new running app, I tracked the colossal amount of calories I was burning off with each run. I'd started a little light reading – a woman's running magazine. It was fantastic with its advice, and healthy eating regimes; and it was normal for new runners to feel tired, but I hadn't expected the exhaustion to be quite so severe. I could quite easily have closed my eyes by eight every night and fallen asleep.

Deciding on a new route in my mind, I went straight past the telephone box, looped back round the lane, over the stile and back home – a little ambitious maybe – but if all else failed I could stride fast.

Life had taken a turn for the better; I pottered around the garden after my morning run, and ambled across the fields with the dog – very pleasant indeed. A few weeks had passed since Penelope stropped out of the kitchen slamming the front door behind her. I had seen neither hide nor hair of her except during the school run. My friendship with Melanie had blossomed; she was a lovely person, very down to earth, and she wasn't in my pocket every minute of the day. Her relationship with the Farrier was going from strength to strength and their children Rosie and Dotty with only a couple of years between them had bonded like true siblings. Matt and I socialised with them on a regular basis.

The following Monday morning was one I would never forget. It was to change my perception of humans forever. Every morning Melanie and I would walk to the school together, past the cricket pavilion, the newsagents and the pub on the corner. It wasn't far and the children kept each other company skipping and chattering along the way. When we reached the main road, which was always congested with cars, and with its very narrow pavements, we had to walk in single file until we reached the pelican crossing, which was only a stone's throw away from the school gates.

That day, Melanie and I were deep in conversation discussing last night's serial drama on ITV. Everyone had been left wanting more, but neither of us could predict the plot. There were so many twists and turns we were willing the week away, ready for the finale, which couldn't come quickly enough. We were about to cross over the road, when we saw BB and her son Lonsdale heading in the same direction as us. This wasn't out of the norm, we usually crossed paths on the school run, but there was something exaggerated in the way she swaggered this morning; something felt different.

'What's up with her?' Melanie whispered under her breath. 'Have you seen the look on her face?'

It was true. BB had a face like thunder. 'That's right, you just walk on like you haven't got a care in the world,' BB barked directly at me with intense venom. I could feel her stare following me while I walked across the pelican crossing; she seemed very unstable, shaking with rage.

This morning, I wasn't in the best of moods, I'd tossed and turned all night with a slight ache under my arm, it wasn't a pain as such, but a small discomfort that had kept me awake. Although I was feeling very drained and short-tempered, I wasn't going to dignify this crazy woman with a response, and I certainly had no idea what she was yelling about. My children had been startled by her actions, even a little frightened. Melanie and I huddled them in closer around the pushchair and told them to carry on walking and not to look behind.

'What is her problem?' Melanie asked.

'I've no idea, but there is certainly something nasty in the wind this morning; look in front of us.'

I felt like I had somehow been transported back in time to my teenage years – a teenager who had been terrified of the school bully, who used to line her army up outside the railings to intimidate and upset the children. There in front of us, blocking the entrance to the school gate was Penelope with her mothers' army. Their arms were folded tightly and their heads swivelled first to me, and then to Melanie. I was a bit shocked, as my eyes took in the mothers that were standing before me, all laughing and staring – I knew this was a tactic – trying to make me feel uncomfortable, trying to isolate me for whatever reason, but I had no idea what that reason was yet.

I was shaking inside. My face was beginning to burn; in fact, I could feel my cheeks were flaming red.

Melanie took control. She cleared her throat, 'excuse me ladies, you seem to be blocking the gateway,' she snapped, and barged straight through them, ushering the kids and me through quickly. It was like a miners' strike, a picket line back in the 80s led by their very own Arthur Scargills – BB and Penelope.

'What in God's name is this all about?' Melanie asked me once we were through the human barrier.

'I've no idea, but look at them all gathered in a huddle staring at us.'

'Since when have Penelope and BB been friends?'

'I wasn't aware they were,' I sighed, rolling my eyes. Amongst the gaggle of mothers, I was shocked to witness one in particular, Harriet Mackintosh, whom I would have described as salt of the earth; a mother who claimed at every opportunity that she would never entertain cliques and bullies. She had one child Clarabelle who had been friends with Eva for a while but without warning, Harriet Mackintosh had ventured over to the dark side. Whatever was going on?

'What shall we do?'

'What can we do? We are standing in a school playground and it's not the time or the place to be acting like them.'

'Let's go for the act natural look, pretend we are laughing and haven't noticed their ridiculous clique,' ordered Melanie, giving a determined smile.

'Why would we do that? I don't feel like smiling. I'm fuming! I want to barge straight up to them and confront them,' I spat, but I took Melanie's lead I gave out a radiant smile.

'What we do is ensure the kids are inside safely then head straight back to mine for a cuppa,' I said.

Mercifully, the school bell rang and the children filed into their classrooms safe and sound. Without even a fleeting backwards glance, Melanie and I were out of the playground quicker than a wannabe WAG trying to bag the local footballer.

Arriving back at home, I was in charge of the teapot. I poured two mugs of tea, and offered Melanie a chocolate digestive. She accepted and we dunked and bit into them at the same time. Matilda and Daisy were quite happily playing on the carpet with jigsaws and dolls.

'I'd heard Harriet Mackintosh had taken up with the clique, fearful her Clarabelle will be left out of the parties and invites for tea,' Melanie stated.

'I'm really surprised; she has always kept a wide berth of the Mafia, constantly refusing to entertain them, until now obviously. Just when you think you've got to know someone, they surprise you,' I grunted.

As I said this, I felt a bubble of fear rise into my stomach. After what we'd experienced at the school gates this morning, I had the feeling trouble was ahead. Fortunately, for me, Melanie was standing like a trooper by my side. Well actually she was sitting slurping tea; neither of us for the moment had any idea what had rattled the mothers.

I refilled the teapot, and we both sank our teeth into another chocolate biscuit.

'Have you had any word from Penelope since her outburst in the kitchen?' Melanie enquired.

'No, absolutely nothing.'

'What about Rupert?'

'Nothing from him either.'

'I've heard he's taken up with the lady in the posh car.'

'Rumour has it she's left her husband; he was abusive or so I've heard from Sandra, at the newsagent. She's taken her two kids and moved in with Rupert, squashed silly in his little flat I believe.'

'I bet that is cramping his style and Penelope won't be happy if he's spending time entertaining someone else's kids.'

'He could have been entertaining 'her' someone else's kid, if you get my drift,' Melanie chuckled trying to make light of the tense situation.

'He's signed the house over to Penelope; she demanded that he provide a stable home environment for Little Jonny and Annabel and with a new baby on the way she didn't want to be uprooting and moving the kids,' Melanie continued.

'That must be a shock for him though, going from two kids to four overnight. Who is the woman do you know?'

'No idea, but Penelope is better off for kicking him into touch, single parent benefit, her mortgage paid, and reduction on the council tax; I bet she thinks she has won the lottery,' Melanie giggled.

Suddenly she went quiet, shaking her head disbelievingly at her phone. The colour drained from her face and she looked up. 'Bloody hell, you are not going to believe this,' she said.

'I'm listening, go on.'

'It appears Penelope isn't playing nicely.'

'What do you mean?'

'It's Penelope and BB.'

I stared at Melanie.

'BB has posted on Facebook.'

'What has she posted?' my voice faltered.

Melanie flipped the phone over to me so I could see.

'That you are a thief,' Melanie reluctantly revealed.

'I'm a thief? What in God's name am I meant to have pinched?' I enquired startled.

'Fifty thousand pounds,' Melanie answered.

There it was in black and white on Botox Bernie's status. As I read the post, my blood started to boil.

'It comes to something when a local mother robs you blind of fifty thousand pounds.'

It didn't stop there.

'Which mother?' – typed by Harriet Mackintosh.

'Rachel Young.' – BB.

'Who has she robbed?' – Harriet Mackintosh.

'Penelope Kensington.' – BB.

'How's she done that?' – Harriet Mackintosh.

'She's been really nasty, fleeced her of fifty thousand pounds. She stole her lottery scratch card.' – BB.

'If anyone robbed from my family I'd do more than slap the cow.' – The woman with the yappy dog dressed in the fake Barbour coat.

'I'm going to sue her.' – Penelope Kensington.

'I'd do more than sue her.' – The woman with the yappy dog dressed in the fake Barbour coat.

The post went on and on and on.

We both sat there amazed at such behaviour from adults. Fifteen minutes later, my temper was wearing thin. 'What the heck is she hoping to gain and why would any other mothers lower themselves to join her pointless crusade – what could it possibly have to do with any of them?' I asked Melanie.

'The answer to both of those questions is very simple. Penelope is miffed she has missed out on the jackpot, more than likely through her own greed. If they'd have offered to pay for the holiday and the car and had actually stumped up the cash in the first place, you may have even considered giving her a share but she didn't! Let her waste her money on solicitors, she can't claim it's her ticket; she didn't even pay you for her ticket!

'The answer to your second question, these types of mothers are obsessed with senseless drama. They are the type of people that love attention and like hanging their dirty linen out in public, and they're usually brought together by gossip and untruths.

What sort of people write on social media sites that they are going to slap people? These dregs of society are simply bullies, the type of people that have nothing going on in their own lives and are very unhappy individuals by the looks of things.'

Melanie had hit the nail on the head; at this moment, I wished someone would hit Penelope and BB over the head – hard with a hammer.

Melanie paused, 'I'm so sorry, this is a horrendous situation, but at least you have found out one thing, Penelope was never a genuine friend, a genuine friend would be happy for you no matter what. It appears she is riddled with jealously at your lottery win. Money does funny things to people; you, my dear, have had a lucky escape.'

Melanie was spot on. For the last twelve months, Penelope had tested my patience to the limit. I had put up with antics for fear of being rejected from village life. But I didn't need superficial friendships. I hadn't done anything wrong. If these mothers wanted to set their children this type of example, and use social media to intimidate people, then frankly, these were the types of people I didn't want to know.

Melanie stood up, threw her arms wide, and gave me a hug.

Taking a deep breath I exhaled, my head was sore and my pulse was throbbing.

'How can she be so bitter about it? Penelope knows that the money has nothing to do with her whatsoever. Do you think Rupert knows about the win?'

'Hell no! If she thinks she will be triumphant in getting her hands on any part of fifty thousand pounds I bet my bottom dollar she won't divulge that type of information to him. If she was ever successful, which she can't be by the way, Rupert would fleece her for half.'

'Good point, except most of the village already knows about her internet crusade. It won't be long before he learns of her actions.'

'They will soon move onto something else, you will be yesterday's fish and chip paper before we know it. Wait until Penelope's scandal is revealed, that she was knocked up by the speed-dating god in a snooker hall toilet, and hopefully, she will soon be too up to her armpits in dirty nappies to even give you a second thought.'

Melanie was talking sense; enough was enough. There is only one thing people like this thrive on and that's confrontation. I didn't need to explain to anyone. I won that money fair and square and I certainly was not having a slanging match with BB over the internet – it was nothing to do with her – it was nothing to do with anyone.

'Here's hoping,' I replied positively.

Melanie had some errands to run that morning so we finished the tea and she headed off into town. 'See you back here for the school run later,' she said as she departed. I settled down for a morning playing with Matilda and Daisy and tried to take my mind off the situation.

CHAPTER 28

At 2.45pm there was a knock on the door, and I found Melanie on the other side. 'Let me in, I have some news.'

Intrigued, I flung the door open wide and invited her in to the kitchen.

'When I left here this morning, I telephoned the Farrier. He was in the middle of shoeing a horse up at the old farm house at the top of the hill.'

'Mr Boardman's place?'

'Yes that's the one, Mr Boardman the solicitor. The Farrier was appalled by the mothers' behaviour; I think his words were: 'damn right outrageous, cruel, malicious and spiteful' to be more precise. Once he finished shoeing the horse, he rapped on Mr Boardman's door. Over a cup of tea the Farrier explained the situation to him. With his thirty-five years' experience in the legal world, Mr Boardman assured the Farrier that Penelope didn't have a leg to stand on; it's all hot air. There is nothing she can do; you paid for the ticket, both tickets in fact. The ticket was in your possession and the money is definitely deposited in your account.'

'That's fantastic! Please thank the Farrier for going out of his way,' I replied, beaming, as relief flooded through my veins.

'However, he has given us some other advice.'

'What other advice?"

'Also in his thirty-five years' experience he has witnessed how times have changed. Due to the advancement of technology, these types of people become brave. They hide behind their computers to voice lies and cause hatred, and influence people who before the age of a computer would have no idea what was going on in anyone's life. A new type of bully has emerged over the last few years. These people judge people on others' opinions, yet in time, their opinions can change, leaving some people with egg on their face. He has advised that you should erase these people from your life. Do not look at their posts; walk away, and remember that no message is always the best message. The best way to keep your dignity is to remain silent. By not reacting to their nonsense, what can they do? People will eventually be fed up with Penelope if she is uttering the same nonsense over and over again and she is only winding herself up. The ones who are shouting the loudest usually have the most to hide. I have to say, my money is on the mothers falling out with each other sooner or later.'

'There's never a dull moment in this village is there? Melanie, I can't believe you would even choose to move back here.'

Melanie smiled, 'If it wasn't for the Farrier I would have never returned. Look at the time; drink up, the school run is upon us. Let the battle commence!'

As we approached the school gates, it was just as we predicted, they were all lurking outside on the picket line again, and I was shocked to see they had recruited two more bodies.

I turned to Melanie, 'have you seen who is with them?'

'Yes, I have noticed them.'

I felt my breath quicken and my chest tighten. What were they hoping to gain by this silly, outlandish behaviour?

I think they needed a reality check. Their offspring were of school age, not them – even though they were giving a very good impression.

Once we were inside the playground, Melanie admitted that she would have felt safer trapped inside the lion's enclosure at the local zoo. These women were brutal; they actually spat venom at us as we passed.

'Remember what Mr Boardman advised, if we don't fuel the fire it will dampen their flames. They will soon get sick of going over the same thing time and time again and move on to the next drama.'

'I was a little taken aback with Denise and Pam's participation in their tribe; I'd always thought they were made of better stuff.'

'Yes, I was somewhat shocked at their involvement especially with their do-good personalities, and running the local kids' groups. Why would they even be listening to Penelope, why would they even care?'

'Onwards and upwards! The question is would you welcome any one of these people into your life if we weren't for the school connection?' I asked.

'The simple answer would be no.'

'Melanie Tate you do talk sense.'

CHAPTER 29

The first day of July, I entered into my official summer style. Soup was ditched as lunchtime fare and was replaced with fresh meats, salads, tomatoes, onions, and cucumber blended together with the finest balsamic vinegar and olive oil accompanied by torn ciabatta bread.

Evening strolls in the warm sun with the family and dog were a must. I pushed the pram while the older children cycled alongside us, jangling their pocket money as we headed to the village pub for a treat of Coca-Cola and salt and vinegar crisps.

A month had passed since we had experienced the wrath of Penelope's gang and fortunately, for Melanie and me, we had survived her and her dithering army. Allegedly, she had been laughed out of her solicitor's office. Apparently, he confirmed she had absolutely no claim to any money from the lottery scratch card and it was more likely that Rachel Young could relieve her of a fair sum of money for spreading of malicious rumours and for online abuse.

The school run was still unpleasant but Penelope's soldiers were beginning to disperse as Mr Boardman had predicted. However, Penelope's feeling of being hard done by was still keeping her grudge burning, it wasn't burning brightly but nonetheless, it was still there.

But the friendships that were thrown together to feed off drama were soon eradicated. The mothers didn't have anything else in common or to talk about once Melanie and I held our heads high and carried on with our business as if they didn't exist. The only people they were winding up were themselves.

Penelope's baby bump was beginning to grow and show, emerging from underneath her tightly clinging tunics. She was happy to encourage the rumours, she herself was circulating amongst her fellow mafia companions, that Rupert had abandoned her and their unborn child.

It was all brought to a head one Saturday afternoon in early July. A Saturday afternoon when the world and his wife, brought together by their children, were trawling around the school summer fair, and being stung for overpriced burgers, or paying extortionate rates for a single ice-cream.

The sun was beating down and there wasn't a single cloud in the sky. I reluctantly left the solitude of my back garden and met Melanie by the front gate. I was feeling a little unwell but I couldn't quite put my finger on why, and school social events made me feel even worse – they were so not on my agenda. We walked along the pavements, with the children, to the fair.

By the entrance to the school field sitting behind their tables rattling their plastic margarine pots, as they collected the 20p entrance fee, were Denise and Pam. Neither Melanie nor I had given them the time of day after they both jumped on to Penelope's bandwagon concerning the scratch card fiasco. Our children had also been affected by their actions since Melanie and I no longer deemed them worthy of looking after them in any of the kids' groups they were associated with. Their behaviour was simply unprofessional.

Entering the field, Melanie and I scanned the area. It was heaving with children running riot with balloons, young children crying over their spilt ice cream, and parents whose voices could be heard reiterating to their children that there was no money left after their excessive spending on absolutely nothing.

All the stalls were looking wonderful though; the brass band was playing and the bunting that weaved in and out of the bandstand brought it to life with bursts of colour. Bridget the headmistress was bumbling around the field welcoming everyone; dressed in her khaki shorts and camouflage sun visor, she looked as if she had just come back from a safari.

'Where shall we go first?' Melanie enquired.

'Who are we avoiding the most?' I laughed. 'Well BB is over in that camp as usual; looks like she has taken over the Pimms and gin on the alcohol stall; Penelope is in the opposite corner supervising hook a duck, and in the northern camp there is Rupert.'

Glancing around the field, I spotted BB first.

'Well, she doesn't leave a lot to the imagination dressed like that does she?' I mused.

BB's skin resembled a tan leather handbag and without a doubt, you could buy dental floss wider than her bikini top. All her 'goods' were in the shop window so to speak and it appeared she was happy to let anyone have a quick sample of her wares. She plainly wouldn't look out of place on the beach of Benidorm. Every time she took a sip of her gin and tonic from the plastic cup, a paper umbrella poked her in the eye.

However, Penelope, tottering on the grass in her high heels, with her hat and matching fancy bag and gloves, appeared to be ready for her debut at the Queen's annual garden party at Buckingham Palace, rather than the primary school summer fair. 'Have you seen Penelope?' I whispered.

'Yes,' replied Melanie, 'she thinks she has wandered out of the paddock on ladies' day but to me it looks like she is late for a big fat gypsy wedding!'

'I'm surprised Bridget has even considered letting her loose near the money from hook a duck after the uniform caper.'

'Hook a duck isn't going to bring in hundreds of pounds though is it? Maybe she is trying to redeem herself, but one thing is for sure, she is definitely taking this event seriously.'

Rupert was standing next to his new flame with his arm draped around her waist. I hadn't clapped eyes on him since the holiday. Rupert wasn't dressed in his usual attire; he was wearing a cream linen suit with the top buttons open a little to reveal a deep purple silk cravat, and poking out of his jacket pocket was a matching silk handkerchief. He was most definitely into colour co-ordination today; the brown leather man bag he was carrying under his arm matched his brown leather loafers on the end of his feet. In spite of all the effort he had gone to, he was flying low, for his shirttail was poking through his fly.

'Rupert thinks he is a dream boat,' sniggered Melanie.

'He's more like a Belgian trawler, does the job, but not much to look at,' I giggled.

'Which way shall we go then? Wherever we choose, we are going to bump into one of them.'

Crossing my arms like the Scarecrow from the Wizard of Oz I said, 'this way! Let's wander over to the drinks stall, the children have run off with their pocket money, we can sit out of the way under the trees at the back of bandstand, it may not be peaceful there but it's tucked out of the way.'

BB was slurring her words when we reached the alcohol stall; it was possible she had sneakily drunk more gin than she had sold.

Standing in front of the table, BB looked up, 'Yes?' she snarled.

Melanie flicked her hair over her shoulder and flared her nostrils; she wasn't in the mood for Botox Bernie's lack of customer service.

'Two gin and tonics please,' Melanie requested politely but firmly.

I fumbled in my purse looking for change but it seemed it wasn't change I should have been looking for. BB slammed two plastic cups down on the table and thrusting out her hand, she demanded ten pounds.

'Are you sure? Is it really ten pounds for two small plastic cups of gin & tonic? That's extortionate, you could purchase a bottle of gin for that price,' Melanie stated.

'Well, you can afford it,' BB nastily fired back nastily in my direction.

'Afternoon ladies, let me get these drinks for you.'

That was music to my ears but instantly recognising Rupert Kensington's voice, I whipped my head round to find him standing directly behind us.

Before I could object, Melanie had already accepted his generous offer. 'Thank-you, that is very kind of you.'

His gaze was fixed on us while he handed a ten-pound note over to BB. She snorted some underhand comment, but none of us paid her any further attention.

'I am glad I've managed to catch up with you,' Rupert said.

'Is everything OK?' I asked.

'Yes, I hope so, I just wanted to apologise for Penelope's behaviour, the holiday, the lack of payment; I am deeply ashamed of the way we treated you. It's no excuse now I know, but I let Penelope influence my judgement mainly because of the children and we should never have gate-crashed your family holiday.'

Melanie raised her eyebrows at me while BB was straining to hear every word.

'What's done is done Rupert, put it behind you, it looks like you have anyway,' I answered, smiling up at the woman who was standing beside him.

'Forgive me, where are my manners? Rachel, Melanie this is Sue, Sue France.'

Standing next to Rupert was a woman who looked approximately the same age as Rupert; she was stunning, petite with flaming red hair that had the most amazing shine I had ever seen. I had seen Sue in the village but I hadn't realised that she was the owner of the posh car.

'Pleased to meet you,' Melanie and I said at the same time.

She stretched out her hand.

'Do you have children at the school?' I asked.

'Yes, two boys, they are running around somewhere I think, they are currently throwing wet sponges at the headmistress in the stocks.'

We all laughed.

'The school has done a fantastic job this year, the bunting and the band are fantastic, and Rupert has been amazing; he was up at the crack of dawn hanging the bunting up.

I thought at this point, BB might pop out of her dental-floss bikini top; she was leaning on her hands, and looking over the table pretending to search for someone on the field when actually she was trying to listen in to our conversation.

'Oh has he now? He's been amazing has he?' came an all too familiar voice from behind us.

All of us spun round.

This was the first time I'd been in touching distance of Penelope since her vile online abuse. I felt sickened by her presence.

BB couldn't believe her luck; she had secured the prime viewing spot of this chance meeting. Entertained and enjoying every second of the floorshow, she tossed her empty plastic cup into the bin and swigged the gin straight from the bottle.

The summer fair was in full swing around us. The brass band was still playing and the sound of excited children's laughter echoed in the air. Bridget the headmistress was demonstrating what a very good sport she was with her arms and head dangling from the stocks whilst the pupils from the reception class chucked wet sponges in her face for 10p a throw.

Penelope was smouldering, her cheeks burning with rage, I could see she was about to let rip.

I began to worry about how this was going to end. I wanted to be anywhere else but here. Flicking my eyes towards Melanie, my look suggested we exit this gathering sooner rather than later, but Melanie had other ideas. She was rooted to the spot, going nowhere fast.

'Yes, he has been amazing,' said Sue strongly, in a voice of grit.

'Not that amazing, abandoning his two children and deserting his wife,' Penelope fired back.

Melanie and I shot each other a puzzled look, neither of us knowing where she was going with this.

'Yes, that's right Rupert, you stand there pretending life is all hunky dory in your linen suit, creating the impression you are off punting down the river. All you're missing is a straw hat,' she sniped.

'You say the nicest things Penelope,' Rupert hissed at his soon-to-be ex-wife's mock outrage.

I felt the urge to scoop Melanie up and run like hell. There was already a crowd of people gawping as they gathered around the verbal war, and BB's view was now obscured. There was only one thing for it, she quickly poured gin into plastic cups and began circulating them free amongst the onlookers, securing yet again another prime viewing spot. Penelope gave the impression she was enjoying every minute of this charade. She was standing tall.

'What sort of man can abandon his wife and family and take up with her?' she jabbed her finger in Sue's direction.

'You've cast aside your own children and welcomed in two more.'

Penelope's voice was becoming higher pitched by the second. I was praying to God she didn't go into premature labour. The last thing anyone needed at this precise moment was Penelope huffing and puffing on all fours while giving birth to a mini Jonny Vegas on the school field.

Penelope needed to tone down her displeasure of Rupert's new relationship; there were three people here who were fully aware that Rupert had not abandoned his kids and a pregnant wife and we were all standing in the vortex of Penelope's outrage.

Judging by the look on Rupert's face, he wasn't going to stand there in front of a field full of parents and be accused of abandoning his family. Granted he hadn't been a saint in the past but to our knowledge he didn't have mini Ruperts running around – well not in the village of Tattersfield anyway.

'I think you are absolutely deluded, kidding yourself, and generating ridiculous rumours in front of all these people here,' he yelled at her, throwing his arms up into the air. 'I tolerated you Penelope; you lured me back into your tangled web of deceit boasting there was a free holiday up for grabs in Spain, and that it wasn't going to cost us a thing. Well it has cost us; it cost us our marriage.'

There was no stopping Rupert now. Penelope had created this situation and there was no escaping it – especially since we were now surrounded by masses of people who had suddenly decided they were thirsty.

I eyeballed Penelope and she glared at me.

'And why has it cost us our marriage Penelope? Please feel free to share your news with all these lovely friends in our midst.'

Suddenly, Penelope seemed lost for words. The brass band was no longer blaring out their noise and the crowd was completely silent. Even Bridget, the headmistress, who had been freed from the stocks, could be seen scurrying over to uncover the cause of the commotion on her turf.

'I'll tell you all why; it's because my lovely wife Penelope has gone and got pregnant with another man's baby.'

Penelope's, secret was out into the open. The onlookers straightened up their shoulders and all eyes turned towards her.

'Man in the loosest sense of the word,' Melanie whispered to me.

The revelation was too much for BB. Not only did her jaw hit the floor, but also she dropped her plastic cup full to the brim with gin, which spilled down her front.

Bridget, the headmistress, who'd finally arrived on the scene, began to clap like a demented sea lion. She wasn't applauding the drama in any way whatsoever but hoping to disperse the crowd. Cupping her hands over her mouth, she yelled, 'free burgers over at the barbecue in the far corner of the school field – first come, first served!'

Within seconds, the swarms of spectators who couldn't resist a freebie could be seen running faster than Olympians, barging past each other and heading towards the open firepit. The unfortunate father from Class One, who'd volunteered his services at the last minute, couldn't throw the meat on the barbecue quickly enough.

BB bent down to pick up her dropped cup,   From out of nowhere, a stranger was standing next to her, and he was smiling at her self-consciously.

The man was tubby with a squashed nose; his rosy cheeks were sunburnt from the afternoon sun. He had thick wiry hair and his brown eyes were taking in the sight before him.

'Oh my Lord, I thought it was you,' he said.

I'd never seen this man before; he wasn't someone I recognised from the playground, but he obviously seemed to know BB. It was our turn to stop and listen.

He removed an old-fashioned handkerchief from his pocket and thrust it towards BB.

Taking the hanky, she wiped the excess liquid from her spilt drink over her body and handed it back to him.

'It's OK, you can keep it,' he smiled.

'Do I know you?' she asked, genuinely flustered by the kindness of the mystery man.

'Not as such but,' he fumbled in his pocket and pulled out a scrappy piece of paper. 'Has anyone got a pen?' he enquired. Rupert reached inside his man bag, retrieved a biro and handed it over.

Forcing the pen and paper into BB's hand he said, 'please can you sign this for me, I am a massive fan.'

'A fan of what?' Melanie mouthed.

'I've no idea,' I mimed back.

BB's face was one of panic, but taking the pen, she signed some illegible scribble on the paper he had given her. I questioned whether she could even write.

'I'd recognise that peachy backside anywhere,' he winked.

Rupert began to grin and turned to the man. 'She was particularly good in 'Saturday Night Beaver,' wasn't she?' he glinted, ushering Sue out of the circle and leading her towards of the cake stall.

'Lovely to meet you,' Sue called back to us, but she glowered at Penelope and didn't even give BB a second glance. Sue France, in my opinion, was a very pleasant woman.

'My favourite was 'Gangbangs of New York'... I think you came into your own in that role. It was very challenging for you indeed.'

The cogs were turning in Melanie's mind faster than mine. However, Penelope's brain was processing all the information faster than any of us.

'It was you; it was you on my telly screen,' Penelope declared.

Melanie and I were rooted to the spot; we were going nowhere.

BB neither confirmed nor denied she was on any telly screen, but all the jigsaw pieces were slowly slotting together.

It was her! Casting my mind back to the night of Rupert's solo 'Strictly Come Dancing' audition, the one that took place after he and Penelope separated at New Year, it all became clear. BB was the woman paused on the television when we busted Rupert, the woman in the porn movie he had been watching.

Melanie sniggered; linking my arm through hers, we rounded up the children and we all headed home for our very own barbecue with Matt and the Farrier. Penelope was last overheard in the distance arguing with BB and the devotee of her movie career was asking them both if they would ever consider a threesome. Glancing back over my shoulder, BB was scurrying away with Penelope shouting expletives as she went. It was the best school summer fair I'd ever attended.

CHAPTER 30

I loved the month of August, the month of no school runs, no buttering of sandwiches or washing of games kits. The long school holidays were upon us and it was pure bliss. The alarm clock was switched off from the early 6 a.m. wake-up calls. There were lazy days, late evenings, and no bedtime restrictions whatsoever.

BB and Penelope's alliance ceased after the revelation that Rupert had watched his porn movie knowing BB was playing the star role. I smiled at the memory of BB exaggerating her career at the Frisky Pensioner's funeral. Divulging the information to the man in the church that she was indeed a movie star, his quick disappearance probably saved his life; either that or he had recognised her too. Melanie's ex-partner Rob really had uncovered the real BB way back at the antenatal class, a few years back.

Melanie and I had become fast friends and so had our children. They spent the sunny days of the holidays hopping between houses. We left our back doors unlocked while they wandered between them, enjoying water fights, playing games and raiding the cupboards of delicious delights.

There was no drama, no playground politics, and I hadn't clapped eyes on the Mafia since the last day of term.

My obsession for running was still very much alive. My old worn-out trainers had been cast aside in exchange for a pair of semi-decent ones, but I was still opposed to wearing a sun visor like the brigade of mothers who trotted past me on numerous occasions. I powered my legs along the same route most days, pushing them harder and faster every time. There was only one major difference in my running regime; I had landed myself a new running partner.

Sue France, now a permanent fixture in Rupert's life, jogged alongside me on every run.

Rupert and Sue traded in the bachelor pad for a part-exchange modern semi-detached on the new estate with bedrooms for Little Jonny and Annabel if Penelope ever decided to let the children see their father again. They were happy. Rupert's love for Sue seemed sincere and genuine.

As friends, Melanie and Sue were worth their weight in gold. No expectations, no judgements, just plain old-fashioned friendship. Melanie, sticking by my side over scratch-card-gate, lost a few of her other friends – but she never batted an eyelid. Her take on the whole situation was one of positivity, why would anyone believe what Penelope was voicing if it had nothing to do with them in the first place? They didn't know me nor had they even bothered to get to know me. It was no loss to her; in fact, her eyes had been well and truly opened to the Mafia playground pettiness. I had managed to keep my dignity throughout the whole episode; I wasn't the one protesting too much, I didn't need to explain myself to anyone.

As the cork flew out of the bottle of the champagne, Melanie and the Farrier, Rupert and Sue, Matt and I clinked our glasses and raised a toast sitting around the open pit of fire in the garden one Friday night.

'What are we toasting?' Matt asked.

'The love of my new lady,' suggested Rupert smiling at Sue.

'Good, honest friendship,' said Melanie winking at me.

'That we have survived the year so far,' I grinned at Rupert.
The Farrier cleared his throat and made us all look at him.

'I've got something worth celebrating I hope,'

'Come on spill, you haven't told me!' responded Melanie eagerly.

We all squealed; as the Farrier flipped, open a ruby red box to reveal the most beautiful diamond any of us had ever seen. He dropped down on one knee at the side of the patio table.

'Melanie Tate, I love you with all my heart. Not a moment, a day has ever gone by without me thinking about you, you have made my life complete. Will you do me the greatest honour of becoming my wife? Will you marry me?'

'How romantic!' Sue mouthed at me.

All our heads turned towards Melanie. She stalled momentarily, the tears were streaming down her cheeks but the sparkle in her eyes and the beam of that smile said it all.

'Yes, Yes, YES,' she cried. Jumping to his feet, the Farrier took the ring out of the red box and slipped it on to the fourth finger of Melanie's left hand. We all gave out a huge cheer followed by heaps of hugs, congratulations and the clinking of glasses.

'And there's more,' the Farrier beamed.

'More? What do you mean there's more?' Melanie questioned.

'I've waited so long for you to come back into my life and I didn't want to wait a moment longer, I know we have already talked about this a little and you have always said you are more of a pint and a pie type of a girl and not one for lavish spending but ...'

'Come on spit it out,' we all shouted.

'The registry office has had a cancellation and if you think it's possible they have reserved the booking for me until Monday.'

We all sat there speechless waiting in anticipation for the date to be revealed.

'And the date?' I asked.

'A couple of weeks on Saturday! What do you think?' He looked at Melanie.

How exciting was this!

'How very romantic,' I was thrilled. 'How absolutely dreamy!'

'Can you run that past me again ... two weeks on Saturday?' Melanie gasped

Smiling at Melanie he said, 'That will be the very one, I would like all the is dotted and the ts crossed as soon as possible, if that is OK with you?'

Melanie was gobsmacked. We were all gobsmacked.

All eyes were on her whilst we waited for her to respond.

All Melanie could manage through her tears of joy was a nod of the head.

We all let out a raucous cheer and Matt popped the cork on another bottle of champagne. Trying to keep her voice steady, Melanie blurted out, 'Jesus Christ, I'm getting married two weeks on Saturday!'

CHAPTER 31

For all of us the next couple of weeks were extremely busy. Pulling together as true friends do, Sue and I spent every spare minute by Melanie's side. Melanie was truly excited; we were all excited. Melanie told us it was like a dream come true; she wasn't one for tradition and couldn't think of anything more romantic then getting hitched in the local registry office with her friends by her side.

With only one week until the big day, we shopped until we dropped – literally – the blisters on my feet were reminders of how hard we worked to pull the wedding together with very little time to do it.

The weatherman had predicted a beautiful sunny Saturday; we were relying on him to be right for once. The wedding was scheduled for 11a.m. at the town hall and once the I dos were all done and dusted we were to be frequenting the local pub for a pie and a pint.

The wedding party consisted of three couples, Matt and me, Rupert and Sue and the happy couple. The children were being babysat for the day by Sue's parents, both retired teachers. Their agenda included an afternoon at the park followed by tea at Frankie and Benny's which gave the wedding party time for ample celebrations.

Melanie had decided she wasn't going to go down the traditional route of a white wedding dress. Comfort had always been her motto and with a crisp white cotton tunic with three quarter sleeves, new skinny jeans and white doc martin boots, her wedding attire was fully complete.

Sue was in charge of the flowers and I was left in charge of the transport. Matt was best man and Rupert's job was to make sure the men were safely at the town hall for 11 o'clock sharp.

The Farrier stayed over at Rupert's the night before the wedding, even though he had never been superstitious in his life; he wasn't prepared to take any chances. He had waited so long for this day to come.

The morning of the wedding was soon upon us and I had never known a couple of weeks fly by so fast. Up at the crack of dawn, I rallied all the children together and dropped them safely in the hands of Sue's parents. Matt, up and out with the larks, had been instructed to collect the freshly prepared buttonholes from the florist in town and deliver them carefully to the nervously awaiting groom who was found to be anxiously pacing up and down Rupert's living room.

Sue and I had the honour of delivering the bride-to-be on time. We were driving Melanie to the Town Hall, and 'Bettie' my old reliable Volkswagen Beetle looked the part with a cream ribbon draped over her bonnet. Beeping outside the house, we were ready and waiting in anticipation for the first glimpse of the bride.

The front door swung open and Melanie looked breath-taking. Her dark hair was curled and pinned loosely into a bun decorated with delicate white daisies, her make-up applied to perfection with subtle au-natural colouring and the skinny jeans showed off her flawlessly toned body. Jumping out of the car to greet her, there was a lot of cooing and hugging. Sue completed the look by handing her the most elegant of bouquets. White and pink luxury roses with frosted eucalyptus sprigs were not only chic, but also perfect for the big day.

Suddenly I paused and leant against the car, I felt unexpectedly light-headed.

'Are you OK Rach?' enquired Melanie as she touched my arm.

'Yes, yes, it must be all the emotion; I became a little light-headed there for a moment. Don't worry, you look exquisite and your carriage awaits,' I smiled, holding open the car door whilst the beautiful bride climbed in.

'Are we ready?'

'Most definitely' Melanie beamed. A quick beep of Bettie's horn and a cheery wave to the onlookers that were now gathering outside their house and we were off!

Pulling Bettie up in the space directly outside the Town Hall, we spotted the Farrier leaning against the wall.

'Oh my, doesn't he look handsome?' Melanie gushed.

'You make the perfect couple,' Sue and I chorused.

The Farrier, spotting the gorgeous woman before him, beamed from ear to ear. His smile never faltered once, and reaching out, he grasped the hand of his beautiful wife-to-be.

'Would you be looking for me by any chance?" he winked. 'You look stunning,' he whispered into Melanie's ear.

He looked so handsome in his dark blue morning suit, pale blue cravat and checked navy waistcoat; so different from the casual horse wear we had always seen him in.

She raised her gaze, 'And you look perfect,'

'Pass me the tissues, I'm already filling up, please God, do not let my mascara run,' Sue said with tears in her eyes.

The town hall was a beautiful old brick building with green ivy trailing all around it; baby pink clematis was entwined between the green leaves that overhung the heavy wooden door forming a striking archway of flowers.

Pushing the door open, a small silver bell tinkled above our heads which alerted the registrar of our arrival. She came scurrying towards us.

'Ladies and Gentlemen are we ready to begin?' She questioned. Matt and Rupert, looking just as handsome as the Farrier did, linked their arms into ours and we followed the registrar down the long winding corridor.

We were led through to a beautiful garden room beyond the Town Hall's mundane offices. The gigantic panes of glass revealed a breath taking view across the lake. Small canoes gently bobbed across the water with couples enjoying the sun.

Directly to the side of the glass panes was a table with six crystal champagne flutes bursting to the brim with delightful fizz. In front of the truly stunning view, there were four gorgeously decorated chairs with white linen covers and a pale blue sash set out before the antique table. The chandelier hung over our heads, glistening in the morning sun.

It was beautiful, every detail a delight, pure and simple. The room was filled with the wonderful fragrance that lingered from the vases of roses scattered around the room.

Matt and I, Rupert and Sue took our seats, already blurry eyed with emotion.

'Wait, I nearly forgot,' the Farrier said fumbling around in his pocket, his palms now sweating from the excitement. Pulling out the most exquisite sparkling silver necklace, he reached forward fastening the clasp around Melanie's elegant neck. It was a beautiful romantic gesture and Melanie was every inch the radiant bride. Kissing the tip of her nose, he made his way to the front of the room.

Melanie appeared to glide along the aisle beside the Farrier and now they stood facing each other. The registrar smiled at the four of us.

'Welcome, everyone, to this very special day.'

She turned towards Melanie and the Farrier. 'Shall we begin?'

Overwhelmed with emotion, the Farrier leant forward and wiped a tear that was trickling down Melanie's face, a very touching moment. I too had a lump in my throat and was blinking back the tears; they looked so perfect standing there. It was so lovely watching my new friends begin the next chapter of their lives together.

'Do you take John Richard Fletcher-Parker to be your lawfully wedded husband?' the registrar asked.

'So that's his name?' Sue whispered.

'I never knew it either, we just called him the Farrier, but he looks like a John; Melanie and John has a lovely ring to it!' I replied softly.

Once the wedding vows were exchanged, there wasn't a dry eye in the room. We could barely wait for the registrar to announce them man and wife. Then as the words were spoken, John Fletcher-Parker, on cue, gathered Melanie into his arms for a long, passionate kiss and the four of us watching let out whoops of delight.

The registrar opened a glass door, which led us out on to a small wooden decking overlooking the pretty lake. We raised our glasses of champagne to toast to the happy couple. 'To Melanie and John,' Matt announced.

'To Melanie and John,' we all chorused.

CHAPTER 32

The long school summer holidays were drawing to a close. In the end, it had been the most fantastic summer ever and a feeling of sadness was creeping through me; I didn't want it to come to an end.

The six of us had become very good friends; the lads wandered around the green most weekends chasing a small white ball, and hacking clumps out of the grass, which kept them occupied for hours. The women, well, we did what most women do best, open a bottle of wine and talk for hours around the patio table in the garden while the children played. Rupert was enjoying life; we'd never seen him like this before. His love for Sue and her boys was his world and the way he looked into her eyes was clear to all of us, he was a changed man.

Penelope was losing friends fast; she used her children as weapons to pull on Rupert's heartstrings. Making life difficult for him, she refused him access to the children. He wasn't going to give up; he was relishing the time with Sue's boys, enjoying the rough and tumble of football in the park, mountain biking and had even bought them each a set of junior golf clubs. Little Jonny was missing out on this fun; he was missing out on a relationship with his father. It saddened Rupert. Looking back, he quite openly voiced his regret in listening to Penelope. Little Jonny was her prodigy; she ploughed everything she had into making him clever, the workbooks and the reading books, while

Annabel never got the attention she deserved. It worried Rupert what would become of them both when Penelope's new baby arrived into this world. He made a decision, he was going to fight for his children; he would fight Penelope in court if he had to, whatever it took he was prepared, he loved his children and both he and Sue wanted them to be a part of their new family.

Melanie and John were still floating on cloud nine since the wedding; they were just the perfect family. John's smile had never wavered since Melanie spoke the words 'I do' when she finally became his wife after all those years. They had their work cut out, completely renovating Frisky Pensioner's house. They ripped out the old-fashioned carpets and surgically removed the woodchip wallpaper; it was a different property when they finished it. Updated and now modern, Melanie had created the most magnificent of homes even down to the soft furnishings which she created all by herself after joining the local sewing club.

The second of September was suddenly upon us, which could only mean one thing – back to the old routine – the school run.

September was also the time of the new mothers to the school. The time when their children, all looking spick and span in their brand new uniforms and shiny black shoes, would enter primary school life for the next seven years.

Melanie and I had become a permanent fixture at the back of the playground. We had every intention of keeping out of the way of the clutches of the new enthusiastic mothers that would start this term. We watched the cliques form, and usually by Christmas when the roles of the nativity play were be delegated to the little five-year olds, the cracks would begin to appear. By the time we reached Easter, there would be a complete shift around, not only in friendships but often of husbands as well.

That first day, alarm intrusion was an unwelcome introduction to the new school term, with everyone feeling sluggish and unprepared for the early start. Even though I was looking forward to a few hours to myself in the day, I would miss the constant chatter and noise that had daily surrounded me for the last six weeks. Sue and I discussed training for a race, maybe a five-kilometre run for charity, and now with the children back at school and nursery we would have more time for running.

Once we were up and dressed and scrambled eggs had warmed our stomachs, the children reluctantly slipped their arms into their coats and feet into their black, shiny no-scuff shoes. We waited for Melanie and the girls to shut their garden gate and gathered outside our house for the short journey to school.

This morning no one was enthusiastic, and Melanie was rolling her eyes at the thought of seeing BB and Penelope again.

BB would be in her element this morning; it was a chance for her to hand-pick her new best friend from the naïve mothers whose children were starting school. She'd be preying upon the ones swinging their Gucci bags, and dressed to the nines in the latest designer gear – the ones with the brand new Range Rovers.

I hadn't clapped eyes on Penelope or BB since the school summer fair. I wouldn't even be looking at them again after the rumours and hatred they had spread on the internet regarding my lottery win. My eyes had been well and truly opened to the mothers in the playground who'd listened to her drama without any evidence of her claims, and I certainly wouldn't give any of them the time of day again. I was extremely lucky to have Sue and Melanie by my side; they were just genuine lovely people.

It was apparent nothing had changed since the day we broke up for the summer holidays except the dog outside the school gates was yapping away, showing off the latest edition in fake coats for pooches.

They were all congregated outside the school gates, that is, Penelope and her clique. BB, having been dropped from the group, swaggered straight past them, shoulders puffed out, and a face like thunder.

'They've definitely fallen out,' Melanie stated.

'I'm not surprised. Penelope and BB were never going to be lifelong friends, thrust together for their love of senseless drama and now it's been revealed that Rupert enjoyed so many of BB's movie roles whilst participating in extracurricular activities, I don't think they will be making up any day soon!'

Penelope was leaning against the school gate, wearing a huge shapeless dress – she was now in her third trimester. Taking life into our own hands, we walked on past the remaining Mafia who were beginning to dwindle in numbers.

All the new mothers were fussing around their children, crying and hugging them as if they were being evacuated to the other side of the country. Most of the children looked relieved to be led away from their hysterical mothers by their smiley teacher to the safety of their new classrooms.

'Well, same old, same old – nothing much changes. How long have we got left of this primary school sentence?' Melanie spurted out.

'Too bloody long!' I laughed.

Sue was always late for everything. This morning was no exception. I was about to ask where she was, when Melanie nodded towards the gate. Running like a lunatic, she was pushing the boys through the gate, their backpacks trailing on the ground. Sue's flustered and red, sweating face was a dead giveaway that her morning was not running smoothly. It was the boys' first day at their new school. Sue and Rupert had decided to relocate them once they all moved into their new home together in the village. Judging by the furious look on Penelope's face, she didn't appear ecstatic at their decision, especially, when she would be bumping into Rupert's new family every day. Sue thrust the boys into the end of the line, and they disappeared through the heavy-duty door that slammed shut behind them.

'This getting-up lark is a killer, it took me nearly thirty minutes to understand why the alarm clock was ringing out and then in my tired, worn- out state I was halfway to the old school before I realised we were heading towards the wrong one!'

Melanie and I laughed at her harassed state.

'I'm being stared at,' Sue suddenly commented.

'Just ignore her, Penelope will move on to the next drama soon enough.'

'Not by her, by him,' she nodded in the direction of a man standing in the corner of the playground.

Melanie and I turned ninety degrees to meet the gaze of the mystery man in question. BB, her arms folded, was loitering on the sidelines of the netball pitch at the far end of the playground, and eyeing up the stranger. I must admit I was casting an appreciative eye over his worn-out converse, and his multi-pocket combat shorts, which no one could dispute showed off his lean tanned legs to the best advantage. His toned, muscled arms stretched out from his white T-shirt, which was sized to perfection across his broad chest. He was tall and his hair blonde, and on his face, a manly gritty stubble. Constantly raking his fingers through his hair and sweeping his fringe to one side, he looked like Brad Pitt's stunt double in a Hollywood movie. 'Wow, that is not the usual type of bloke we encounter in this playground,' I stammered, mesmerised by his sheer presence.

'Oh my God he is coming over. Who is he?' Sue gasped.

Rooted to the spot, we gawped at him as he sauntered over to us.

'I feel like a dithering school girl with my first crush on the captain of the football team,' Sue wittered.

'Be quiet, he's nearly here,' I whispered.

She nodded, her eyes watching his every move. 'Handsome, isn't he?"

I felt myself blushing; I really hoped he wasn't a mind reader.

Sue and I were so captivated by his presence; we didn't notice the lack of response from Melanie who'd avoided joining in with our chitchat regarding the enchanting looking stranger. Her expression indicated that her only thought was 'could he be looking for me?'

'Hi,' he grinned at Melanie. 'Long-time no see.'

Both Sue and I spun our shocked faces towards Melanie. She knew him! So who the hell was he? We wanted to know.

'You're back, then?' Melanie spat at the delicious stranger.

'You know each other?' I asked, baffled.

'Ladies, let me have the pleasure of introducing you to Rob, a poor excuse of a man, but Dotty's father, the ex-bastard.' she snorted.

Wow! I stared at him open-mouthed, but he didn't seem shaken by Melanie's introduction. Both Sue and I knew of the unfortunate moment Rob had been caught with his trousers around his ankles with another woman in the hospital toilets at Dotty's birth. I was slightly jealous of Penelope, who had witnessed that moment. She was luckier than me, who got lumbered with the eyeful of the Jonny Vegas look-alike banging her in the disabled bogs of the snooker hall.

'Well hello, ex-bastard, don't you just love a good ice-breaker!' Sue laughed.

I was speechless; I wasn't sure whether that was down to the situation we were faced with, or the fact he was one extremely handsome guy. It was evident by Melanie's reaction that she wasn't impressed one little bit. I think it was the stony- faced stare that gave it away. She looked murderous.

Rob wasn't going to let Melanie's frostiness put him off.

'Can we talk? Is there anywhere more private we can go?' he asked.

His question had come out of the blue. Melanie didn't know how to answer and she didn't want to answer. This was not what she was expecting on the first morning of the new school term.

'Well ... I don't know. I mean ...' she shrugged.

Melanie looked at me expectantly. I wasn't sure what she wanted me to do or say.

'You still look the same,' he smiled.

'Cut out the pleasantries,' she spat back; her brows arched, as she looked daggers at him.

'Please, Melanie, at least hear me out.'

Melanie didn't answer.

'You could borrow my kitchen if that helps?' I offered. I didn't know what to do for the best, I wasn't sure whether I should have got involved or just kept quiet.

'I could easily make myself scarce for the next hour.'

Already dressed in my running gear I had every intention of taking myself off for a run after the school bell sounded and had already been early enough to drop the younger two at nursery first.

'Would you come too Rachel?'

'Me?'

'Please, whatever he has to say he can say in front of you too, I have nothing to hide.'

Looking at Melanie I could see her eyes widen. I didn't mind being there, I didn't know him and if my friend felt safer with me there I was happy to help her out.

CHAPTER 33

Opening the front door to my house Melanie and Rob followed me in silence into the kitchen.

'Tea or Coffee?' I asked Rob.

'Tea please, have you got a toilet I can use?' he asked.

'Yes, just through there,' I nodded my head in its direction.

Once he was safely out of earshot, Melanie spoke.

'I cannot believe after all this time I find myself in your kitchen about to share a cuppa with the father of my child, a man I thought – hoped, I would never set eyes on again.'

'Are you OK?'

'Yes, I will be. I'm sorry for dragging you into this Rachel but I didn't want to be alone with him and I think it would be disloyal to John if I didn't have a witness.'

I didn't think I would ever get used to the Farrier being called John.

'Don't be daft, I fully understand, it's not a problem, but I'll sit in the conservatory with the door open so I can still see and hear you but won't directly under your feet.' I was thankful for the sit-down; the earlier morning alarm was already taking its toll.

'Good plan and thank-you.' Melanie looked momentarily relieved.

'I wonder what has brought him back.'

'I have no idea but his infidelity, his mind games, and his controlling nature left my self-esteem destroyed for many years – something I will never forgive him for.'

Rob came back into the room and seated himself down at the table. I placed a mug of tea in front of them both. 'I'll just be out there,' I said.

Melanie decided to broach the question that was obviously burning inside her.

'How the hell did you find me?' I could see Melanie was scrutinising him curiously.

'I was driving through Tattersfield back in July. For years, I've been visiting places with masses of people or in crowded shopping centres thinking I had caught a glimpse of you and each time it was just someone bearing a resemblance to you. This one morning I spotted you walking up the main road with a child. It was purely by coincidence; I was on my way to a business meeting and had never driven through this village before. I slowed right down, parked in the lay-by opposite the school, and watched you walk by. I couldn't believe my luck when I saw you that day.'

'What you did to me was unforgivable – the day I gave birth and Laura, and how many others I never knew about. You never treated me with the respect I deserved.'

'Part of me knew what I was doing to you, I am so sorry; I regret everything.'

I saw Melanie shut her eyes probably in a vain attempt to block out the tears. She was a strong person; single-handed she'd looked after Dotty from the day she was born and was more than likely determined not to show her emotions. I could see her legs shaking under the table.

'You made me feel like a complete and utter failure.' Melanie said. The pain in her face was visible and she wiped her hand across her face to dispose of an angry tear that had escaped.

'If I could turn back time and do it all again differently, I would,' Rob said.

'Well luckily for me you can't,' she answered wearily.

'Please, let's give it another go. I am nothing without you; we are meant to be together.'

'Shame you didn't realise that when you had me.'

'Please Melanie, I've made a huge mistake; we have a daughter together and I really want to be a part of her life too.'

'So do you even remember I gave birth to a baby girl then?'

I witnessed an exchanged glance between them.

'Our daughter is beautiful; I watched her amble along at your side walking through the school gates.'

'Tell me Rob, what's happened from July to now; there have been a fair few weeks that have gone by.'

'I drove the same route the next morning and nothing; there was not a soul in sight, no mothers, and no children. The street was stripped of people and the school gates padlocked shut. I plucked up the courage to nip into the local newsagent to enquire why the school was closed; the guy behind the counter stated the school had broken up for the summer holidays. I checked their website and here I am the first day back after the holidays.'

In the conservatory, I watched and listened to every word. I felt sorry for Melanie. The man before her had mentally abused her and was a distant memory, yet here he was back again, begging for another chance. All this just didn't seem real.

'Can't we leave the past behind us? I'm a changed man.'

Suddenly he became serious, taking a deep breath and I could see he was staring straight at her, 'I love you Melanie, I always will, I'm sure we could work it out.'

'It's too late,' Melanie replied firmly.

'It's never too late,' he whispered. Rob stood up from the table and moved gently towards her; she pushed out her hand, holding him at arm's length.

'Do not touch me,' she said firmly.

'Remember when I used to moan that the bed wasn't big enough for us both? Well now, I can stretch out my arms and legs; it's cold and lonely without you there. I miss you Melanie.'

'Miss me? It's taken you all these years to decide you miss me?' she fumed. 'It really is too late; I have buried the past well and truly. I got married last month to the most wonderful man on this planet and you aren't a patch on him. I love him, not you.'

Frustrated, Rob banged his fist down on the table and a look of anguish flashed across his face. For a fraction of a second, Melanie looked sorry for him, but no doubt all of his lies filtered back through her mind.

'What happens now? Where do we go from here? What about Dotty?' he asked sadly.

'It's simple, Rob. You go back to wherever you have come from; I have slipped through your fingers, and you are no longer a part of my or Dotty's future. I made that decision the day she was born. I will never be burnt by the same flame twice. Goodbye, Rob.' And with that, she boldly stood up and opened the door.

Knowing he was beaten, Rob looked gutted.

'Melanie, you are a wonderful person and deserve the very best that life can offer you. Your husband is a very lucky man.' And with that, he walked out.

Melanie watched the man who was once the love of her life disappear up the path – gone from her world for a second time and forever. 'You can come out now,' she shouted to me.

Going back into the kitchen I held out my arms and she crumbled inside them. I hugged her tight.

CHAPTER 34

I was standing patiently in the queue at the Doctor's surgery waiting to check in with the receptionist. Well, when I say queue, there was one patient in front of me. He was an elderly man who was wrapped up tightly in his grey duffle coat with a tartan scarf draped around his neck. The receptionist was in a battle of wits arguing over an appointment that he appeared to have missed. He wasn't going to budge until she allocated him a further appointment and preferably one today. She led him into the nurses' waiting room out of earshot of the onlooking, nosy patients, and calm was finally restored. I didn't like these places; I didn't like them one little bit.

'He needs sectioning,' one woman bristled. I tried to drown out the cries of a screaming baby with a raging temperature; the tired distraught mother rocked the baby incessantly while apologising profusely to the faces that were staring at her.

'Name,' the receptionist bellowed at me. She didn't even look up at me.

'Rachel Young,' I replied politely. I smiled, but it was wasted on her; still not making any eye contact with me, she continued to tap on the keypad in front of her.

'Take a seat,' she commanded.

Unwillingly, I plonked myself down on one of the uncomfortable plastic chairs in the waiting room, the furthest away from the artificial Japanese fruticosa tree and the man that was coughing profusely into an oversized hanky. Picking up a maga-zine from the pile on the table, I flicked through an ancient copy of Heat. I wondered how many thousands of hands it had passed through since its release back in 2007. A minute later, the double doors flew open and a couple emerged hand-in-hand from the doctor's room.

'Rachel Young, you can go in now.' Thankfully, the doctor was only running half-an- hour late, which by any doctor's stan-dards is a miracle in itself. All eyes in the waiting room watched me push open the double doors with force. Like an episode of 'Stars in your Eyes,' but lacking the drum roll, I disappeared through them without so much as a puff of smoke.

I knocked on the doctor's door, and he bellowed, 'come in!'

I entered his room to find him looking up at me from behind his desk – smiling – which was more than I could say for his re-ceptionist. Gesturing with his hand towards the seat, I sat down opposite him. 'What can I do for you, Mrs Young?' he enquired.

I didn't really know what he could do for me. The reason for my visit was one of gut instinct. Something inside me had been niggling away for a while and I couldn't quite put my finger on what it was. My health, as far as I was concerned, was good. I rarely suffered from colds, chest infections, or even my water works, unlike Sue who struggled to hold onto the contents of her bladder every time we went running or she sneezed – we of-ten joked she should seek shares in TENA Lady. Recently I had been feeling even more drained than usual, and remembering my mental note to myself I thought it was about time to find out if my body was lacking iron.

For a couple of months, I'd put it down to my increased activity on the running front; Sue and I had been pushing our running routine harder and faster each time we went out in preparation for our first race in February. On top of that, the mental exhaustion of having four children had tired me out completely even though I was lucky they were good kids, and no trouble at all. I was certain a bottle of iron capsules would put me right back on track. Explaining to the doctor I was probably wasting his time, it was more than likely down to the trials of family life, he suggested a couple of blood tests to see what they would discover. Flicking through my medical records he asked me a series of questions, the usual ones concerning my weight and did I smoke but the question I most dreaded was how many units of alcohol did I normally consume on a weekly basis.

'Too many,' was my answer to that personal question; way too many. In my defence, I was thirty-five now and a few small glasses of wine each evening helped me to relax; well that was my story and I was sticking to it.

The only change in my body that I had recently noticed was a slight tenderness under my left arm at the side of my left breast when I pushed myself harder with the running. To be precise, it was more of an ache and on the odd occasion, it caused me slight discomfort. Sharing this information with the doctor, I assured him that I checked my breasts on a regular basis and there was nothing at all unusual. I'd never felt any lumps or bumps. All the same, erring on the side of caution he thought it was best to arrange a mammogram, which he scheduled for the following week.

Leaving the surgery, I sent Melanie a quick text to see if she was free for a cuppa. Smiling down at my phone, I laughed at her reply, *'only if you have cake!'*

Luckily for her, I hadn't been able to resist the magnificent Victoria sponge with oodles of cream oozing out of its sides that was screaming 'eat me' when I cycled past the local bakery window that very morning.

'I have cake! See you in five.'

Arriving back at the house, I kicked off my shoes and flung my coat and scarf over the banisters and went straight into the kitchen. Flicking the switch on the kettle and removing the cake from the fridge, I retrieved the mugs from the cupboard while pondering over my morning appointment at the doctor's. I debated discussing it with Melanie, but what was the point? I didn't really have anything to tell her. It was probably something or nothing and obviously, I hoped it was nothing. Before the water had come to the boil, Melanie flew through the kitchen door faster than a bird escaping the clutches of a ferocious cat.

'Come in why don't you!' I laughed.

Melanie was looking frazzled which really wasn't like her and I could tell she had a bee in her bonnet about someone or something.

'Have you seen this? The absolute cheek of the woman.' She thrusting a letter in my hand, and I glanced down to see what all the commotion was about.

'It looks like a party invitation to me?'

'Oh yes, it is that all right.'

I wasn't sure what I was missing, but I was missing something.

'It's from that Charlene, her son is in Dotty's class, you know the one, the mother we joke about being Supermum.'

I knew exactly who she was talking about; the child spoke like Prince William with his very posh and proper accent, way too aristocratic for our local village school.

Charlene is the most prepared mum you would ever have the pleasure of meeting in the school playground, an extremely organised individual. She became worthy of her nickname 'Supermum' the afternoon of bikeability. Supervising numerous kids wobbling on bikes down a main busy high street was enough for any teacher to consider phoning in sick for day. Bundled up in layers of clothes to keep warm, the children had faced the day being swayed by the high winds and dodging the scattered rain showers which for once was correctly predicted by the weatherman.

On this particular day, Melanie and I had passed the school gates at lunchtime while out for a stroll with the dog. We clocked Supermum running hell-bent towards the rows and rows of bikes that had been propped up or dropped in the school playground before the lunchtime bell. With the black clouds lingering above us, the raindrops had started to belt down heavily when we noticed her locate a bike and rest it up against the wall of the classroom. Whipping out a plastic carrier bag from her coat pocket she placed it neatly over the saddle and secured it with string, there was no way on this earth that she was going to let Frederick sit on a wet saddle when returning from his delicious packed lunch, which by the way, would also be fit for a prince.

I knew Melanie well, and she was still seething from the incident at the Easter Bonnet parade back in April. The school hall had been set out with long trestle tables covered in sugar pink paper tablecloths. Each class had been allocated their own stall of honour to show off their Easter extravaganza creations. There was a raised platform placed in the centre of each table where the winning bonnet from each class would be displayed with pride.

Melanie was a no-mess mother and by this I mean *no mess*. All gluing, painting and any cake baking, and other messy activities were on a permanent ban in their house – it was non-negotiable. I knew where she was coming from. The year before, I had the doubtful pleasure of opening the front door to a bunch of God-botherers, and while I was plotting a polite escape, my standard poodle bolted like the speed of light straight past us out of the front door with the contents of a whole packet of sanitary towels stuck down with superglue to the length of his curly back. It was at that point that I realised I could not leave Samuel unattended for one minute.

On this occasion and after constant nagging from Dotty, Melanie had decided to throw caution to the wind or should I say chicks to the hat and Mission Easter Bonnet was underway. Braving the aisles of Home Bargains her shopping basket was overflowing with 'anything Easter' that could be glued firmly to a pink straw bonnet. With the kitchen table laid out with newspaper and gluepots, Dotty was having a whale of a time decorating her bonnet. There wasn't any part of her hat left un-covered, without a doubt it was all her own work and Melanie was gushing with pride.

Carefully wrapping the Easter bonnet in a black bin bag, they had cautiously carried it to school the next morning, mak-ing sure none of the glued-on chicks flew the nest.

The Easter Eggstravaganza was always well received at school, when all the parents and even Grannies attended to view the children's wonderful creations of decorated bonnets and sample the delicious toasted hot cross buns while enjoy-ing a cup of tea. This is when the tension began to surface, not from the kids I may add, but from the mothers. Once the toasted buns had been devoured a crowd of children, moth-ers and glamorous grannies quickly gathered at the front of the stage. Bridget, the headmistress, took the opportunity to announce the winning bonnet and present the child with a Cadbury's crème egg.

The winner from Dotty's class was about to be declared. Bridget, hushing the eagerly chatting mothers, was waiting to reveal the winning bonnet covered over with the cloth. Melanie knew it was in the bag. Scanning the table of hats, Dotty's was nowhere to be seen; it must be that hers was the winning creation – in pride of place – on the winners' podium.

'The winner of the Easter bonnet is Frederick Pontington-Smythe; congratulations Frederick! Can we all give him a round of applause,' she announced.

'Ta da!' She flung the cover off the concealed bonnet, and it was immediately apparent that no way a child in the infant school could have decorated that bonnet, unless he was child genius sculptor. Enraged, Melanie marched straight up to Bridget. Unable to control her anger and standing with her hands firmly on her hips, she spluttered out in front of a hall full of people, 'Fix! It's a fix! I'd eat my hat if that entry has been decorated by a child.'

Melanie was correct; Supermum AKA Charlene was applauding her own work while Frederick shovelled his winning cream egg down his gullet. Glancing down at the floor, Melanie noticed Dotty's bonnet squashed on the floor underneath the metal legs of the trestle table.

'Well?' said a breathless Melanie, back in my kitchen.

'Well what? What am I looking for?' I replied. Puzzled, I flipped the party invite over to inspect the reverse.

'Look at the small print underneath the RSVP telephone number,' she demanded, pointing to the bottom of the invitation.

Glancing down at the invite from Frederick Pontington-Smythe I focussed on the minute writing and then laughing, sprayed my tea all over Melanie!

'No way, that's ridiculous! Surely no mother could possibly get away with that?'

'Told you so; she has a cheek!'

'She can't do that!'

'Well she has, and I shouldn't mind as they must be the richest family in the school.'

There in black and white it read, 'Frederick would like to invite his classmates to dine with him on 1st November at 5 p.m. sharp. The venue – Quince Kids … decadently delicious. Please dress to impress! Boys are to wear dinner suits and girls party dresses. Your meal will be at the cost of £15 per child, please pay me direct into my PayPal account before 25th October, details below. Kind Regards Charlene.

'That is absolutely bonkers, the world has gone mad! Can you really invite a child to a birthday party and demand they pay for themselves?' I blurted.

'No you bloody can't! Next she will be demanding money for the present because I bet Frederick is saving up for his first Porsche and will be collecting donations in the playground no doubt!'

'Whatever happened to good old parties at home with pass the parcel and egg sandwiches?'

'Charlene Pontington-Smythe is what happened!'

'I take it you won't be lining Charlene's PayPal account with £15?'

'Damn right I won't! The absolute brass neck of that woman, who does she think she is, a Hollywood superstar?' We both laughed and bit into the large slices of Victoria sponge. There was only one thing I would ever have in common with the likes of Charlene Pontington-Smythe and that was we gave birth to a child in the same class, but knowing her, she would have been too posh to push.

Melanie was comical with all her huffing and puffing through the scoffing of the cake. The hilarity of the situation was just what the doctor had ordered. It had taken my mind off my morning appointment at the surgery, well for the time being any way, but there was still a niggle in the back of my mind that just wouldn't go away.

CHAPTER 35

The year was flying by and I couldn't quite believe we were near the end of October already. The temperature had dropped sharply and the bleak mid-winter was upon us once again. I did quite like winter, and the dreary state of it all; it was a time of slow-cooked stews, homemade bread and oversized sloppy jumpers to snuggle up in and of course, X-factor was back on the television every Saturday night, which meant the run up to Christmas was well and truly underway. Each afternoon I would hurl the logs from the woodshed, pack the fire full of kindling and logs and toss in a firelighter. Watching the flames ignite, I would leave it burning furiously, ready and warming on our return from the school run. Once I'd collected the children from their tiring day, we would batten down the hatches; kick off our shoes, hang up our coats and make ourselves comfortable in our toasty living room while supping hot chocolate.

On the first of November, the letter from the hospital confirming my appointment dropped through the letter flap onto the mat. Not ready to read it, I scooped it up and hid it carefully behind the kitchen telly. Although extremely tired, I had a restless night and could not sleep. Trying not to wake anyone at two in the morning, I tiptoed downstairs to make myself a cup of milky tea. I retrieved the letter, and sank down quietly into the chair, trying not to scrape the legs across the floor or make any kind of sound. Luckily, for me the dog didn't wake and the only noise I could hear was the soft sound of him snoring from his basket.

Finally having the courage to tear open the envelope, I noted the appointment was scheduled for the following Thursday. I pencilled in the 'appointment' and the time on the family organiser pinned to the kitchen wall. I was beginning to feel apprehensive and I wasn't entirely sure why. Telling myself, I was being daft and there was absolutely nothing to worry about, I quickly drank my tea and returned to the warmth of my cosy bed. Snuggling back down into our bed and pulling up the duvet around my chin, I was positive that once Sue and I ran the race we were rigorously training for, my energy levels would slowly increase. I'd also put myself on a strict eating regime which included no alcohol, no chocolate and no crisps, which should help

I lay awake for a short time longer and watched the shadows of the trees dance across the bedroom ceiling, and then I finally closed my eyes.

I hadn't told Matt about my trip to the Doctor's. I didn't see the point, as there wasn't anything at this stage to tell, so there was no need to worry him. By the time I eventually drifted off to sleep, I'd convinced myself my increase in tiredness was down to a lack of iron and a surge in exercise.

Life in general at the moment was pretty damn good. There were no more trials or tribulations from Penelope or BB, and my friendship with Melanie and Sue was going from strength to strength; both friendships I treasured dearly.

The morning of my appointment I was in a complete flap, not only was I running late but also I'd forgotten to make the children's packed lunches. Matt, noticing how on edge I was, quickly gathered some change from his pocket. Dividing it up equally between the children, they each received a handful of coins so they could purchase a school dinner.

'Are you OK? You didn't sleep last night; you spent the whole time tossing and turning,' he enquired, kissing my forehead before picking up his laptop and heading towards the door. 'No, not really,' I replied.

Matt turned swiftly and immediately placed his laptop bag down on the floor.

'Why, what's up?' he asked eying me suspiciously.

'Oh nothing, I'm just being silly it was probably one of those nights where my body is lacking in alcohol or something like that.' I laughed nervously.

'You can't fool me Rachel Young, come on spit it out, I'm not moving until you tell me.'

'You'll be late for work.'

'And work can wait,' he replied firmly.

'I've got an appointment, it's probably nothing, just a routine check-up at the hospital but I'm feeling a little nervous now.'

Matt's eyes widened, 'at the hospital, and you didn't think of telling me?'

'I didn't want to worry anyone, its only routine, I've been feeling a little tired of late and had a small ache under my arm they are sending me for a scan this morning to make sure everything is just as it should be.'

'This morning? You are going this morning?'

'Yes, straight after the school run.'

'Rach, why on earth didn't you tell me,' Matt replied, rather annoyed. I knew he was annoyed because his cheeks began to redden, a sure sign he wasn't happy.

'Please don't be angry with me, I'm feeling anxious enough.'

'I'm coming with you.'

'But ...'

'No buts Rachel, I'm not letting you go alone.'
'Thank you,' I replied, relieved.

Matt accompanied me on the school run and we didn't hang around once the children were safely in their lines. This morning I gave each of them an additional squeeze. After dropping Matilda and Daisy at preschool we began the journey to the hospital.

The drive was quite straightforward and we sailed through the rush-hour traffic with no delays whatsoever, and we arrived at the hospital twenty-five minutes later. Removing the ticket from the machine at the side of the barrier Matt pulled my car into a vacant space outside the hospital building.

We located the unit from the specifics in the letter, and headed off in the right direction, following the arrows on the signs down the long white corridors. I noticed numerous groups of people congregating around the coffee machines; this seemed to be the norm in hospitals. Whenever anyone didn't know what to do, they would go in search of a coffee machine. I was feeling slightly undressed. It was silly really but the advice in the additional information stated to stay clear of all deodorant and perfume as they can play havoc with the mammogram, showing up as white spots if detected.

I handed my letter over the counter to the receptionist; she was extremely polite and put me at ease straight away. After confirming my personal details, a nurse took me through to a separate room. Matt waited patiently in the waiting room. My mind was elsewhere as I was trying to think of everything and anything that was positive. I filled my head with my children's faces, their smiles and their voices.

Handing me a gown, the nurse asked me to undress from my waist up. Pulling the curtain around the rail, she asked me to let her know when I was ready. Feeling nervous, I disappeared behind the curtain; it was deadly silent except I could hear the nurse breathing whilst she waited patiently for me on the other side. Removing my blouse and bra and folding them neatly, I placed them on the chair at the side of me. Taking a deep breath I managed to call out, 'I'm ready.' The nurse pulled the curtain back, and led me through another door into a room with a lot of machinery. There was another person present in the room, a technician who was colour co-ordinated with the bright white clean clinical room we were standing in, even down to her clogs. She looked over at me and gave me a reassuring smile, making me feel at ease, well as much as anyone could feel at ease in a situation like this. Signalling to me to come over, I stood next to her and the machine. Her voice was comforting and sooth-ing while she explained clearly, what was going to happen next. There was nothing at all to worry about and it was simple.

'You will stand in front of this special x-ray machine. Each breast will be placed onto a plastic platform and then pressed by another plastic plate. You may feel some pressure, but that's nor-mal, do not worry and keep still. Pressing the breast in this way spreads the tissue and prevents any sort of movement; it helps to get a sharper image. The steps are then repeated to get a side view. The compression for each breast only lasts a few seconds and the overall procedure takes approximately fifteen minutes. Do you have any questions?'

My mind was whirling; there was only one thing I could honestly say about myself and that was Rachel Young doesn't do pain.

'Is it painful?' I queried.

'Most women feel uncomfortable when their breasts are being pressed and some women find it painful but the discomfort only lasts a few seconds each time. Once the mammogram is finished, some women feel sore; does that answer your question? Are you ready?'

'Ready as I'll ever be.' I just wanted it to be over.

It was exactly how the nurse and technician had described it, and within fifteen minutes, I was relieved to be back behind the curtain and reunited with my bra and blouse. I felt a little sore, but I was thankful it was over. I was asked to return to the waiting room while the technician examined the x-rays to make sure none of the images needed retaking. Matt was still sitting patiently on his chair. I glanced round at a sea of women, their faces anxious, likely fearing the unknown. I sat in the chair next to him.

'Everything OK?' He asked.

'Yes, I've just got to wait until they tell me I can go.'

Hearing footsteps in the corridor, the technician popped her head around the waiting room door and gave me the thumbs up, 'We have everything we need,' she confirmed. 'We will be in touch as soon as the results become available,' she continued with a reassuring smile.

Matt and I decided not to tell a soul until there was anything to tell. Life went on as normal for the next two weeks. It was just a waiting game, a game I wasn't in control of and a game I didn't want to play, but wanted to win. I was occasionally worried but there was nothing I could do until the results were ready. Pushing it to the back of my mind, I tried to carry on as normal.

For the next week I put my heart and soul into training with Sue for our upcoming running race, we were covering a hell of a lot of kilometres on a daily basis. Running for an hour every morning provided me with headspace – time to myself and to relieve any stress and clear my mind. I didn't think about anything in particular when I was running, but enjoyed the wind rushing in my face and the scenery all around me. There was one thing I loved in particular about running with Sue was that we didn't talk. Sue provided enormous calm in my life and that was what I needed at this moment in time. It was great to know she was at my side but no forced conversation was needed.

We were running faster and stronger each day and this one morning in particular, we noticed the mothers' running brigade up in the distance. They were kitted out in new running outfits every day, and were still wearing their sun visors even though we were in the middle of November and hadn't seen any sun for a while.

Sue, winking at me, patted my back and said, 'come on, let's leave them for dead.'

Powering our legs harder up the hill, they hadn't noticed us sneaking up behind them. They were too busy gossiping about a mother from school who was having a secret affair with her landscape gardener; according to them, there was something impressive about his enormous chopper. We were hot on their heels and caught them up in no time at all. Sue bellowed, 'good morning ladies,' and we left them jumping out of their skins and gasping with fright.

'You are terrible, you are,' I smirked at Sue. It was simple things like that which helped me get through the days and made the waiting easier.

CHAPTER 36

Matt and I paused outside the old imposing hospital building, admiring its magnificence. Looking up at the impressive architecture that surrounded us, I imagined the millions of people that must have passed through those doors over the years. The telephone call I had been waiting for had arrived earlier in the week, the diagnosis results were available and an appointment was scheduled with the surgeon. After dropping the children at school and pre-school I couldn't even remember travelling to the hospital that morning; Matt drove. I was dazed and must have been on auto-pilot.

Taking a deep breath, we entered the hospital, which held all the information to my future. Matt squeezed my hand for reassurance. After the receptionist had punched my name into the computer, we were told to take a seat and we would be shown through into the surgeon's office in a moment.

With my backside firmly wedged in the plastic chair, I really didn't know what I was thinking; biting hard on my bottom lip, I tried to keep my emotions under control. My palms were sweating and my head throbbing. Matt sat next to me with a reassuring hand on my knee but in complete silence.

'Rachel Young,' the voice echoed all around me. I didn't move, I couldn't move.

'Rachel Young,' the voice sounded again.

Matt touched my knee. 'That's you.'

I looked up and caught the nurse's eye. 'Are you Rachel?' I could only manage a nod of my head.

'This way; would you both like to come through?'

I didn't want to go through anywhere, but somehow my legs moved and my body followed the nurse into the examination room, Matt followed me.

'Take a seat, the surgeon will be with you in a moment.'

Pulling out a chair, I glanced around the room, still biting hard on my bottom lip as a tear slid down my face. I had no idea what the diagnosis was going to be, but hopefully in a couple of minute's time the tears would be ones of relief. Matt sat down in the chair next to me. Another door into the room opened slowly and the surgeon accompanied by a Macmillan nurse entered. After introducing themselves, they too sat down and checked over my personal details.

It was at this moment I knew exactly what they were going to say.

'I'm really sorry, but the mammogram has revealed you have two tumours in your left breast.'

Nothing in this world prepares you for this type of news. Sinking down heavily into the chair my head was spiralling out of control; it was telling me not to panic. My eyes filled with tears and I tilted my head backwards trying to blink them away. This didn't feel real; I felt as if I had been kicked in the stomach. Every emotion surged through my body. I was hearing words all around me but I couldn't absorb any of them.

I was in utter shock; faced with my own mortality I wasn't ready to hear this. There had to be a mistake, I hadn't even felt sick. How could I do this to my wonderful family and my children? Looking at Matt the only words I could say were 'I'm sorry.' His face too was in utter shock; his eyes too were blinking back the tears.

'I love you and there's no need to be sorry, we will fight this.' He grabbed my hand and gripped it tightly as if his life depended on it.

The next few minutes were all a bit of a blur. I watched the surgeon's mouth move and heard words such as malignant, scans, lymph nodes and chemotherapy but I couldn't digest any of the information. I had grade three evil inside me; I could remember that much, an aggressive kind they said.

I was to commence chemotherapy as soon as possible. I'd heard the word and read about it in magazines but never quite understood was it was. It was going to be injected directly into my vein. The surgeon and nurse were positive; there was a chink of hope. They explained that chemotherapy was more advanced these days and was a very effective treatment that had helped save millions of lives. The surgeon explained the side-effects of the poison that was to be injected into my body; it might cause nausea and vomiting, and I possibly would feel tired and weak all the time. There would be six sessions of chemotherapy altogether, one every three weeks. Living with and adapting to the side-effects could be very challenging.

Then I heard the words, the words that made me sit up and focus.

'Three weeks after your chemotherapy starts there will be complete hair loss.'

It was at this point reality smacked me round the face and I didn't think I would ever recover from the shock.

My mind transported me back to the summer of 1995. This was the time when the joys of home perms were all the fashion. My mother borrowed her friend's hairdresser's rollers, and bound my hair into the tightest corkscrew curls that you could ever imagine; I was talk of the town and probably not for all the right reasons. I wanted to be back in 1995, I wanted a wig of curls again.

On the way home from the hospital, I was in complete meltdown. Matt drove me home with one hand on my knee and the other on the steering wheel.

I needed to share my news with my two best friends, I wanted to share the news with Melanie and Sue but I had no idea what I going to say or how they were going to react.

I decided to send them both a text; if I phoned them, they would automatically detect the upset in my voice and it wasn't something I wanted to do over the phone.

It read … *'Can you both meet me at home in ten minutes it is very urgent x '*

As we pulled onto the drive, Melanie and Sue were already standing outside the front door waiting anxiously. I got out and I was physically shaking as I staggered towards them, my legs were barely able to carry the weight of my body. I opened the front door and my two close friends followed me in silence. They knew there was something seriously wrong. Matt waited in the car. He wanted to give me time to tell my friends, and not surprisingly, needed time to compose himself as best he could. On the way through the hall, I glanced at my reflection in the mirror hanging on the wall. I knew it had already been a long traumatic day and we were only on lunchtime. My mascara had slipped so far down my face it was no longer accentuating my eyelashes. Instead, it was highlighting very successfully the bags under my eyes. I looked like I had been in physical combat yet it was nothing compared to the battle I was about to fight.

I'd always dreamt of living happily ever after by the sea. That was my dream and I wasn't about to let my dream be taken away from me and certainly not by this evil thing living inside me. I was a fighter with everything to fight for.

Melanie and Sue followed me in to the kitchen.

'Rachel, whatever is the matter, what's happened?' Melanie asked softly. Tears were already sliding down Sue's cheeks before I even spoke.

Both friends stood in front of me their eyes searching mine for answers. Melanie took a step closer and placed her arm around my shoulder.

'What is it? You can tell us.'

I wanted to tell them but the lump in my throat got in the way and I lowered my head into Melanie's shoulder, her eyes now pricked with tears.

'Tell us Rachel, you are beginning to frighten us now,' their eyes were studying me intently.

I took a deep breath, but words failed me; they wouldn't come. I tried again.

'Something terrible has happened.' There, I had started and I needed to continue.

I knew from the look on their faces their minds must be racing with all sorts of scenarios but my guess was that this one hadn't even crossed their minds. I wished I could turn the clock back but I couldn't. I wished this wasn't happening to my beautiful family but the evil was taking over my body no matter what I wanted.

'I have cancer, I have cancer.'

There, I had said it. The hardest words I ever had to say.

CHAPTER 37

Nearly four weeks on, it was beginning to look a lot like Christmas. You could tell it was just around the corner because in every department store known to man, 'I Wish it Could be Christmas Every Day' was blasting out of the speakers, providing the busy aisles with abundant festive cheer.

I loved this time of year; everything felt magical and everywhere I looked or walked there were jolly Santas and reindeers hanging above my head, wrapped up with colour-coordinated baubles and tinsel that had spiralled out of control.

Matt on the other hand was always 'bah humbug' when it came to Christmas and the spending of money – being the original Scrooge. With four children, the expense of it all nearly gives him a heart attack. For the sake of marital bliss, I always promised to cut back but I never did.

He does however, love the seasonal foods. My bone of contention is that each year he dances up and down the supermarket aisles filling his trolley with mince pies and twiglets – which the rest of us can't stand – so I can guarantee they will still be gathering dust in the kitchen cupboard in June. But it wouldn't be Christmas without his quirky ways.

Since the first week in September when the children returned to school, I had been putting away a few Christmas presents, well you have to with four children otherwise it becomes a very expensive time of year. I'm glad that I used my initiative and got started early because the last couple of weeks had been traumatic to say the least.

Christmas is always the perfect time to lose myself in family life. I cast my mind back to Christmas as a child; it was a very different time. Every year my Mother would stress over decorating the Christmas tree. The decorating of the tree is usually a family ritual but not when I was growing up – we were never allowed to get involved. We would be sent to bed but could clearly hear her muttering that the baubles didn't hang symmetrically or the tinsel didn't trail evenly. To add insult to injury, there were never any chocolate novelties hanging from the fake plastic branches because they had all been devoured by my mother. In the morning when we awoke, there was usually an empty bottle of sherry lying under the tree which my mother always swore blind had been used in the trifle. Sometimes the tree wouldn't appear until Christmas Eve, despite our constant longing but my father, who had to take life into his own hands by climbing into the loft for the moth-ridden thing, used to put it off until the very last moment.

My mother was never a Christmas person; her entire day was filled with worry. She spent the most of the day huffing and puffing whilst peeling vegetables, before attempting to saw the turkey in half which was always too large to wedge into the oven. My father did what he did best and disappeared to the local pub to stay out of the way. It was only after dinner had been consumed that the stress began to lift for my mother and usually when gallons of alcohol had been consumed.

Smiling to myself while I recalled those memories, I caught my reflection in the mirror. The image that was looking back at me was not one that I recognised. The chemo had taken its toll and as predicted, my hair was starting to thin, Apart from that though, I didn't scrub up too badly. I couldn't describe myself as glamorous but there was a positive twinkle in my eyes.

Matt had been fantastic; although devastated by the initial diagnosis, he soon went into positive overload. Cutting his hours back at work, he took over all the household duties and I didn't need to lift a finger, which was a relief as the sickness had taken over my life. The hardest part had been telling the children. Trying to keep as normal a routine as possible, we kept calm, encouraged them to ask questions and frequently reassured them of our love. We didn't hide anything from them and Eva and Samuel were involved in some very important duties, which included the selection of my wig. I wanted to be ready for the hair loss and even before my hair fell out, I wore the wig around the house so everyone could get use to my new hairstyle.

The first time I took my wig out of the box and placed it on my head, I was immediately transported back to 1995. I was certainly no square with my corkscrew hair and I didn't doubt for a moment the sniggers I would hear from the Playground Mafia once they clocked my new hair style. But I didn't care, the only people that were important were my family and friends, these people and what they thought no longer had a place in my life.

Sue and Melanie were sworn to secrecy. They were brilliant, rallying round to support me by taking the children to and from school. Once they were over the initial devastation of the situation Melanie with her wicked sense of humour made me laugh on numerous occasions 'Well, Young, if we can survive Penelope, Botox Bernie and the Playground Mafia we can survive anything. This cancer thing will be a doddle!'

Melanie and Sue were wonderful friends, shielding me from stress and lifting my spirits at every opportunity; and Matt –

well he was the best husband in the world that anyone could hope for.

The year was drawing to an end. It had flown by so fast and I couldn't quite believe I had survived another year of village life. The holiday with Penelope and our lottery win seemed like a distant memory; the money was still sitting in the bank with hardly a penny spent.

Christmas was an enjoyable family affair; Matt, inspired by Jamie Oliver, dished up a succulent mouth-watering turkey with homemade cranberry stuffing and all the trimmings and as usual, the children polished off their selection boxes for breakfast. He was fantastic; he did everything, the cooking, the cleaning and entertaining the children whilst I, exhausted, rested on the couch, but still involved, loving to watch my excited children.

After dinner, the dog's bowl was filled with leftover sprouts. No one in our family were sprouts' fans – like the mince pies and Twiglets – I'm not sure why Matt insisted on buying them every year. He says that it isn't Christmas if there are no sprouts, unfortunately for the dog, for no one will go near him until he begins to smell less sprouty.

This year's Christmas Day had been as perfect as it could be. Both Matt and I tried to keep everything as normal as possible for the children's sake. Coronation Street played out from the television and yet another Christmas Day baby was born – clearly a must at Christmas for any soap opera.

Out of all the children, Eva was the most affected. Matt and I could see in her eyes how frightened she was. Being the eldest she knew what having cancer meant but, she was on a mission and fussed around me continuously, making sure I was always comfortable. I was so proud of the way she handled everything, I was so proud of them all. She never left my side all day. Every time I fell asleep, she held my hand, waiting for me to wake.

The nausea had been simply awful, there is no other way to describe it and Eva was the perfect nurse reminding me to take my anti-sickness drugs. As a family we kept everything positive, there was no other way and cuddles with the children were dished out at every opportunity.

Once Christmas was behind us, the countdown to my birthday began again. It only seemed two minutes ago that we were stood watching Frisky Pensioner leave his house one last time on the paramedics' trolley. This year, birthday celebrations would be low key, I wasn't up to hosting any New Year parties but I did want to spend quality time with my family and close friends.

We couldn't believe how things had changed for us and for our friends too over the past year. Rupert was all loved up with Sue and they made a perfect couple. He had finally changed his ways, and with full support from Sue, he was fighting Penelope for custody of the children. Sue was simply a lovely person and I was very fortunate she had come into my life at such a difficult time.

Melanie and the Farrier – I couldn't get used to calling him John – were still besotted with each other and were clearly meant to be together. Melanie had news of her own – she and the Farrier were expecting a baby and she was certainly outdoing me on the sickness front – her morning sickness was definitely taking its toll.

The six of us had decided there would be no madness this year. However, Rupert suggested if I could manage an hour, that as it had been a hell of a year for all of us, a small tipple wouldn't go amiss on New Year's Eve. So with a little persuasion, Sue's mother kindly agreed to babysit all of the children at our house so we could take the short walk down to the local pub to soak up some of the atmosphere.

CHAPTER 38

New Year's Eve in 'The Queen's Head' was nothing special. The pub could definitely have done with a bit of a sprucing up; the main entrance was usually surrounded by smokers gathered to get their fix of nicotine and it felt as if you had passively smoked ten cigarettes before you had even made it inside. The ladies' toilets appeared to have been painted so many times that there was a kaleidoscope of colour in the areas where the paint had peeled. Despite its many shortcomings though, it was a convenient place to drink with no taxi costs.

Pushing our way in through the crowds of people, the atmosphere was jovial. It was fast approaching 11.30 p.m. The live band in the corner was belting out tunes from the eighties and requests were encouraged. Most drinkers had long abandoned all sense of decorum and the dance floor was full of inebriated youths, enjoying their night with no intention of going home any time soon. Every one of them were eyeing up the remaining members of the opposite sex on the dance floor in the vain hope of copping off with a stranger before the clock struck midnight. I was glad those times of my life were over; it made me exhausted just looking at them.

Rupert managed to grab us a vacant table in the corner of the pub while Matt and the Farrier fought their way through the crowd of people gathered at the bar. The majority of them were swaying from side to side and slurring their words shouting

'Happy New Year' even though there were still thirty minutes to go until we linked arms for the traditional Auld Lang Syne.

There seemed to be some kind of additional frenzy in the corner of the bar. Melanie, Sue and I turned swiftly towards the raucous cheer. Our eyes widened and our mouths fell open as we identified the person causing the commotion. There was no mistaking BB, who no longer had her feet on the ground – which was an occupational hazard for her – as she stood brazenly on the polished oak bar high above the punters waiting to be served.

She looked as if she was laced with every type of alcohol available, right down to her knickers which she was parading for the world and his wife to see. Melanie mouthed over the loud music, 'I'm just glad she is actually wearing some,' and winked.

It was cringe city, and judging by the hysteria that was going on around her, she was clearly arousing the majority of slobbering excuses for males, who were standing in front of her videoing her little performance on their phones which no doubt would provide them with additional entertainment when they returned home.

One bloke zooming in on her chest could be heard slurring, 'look at those beauties,' then 'damn,' when the battery died and the phone shut down. She was a party animal – there was no denying that – but I was momentarily lost for words. BB was now swinging her arms around in circles like she was about to launch a shot-put.

Melanie, Sue and I exchanged a knowing smile; we knew the lyrics to the next song very well and it was only a matter of time before BB took a tumble. She put her hands on her hips and brought her knees in tight – which was an unusual position for them to be in.

'Here goes,' Melanie laughed as BB launched exuberantly into the pelvic thrust – which was much more up her street – and slipped off the edge of the bar, toppling onto the beer swilling gawping males below.

The lads returned with the drinks, which was my cue to fight through the crowds and nip to the toilet before the clock struck midnight. Stepping over a few comatose bodies on the floor and numerous strangers that were in very compromising positions, I was relieved to find there was no queue for the ladies'.

Looking at myself in the mirror, I admired my wig, which didn't look too bad and was genuine enough so nobody on the school run had guessed I was wearing one. Still studying my reflection in the mirror, the cubicle door flung open behind me and I couldn't believe my eyes. There standing in the doorway was a very pregnant Penelope.

I'd managed to avoid any contact with her since the episode at the summer fair. She was hanging on to the frame of the door looking completely shell-shocked, her talons digging into the flaky paintwork.

'It's coming,' Penelope panted, 'the baby is coming.'

It was just my luck that I had needed to go to the toilet at this very moment. Why me? Why bloody me?

The look on her face told me this was no exaggeration and the time between her contractions suggested the baby was well and truly on its way.

'BB isn't answering her phone; I've tried to ring her but there is no answer.'

I knew very well that it was highly unlikely that BB would hear her phone, never mind answer it. She was too busy putting it out at the bar for the men who were drooling over her.

I hadn't known they had patched their friendship up, but since neither of them had anyone else in the village, I guess it was no surprise.

Neither of them had moved on since last year; at the very start of this year, BB was entertaining more than one frisky pensioner in the pub and Penelope was about to give birth on a reeking pub toilet floor. I supposed it was a step up from the disabled toilet in the snooker hall where the conception had taken place.

I took off my cardigan and laid it over a patch of the beige dimpled tiles, trying not to imagine the delights it would absorb. The practicality of trying to move Penelope was too complicated and it was way too late. Clutching her bump in agony, the contractions were becoming more frequent and it was clear she wasn't going to hold the child in for much longer. She lay down on my cardigan on her back, raised her knees, and begged me not to leave her. I prayed someone else would venture into the toilets soon so I could send them for help; I had never known a ladies' loo so empty before – ever.

'Take off your tights,' I instructed bravely, 'I'll have to have a look at what is going on down there.'

For once Penelope didn't protest and did as I asked; she was breathing very heavily now and she wasn't the only one. I had no clue what it was like at the other end until now. Struggling out of her tights and knickers, she lay back down on the toilet floor.

Penelope was becoming panic-stricken. 'Can you see the head?' she yelled at me. She held on to my hand and squeezed tight, in fact so tight, that I started to lose feeling in it.

To be honest, I'd done some things in my time but looking at Penelope's nether regions was certainly beyond the call of duty. I had found it difficult living with the image of her bonking the Jonny Vegas look-alike the night of the speed-dating incident and never in a million years had I ever anticipated I would be present at the birth.

Marjorie would have a field day if she got wind of this little gem. I cast my mind back to the wannabe Cilla Black, who for four years – according to her – had successfully run her speed-dating business from the snooker hall. In all that time, she hadn't managed to fix up a single, solitary date, but a speed-dating baby would certainly put her back on the map; the publicity she could milk from this would be very beneficial. Penelope had her first potential candidate for the role of godmother.

Penelope cried out in pain. 'It's coming, it's coming,' she panted.

'Just keep calm and breathe through the contractions,' I replied.

'I DON'T WANT TO KEEP CALM!' she yelled. 'I WANT IT OUT NOW.'

Believe me; I wanted it out just as much as she did. Where the bloody hell were Sue and Melanie? Surely, they must have noticed I was missing by now.

'You are doing really well, not long left now,' I reassured her. I actually had no idea how much time was left.

'I want to push, it's coming,' she insisted.

I wished someone would come and help; where was everyone? Apart from Penelope screaming, the only other thing I could hear in the background was the sound of the hokey-cokey playing out from the jukebox.

'I can feel the head.'

'Are you sure?' I enquired.

Penelope nodded. She was pale and sweating heavily.

I thought how ironic it was that after the crap Penelope had put me through for the last two years, I was the one to deliver her baby.

'I don't want my baby to be born in a toilet,' she screamed.

I wanted to remind her that it was conceived in a toilet but then I remembered she was entitled to be a bit tetchy giving birth with no pain relief in sight.

Glancing down I could see the head.

'The head is crowning, I can see the head.'

'I know, I can feel it, I need to push again.'

'Penelope this baby isn't hanging about, it's nearly here, on the next contraction push as hard as you can.'

The contraction was coming; I could tell by the pain in her face.

'You bastard,' Penelope started screaming. 'You bastard, I hate you.'

That was a bit rich coming from her by anyone's standards. Her eyes were black with hatred, when I realised the door had opened behind me.

I couldn't believe my eyes; it wasn't me she was calling a bastard but Clive, the Jonny Vegas look-alike who had just so happened to have entered through the wrong toilet door, and was now faced with the result of his one-night stand being born on the toilet floor. What were Paddy Power's odds on that?

I had never been so happy to see another individual in my life. Clive on the other hand, who pretended not to recognise Penelope, turned to me and said, 'you've changed your hair. Curly suits you,'

'Never mind my bloody hair; I hope you two remember each other. Clive I need your jacket.'

'Come on Penelope, one last push, this is it, this is the one.'

She nodded and despite the pain in her eyes, gave it everything she had, gaining leverage by pushing one leg against the frame of the toilet door and one against Clive. The perspiration was running down my body and I felt as if I had run a marathon. I could hear the crowd in the pub counting down, ready to welcome the New Year in. Where the hell was everybody and why hadn't Matt come looking for me?

'Ten,' the crowd roared in the pub.

'I'm not comfortable,' Penelope wailed.

'Nine.'

'Stay calm, you have done this before.'

'Eight.'

'Not without pain relief!'

'Seven.'

'Too late for that now, far too late.'

'Six.'

'Rachel, are you in there, can you hear me?' came the voice of a concerned Matt from the other side of the toilet door.

'Five.'

'About bloody time, Matt. Hurry up we need help.'

'Four."

'I can't come into the ladies'

'Three.'

'You can and come now! For God's sake, hurry.'

'Two.'

The crowd in the pub had reached the heights of raucousness when Matt flung the door open to find Penelope's legs akimbo with a Jonny Vegas look-a-like and me about to deliver the baby.

'It's here!'

'One.

Happy New Year!' The pub erupted. All around us, party poppers were being let off, and the fireworks in the distance could barely be heard as Penelope gave out a last scream and with one last push, a slithering bundle of slimy life slid straight into my hands.

Matt quickly rushed over to the paper towel dispenser, grabbed a handful of towels and wiped the mucus from the baby's mouth and nose. The baby let out a cry and the relief was instant.

Wrapping the baby up in Clive's coat, we placed it onto Penelope's chest. Matt finally obtained a signal on his mobile phone and was able to call the paramedics.

'Don't touch the cord or the placenta,' Matt relayed back to us, help will soon be here.

'Mother and baby appear to be doing well,' Matt announced down the phone before hanging up.

'And who's this?' Matt directed at Clive.

'Clive, meet Matt and Matt, meet Clive, the baby's father.'

Penelope was worn out; tears of relief were streaming down her cheeks. 'What have I got?' she asked, exhausted.

'You've got a little girl,' I told her. 'A beautiful little girl. Just stay still now, help is on its way.'

Hearing the sirens in the distance, we knew it wouldn't be long before the paramedics arrived. The toilet door opened again and we had some extra company. BB, finally realising that her sidekick had disappeared, had come in search of Penelope. She appeared to sober up immediately and rather than congratulate her friend on the arrival of her baby daughter, she could only stare intently at the man crouched down at Penelope's side.

'What the fuck are you doing in here?' she yelled at Clive.

That was the second time tonight that poor Clive had had a woman hurl obscenities at him; all he'd done was to take the wrong door and it had changed his life forever.

'You bastard, I can't believe you've turned up after all these years.'

'Do you two know each other?' Penelope enquired quite innocently, clutching her bundle of joy.

'Know each other,' BB spat. 'This is the bastard who left his rancid Lonsdale boxer shorts on my bedroom floor – the bloke who did a runner never to be seen again. This is Lonsdale's father!'

I could hear Sue and Melanie behind me, taking in all the commotion.

'Well, you know what that means then don't you ladies?' Melanie smirked, joining the dots much quicker than me.

'You Penelope and you, BB have children by the same man, which means your kids are half-brother and half-sister!'

I hadn't even thought of that. I felt sorry for poor Clive; this morning he had woken up with no children and now he had gained a son and a daughter in a matter of minutes!

'Have you got a name for the baby, Penelope?' I asked, changing the subject quickly.

'I'm going to call her Lulu,' she gushed.

'Very apt,' Sue whispered behind me. 'Made in a loo, born in a loo!'

'Come on, you,' Matt said gently, grabbing my hand and helping me off the sodden wet floor. 'The paramedics are here now, let's find Rupert and the Farrier and get you a drink before we head home.

Returning to the comfort of the chair in the corner of the pub, I was covered in every bodily fluid known to man. It felt like hours since we had arrived and I had ventured into the toilet. Everyone returned to table and Rupert handed me a glass of water in a champagne flute.

'Come here Rachel Young, I need a kiss,' declared Matt. 'Happy New Year,' he whispered, and taking me in his arms, Matt's lips tenderly touched mine.

'But that's not all! I have an announcement to make. We all know how much I love Rachel and what a fighter she is, I know we aren't out of the woods yet but I am certain we will win this fight but Rachel has always dreamed of owning her own vintage tea shop on the beautiful Devon coastline of Hope Cove,'

'Ooh I have,' I interrupted.

'Well, my gorgeous wife,' Matt exclaimed, dangling a set of keys in front of my stunned eyes. 'Your wish is my command, we are on the move! Happy birthday!'

Everyone looked at each other in amazement.

I was lost for words.

Rupert and Sue, Melanie and the Farrier and Matt and I lifted our glasses and clinked them together, raising a toast to a new life, new adventures, true friendships and good health.

LETTER FROM CHRISTIE

Dear all,

As the writing of *The Misadventures of a Playground Mother* has come to an end, I must confess I will miss the characters Rachel Young, Melanie Tate, Penelope and Rupert Kensington and not forgetting the Farrier. I just want to say a heartfelt thank you to everyone that has been involved in this project - my family, friends, book bloggers and readers for all of your lovely messages, tweets and emails along the way. Writing fiction is certainly a lonely job and ninety-five per cent of that time is spent on my own, tapping at the computer with only a mad cocker spaniel named Woody for company.

I hope you enjoyed both *A Year in the Life of a Playground Mother* and *The Misadventures of a Playground Mother*. **If you did, I would be forever grateful if you'd write a review.** Hearing what readers think is a true joy and makes all the hours of writing truly worthwhile and your recommendations can always help other readers to discover my books.

To keep right up-to-date with the latest news on my new releases just sign up using the link below:

www.bookouture.com/christie-barlow

Please remember this book is fiction and I hope the tales of Rachel Young hasn't put you off moving to a country village or joining the PTA! There are some wonderful people that frequent the playgrounds and all the teachers and assistants do a magnificent job.

I would love it if you would all keep in touch,

Warm wishes

Christie x

@ChristieJBarlow
ChristieJBarlow
www.christiebarlow.com

A Year in the Life of a Playground Mother

Ever had the pleasure of collecting your children from the school playground? Even if you haven't, this is a hilarious must-read.

Fed up with the playground mafia at her children's school, **Rachel Young** is desperate for a change.

With her family and various pets in tow, a picture-perfect village in the countryside beckons. There, Rachel's children will be able to keep chickens and skip through fields and she'll bid farewell to the botoxed, fake-Gucci wearing Mumzillas forever.

But at the new school the mums are even worse, and before long, Rachel finds herself fighting for her place amongst the playground mafia.

While the children are practicing their sums and perfecting their reading, Rachel is learning some harsh lessons on the other side of the school gates, and ruffling plenty of feathers along the way…

An entertaining, heart-warming and funny tale, perfect for fans of Fiona Gibson, Kerry Fisher and Katie Fforde.

'**Well-observed, highly-relatable and wickedly-funny.**' Cathy Bramley

Printed in Great Britain
by Amazon

44674295R00163